studies in jazz

Institute of Jazz Studies
Rutgers—The State University of New Jersey
General Editors: Dan Morgenstern and Edward Berger

RED HEAD
A Chronological Survey of "Red" Nichols and His Five Pennies

by
STEPHEN M. STROFF

Studies in Jazz, No. 21

Institute of Jazz Studies
Rutgers—The State University
of New Jersey and
The Scarecrow Press, Inc.
Lanham, Md., and London

SCARECROW PRESS, INC.

Published in the United States of America
by Scarecrow Press, Inc.
4720 Boston Way
Lanham, Maryland 20706

4 Pleydell Gardens, Folkestone
Kent CT20 2DN, England

British Cataloguing-in-Publication Information Available

Library of Congress Cataloging-in-Publication Data

Stroff, Stephen M.
Red head : a chronological survey of "Red" Nichols and his Five
Pennies / by Stephen M. Stroff.
P.   Cm.   —(Studies in jazz : no. 21)
Includes bibliographical references, discography, and index.
1. Nichols, Red—Criticism and interpretation. 2. Five Pennies
(Musical group). 3. Jazz—United States—1921–1930—History
and criticism. 4. Jazz—United States—1931–1940—History and
criticism. I. Title. II. Series.
ML419.N36S77   1996   781.65'092—dc20   [B]   95–35652

ISBN 0–8108–3061–2 (cloth : alk. paper)

☉™ The paper used in this publication meets the minimum requirements of
American National Standard for Information Sciences—Permanence of
Paper for Printed Library Materials, ANSI Z39.48–1984.
Manufactured in the United States of America.

To Ralph Berton (1910-1993), who first introduced me to the records that Red and Vic made together; to Frank Powers, who taped over one hundred rare titles for my inspection; to Stan Hester, who double-checked my discographical data and provided two rare photographs; and most especially to Ernest Nichols, a man who took far more abuse for being good than any jazz musician past or present.

When I first saw *The Red Nichols Story* in 1959, I complained to Red that the film left out too much of his real musical history. "Hell, Ralph," he said to me, "that's Hollywood—what did you expect?" Now, finally, Steve Stroff has given us a book that does full justice, not only to Red, but to Miff, JD, Lang, Pee Wee, Artie [Schutt], Glenn Miller, my brother Vic, and the whole gang. A much-needed piece of jazz scholarship, and it's the whole truth!

–Ralph Berton (1993)

Contents

Acknowledgments

Grateful acknowledgment is made to the following persons or institutions for permission to reprint excerpts from various sources:

Ralph Berton for the excerpt from *Remembering Bix: A Memoir of the Jazz Age* (Harper & Row, 1974).

Richard M. Sudhalter ahd Philip R. Evans for the excerpt from *Bix: Man and Legend* (Arlington House, 1974).

Penguin Books Ltd., London, for the excerpt from *Recorded Jazz: A Critical Guide* by Brian Rust and Rex Harris (Penguin Books, 1958).

Macmillan Publishing Co., New York, for the excerpts from *The Big Bands* by George T. Simon (Macmillan, 1967).

Henry Holt & Co., Inc., for the excerpt from *Hear Me Talkin' to Ya* by Nat Shapiro and Nat Hentoff (Holt, Rinehart & Winston, 1955).

John Chiton and CBS/Sony Records for the liner note excerpt from *Louis Armstrong: Hot Fives and Hot Sevens, Vol. II* (CBS Records, 1990).

Max Kaminsky for the quote from *My Life in Jazz* by Max Kaminsky with V.E. Hughes (Harper & Row, 1963).

Edward F. Polic for the photograph of young Glenn Miller, previously published in George T. Simon's book *Glenn Miller and His Orchestra* (Thomas Y. Crowell, 1974).

Editor's Foreword

This welcome book sheds new light on a once-celebrated but long-neglected figure in jazz history. Ernest Loring "Red" Nichols (1905-1965) was active in music through five decades, but Stephen Stroff has rightly focused on the cornetist's most important work: his jazz-oriented recordings made between 1925 and 1932. Stroff has listened well to this prodigious output and has much to tell us about this almost always interesting and sometimes brilliant music, which (with the notable exception of England's Max Harrison) has been almost completely ignored by contemporary jazz criticism and historiography.

I first encountered the lively and discursive mind of Stephen Stroff in a compact survey of recorded jazz, *Jazz In a Nutshell,* later expanded into *Discovering Great Jazz,* the work of a surprisingly open-eared and commendably enthusiastic listener clearly well-acquainted with all facets of jazz. Subsequently, in the pages of *The Music Box,* an excellent but, alas, short-lived journal Stroff edited and published from 1991 through 1994, I found him equally knowledgeable about classical music.

Wide-ranging and unpredictable, this was a publication in which one could read about Joseph Schmidt and Harry "The Hipster" Gibson—to pick two totally different (and obscure) artists for whom Stroff had an informed affection. This book, then, is not the work of a boring specialist but rather of a genuine connoisseur and music lover who comes to his subject with a fresh perspective. It is clear that Stroff cares about this music, and it is to be hoped that his informed advocacy will bring new listeners to the old records (not enough of which are currently available— a state of affairs that this book might help to remedy) and cause veterans to revisit them.

Those who do will be in for a pleasant surprise. This work closes a gap in the appreciation and understanding of the multifaceted and ever-fascinating music called jazz, and thus fulfills one of the purposes of this series, to which it makes a stylish addition.

Dan Morgenstern

Preface

Red Nichols was unquestionably the most prolific jazz artist of the 1920s and early 1930s. He made thousands of records with various dance bands, including those of George Olsen, Sam Lanin, Joe Candullo, Jack Stillman, Lou Gold, Paul van Loan, Ben Selvin, Mike Speciale, Al Jockers, Fred Silver, Barney Rapp, and Bob Haring. With few exceptions, however, neither the text nor the selected discography of this book is concerned with those "commercial" dates. The recordings discussed and listed here are, for the most part, jazz recordings made with other bands, and jazz and popular recordings made under Nichols's name. This is even true in the case of those commercial dates where Nichols or his colleagues may have turned in a jazz solo. The same, more or less, goes for Miff Mole who, though not quite as prolific as Nichols, certainly recorded more sides than are covered in this volume.

Regarding said discography, the information therein was drawn from several sources, but primarily from Brian Rust's *Jazz Records 1898-1942*. In some instances my listing of dates and personnel varies from Rust's book; this information is based on later research into who the players were, either by Rust himself or Nichols expert Stan Hester. In all cases where a discrepancy existed, I tried to decide who were the most likely players on any given session. As a result, I may sometimes have been wrong in my choices, but only in two instances did I impose my own feelings upon the personnel listing. All other choices were made by others more skilled than I in this matter.

Introduction

The question of what is great and what is merely ephemeral in musical art may never be answered. There are, of course, objective criteria that we may apply to such standards, but in many instances subjective elements enter into it. Nor are the choices made always reflective of a person's lack of experience or education. Benjamin Britten, considered by many England's greatest opera composer, certainly was not an ignorant or undereducated man; yet he went completely against the accepted grain that Ludwig van Beethoven was a great composer, preferring instead the music of Beethoven's younger contemporary, Franz Schubert. Britten viewed Beethoven's music as somewhat contrived, calculated, and lacking the passion and aesthetic creativity he perceived in Schubert. Other critics see it entirely differently, elevating Beethoven to the stature of genius and considering Schubert a melody-writing hack; and still others recognize greatness in both, while admitting that their aesthetic was by no means identical.

This discourse is, I think, entirely apropos to the subject at hand. During his career, Red Nichols was praised extensively by several critics—both French and British—who saw in him a realization of pure, uncluttered jazz expression, at least until his band's style changed in 1929. Later, some French critics disowned Nichols completely, in fact apologizing for having once liked him at all, in favor of black jazz artists they had previously neglected. By and large, the British have maintained their fascination with Nichols's structures, while American critics—some of whom missed the forest for the trees—insistently compared him unfavorably to one of his prime inspirators, Bix Beiderbecke.

There were reasons for all of this, which we shall now proceed to discuss. First and foremost, of course, jazz was *not* considered anything like an art form, at least by Americans, until some thirty-five years after it first appeared on records. Part of this is attributed to the fact that it had an "unsavory" childhood, born in the streets, saloons, and bordellos of Louisiana and Texas. In addition, even as it was "coming of age" in the 1920s it remained a *popular* art, and as late as the 1960s its primary venue was not the concert hall but the nightclub. Certainly, anything this vulgar could not be true art; and as a result, many critics and musically-cultured Americans looked down on, and continue to look down on, jazz as a form of "musical perversion" (to quote one of them).

Curiously, this attitude was often fostered by the musicians themselves. Though nice people and generally bright, many of them were not intellectual heavyweights, and they mistrusted any intellectualization of jazz as a form of "cultism." Primary among these was banjoist-guitarist Eddie Condon (1905-1973), who in 1953 described the work of archivists as "very good for those who like surrealism,"[1] insisting that most jazz musicians simply pick up their horns and blow without pre-planning. Of course, Condon was just one man, and in fact his failure to grow musically or emotionally eventually caused a rift between himself and such early followers as Bud Freeman and Pee Wee Russell. But, unfortunately, he both represented and controlled a large segment of the "trad jazz" market, and by his words and actions did his best for forty years to separate his view of jazz from that of planned structures (i.e., arrangements) or any group larger than a septet.

The richest joke is that classical musicians often admired and envied jazz players. As early as 1919 Ernest Ansermet, who conducted the Suisse Romande Orchestre well into the 1960s. wrote the first legitimate jazz review, proclaiming clarinetist Sidney Bechet a musical genius. Donald Voorhees, who later conducted the Bell Telephone Hour Orchestra, led a dance band in the 1920s. Jan Savitt, a child violin prodigy who was concertmaster of the Phila-

---

[1] Condon, Eddie & Gehman, Richard, *Eddie Condon's Treasury of Jazz* (Greenwood Press, 1956), p. 24.

delphia Orchestra at the incredible age of eighteen, completely jettisoned his classical career in the late 1930s to
lead a jazz band (the Top Hatters). Franz Schoepp, a
clarinetist with the Chicago Symphony under Frederick
Stock, was as proud of his two "jazz" pupils—Buster Bailey and Benny Goodman—as of any classical clarinetist he
ever taught. Vladimir Horowitz was fascinated, at a party
thrown by George Gershwin, watching Art Tatum play
piano. And B.H. Haggin, one of the fussiest and most
demanding of classical music critics, loved jazz, which he
described as "the moment-to-moment working of a mind
which we observe this time in the very process of creation,
operating with an inventive exuberance that is controlled
by a sense for coherent developing form."[2]

Secondly, there are those who rejected Nichols after first
accepting him. Primary among these was Hughes Panassié, whose 1942 sequel to his groundbreaking book *Le
Jazz Hot* was prefaced by an astounding apology. "It
should be confessed," he wrote, "that I had the bad luck,
in a sense, to become acquainted with jazz first through
white musicians, through the recordings of Red Nichols,
Frank Trumbauer, Bix, Ben Pollack, whose music, because it differed enormously from that of the great colored
musicians, could not give an exact idea of authentic jazz...
I did not realize until some years after the publication of
my first book that, from the point of view of jazz, most
white musicians were inferior to colored musicians."[3]

Here we run into that Great Barrier Reef, the oft-raised
black vs. white question. There are, of course, two ways
to look at it. We can ignore it and pretend it doesn't exist
(as most modern critics do), or confront it. I have chosen
the latter course, primarily because I am sick and tired of
having myself and every other writer who dares to pro-

---

[2] Haggin, B.H., *The New Listener's Companion and Record Guide* (Horizon Press, 1974), p.
186.

[3] Quoted by Richard Sudhalter in his notes for *The Jazz Age* (RCA Bluebird 3136-2-RB).

mote early white musicians as racist.

According to *The American Heritage Dictionary,* racism is "the notion that one's own ethnic stock is superior." But I do not claim that white jazzmen of any era were, or are, *superior* to blacks; I simply find them at best equal, at worst inferior, more often simply different aesthetically— just as Schubert was different from Beethoven. My father has many bad habits, but racism was never one of them. I was taught, from a very early age, to judge people by *what they are like* rather than *what they look like.* Indeed, I daresay that in our beauty-conscious society, overweight or deformed people are more subtly prejudiced against that people of varying races. It is an irony, in fact, that though we are not allowed to openly discuss another's physical misfortumes, nothing prevents us from laughing at them when stand-up comics launch into tirades against "fatties" or "cripples in wheelchairs."

As for white jazz, it had its place almost from the very beginning. As it evolved in New Orleans it was an amalgam of black soul and swing, the French Caribbean touch of the Creoles, and the formality of white European concert-band music. Prior to the 1960s, when he became something of a household name, I doubt that anyone could tell just by listening that Scott Joplin's ragtime pieces were written by a black man; and there was never a more form-conscious or prejudiced jazz musician than Jelly Roll Morton, the black Creole who thought himself a white supremacist. Moreover, the early style of Fletcher Henderson's Orchestra, and in particular the playing of its tenor-sax star Coleman Hawkins, was as stiff and formal as any white band of its day; the four most influential jazz musicians of the 1920s were equally divided between black and white—Louis Armstrong, Jimmie Noone, Bix Beiderbecke, and Frank Trumbauer—and, moreover, these four musicians influenced players of all races.

There is no doubt that, because of the racism prevalent in America during the 1920s, 1930s, and 1949s, white music- ians almost always found the better venues for their music.

Yet, though public segregation existed, and while some white musicians remained racist, barriers began to break down in the face of jazz's advancement. They almost had to. In the complex socio-economic system that existed at the time, blacks needed white patrons to help them break into bigger markets and achieve greater fame, while whites needed the musical give-and-take in order to nourish themselves and evolve. Though the white jazz style continued into the 1930s, particularly through the bands of Phil Baxter, Joe Haynes, and the better-remembered Glen Gray and the Casa Loma Orchestra, they came to be regarded (erroneously) as "pale imitations of jazz" by racial revisionists in the years after World War II, mostly because those writers detected the black jazz roots in the rich crops they harvested. Very few white jazzmen were as independently creative as Red Norvo, the man who single-handedly invented "third stream" music with *Dance of the Octopus* in 1933, and then evolved an entirely white but wholly valid jazz style in his big bands of 1936-39 and 1941-42. Most of them built their styles, both in solo improvisation and band arrangements, on the dialects and accents that black musicians spoke through their "axes."

What's more, this musical influence worked both ways. Just as Beiderbecke was dazzled by Armstrong's "heavy" swing and fractioning of time in the 1925-26 Hot Five recordings, so was Armstrong influenced by Beiderbecke's logical structuring of a jazz chorus into two-bar and four-bar cells. Just as Charlie Christian admired Django Reinhardt's whirlwind speed and harmonic audacity on the acoustic guitar, so did Reinhardt admire Christian's more streamlined phrasing and bluesy inflections on the electric —and this was a cross-influence that existed solely via records, as Reinhardt and Christian never met one another! Some jazz instruments, notably the piano, almost had to be developed along white, "classical" lines in order for a technique and a vernacular to evolve.

And so it went, through most of jazz's history: a give-and-take of the races, adapting and evolving—until today when, sadly, musical segregation seems to be setting in once again. The current state of jazz, in which there seems to be no actual evolution but rather a sense of retrenchment, is sad testimony to the lack of cooperation between races. The white neo-swingers don't talk to the black neo-boppers, the white avant-gardists are rebuffed by the black funk and rap crowd, all instrumental music is called "jazz," and the public is confused, polarized, or both.

The above discussion may seem a diversion from the main subject of this text, but in point of fact it is the crucial core. Nichols, Mole, Schutt, Lang, and Berton were questioned in their time as "real" jazzmen because their music was technically brilliant, tightly arranged, and lacked the "low-down" quality of black players. Today, and for the past thirty years, they are questioned as real jazzmen because they were white and successful.

The "white and successful" aspect must simply be overcome by listening. As for the technical and pre-planned aspects, they must be overcome by education. Despite popular beliefs, very little jazz is actually improvised on the spot. Most jazz musicians work from a vocabulary, and its dialects, which are well-learned in their travels and experiences. Their worth is more often judged by the originality with which they put those materials together, in a solo or composition. Even the redoubtable Armstrong, once he had "found the way" in a number of his most impressive musical ideas, rarely deviated from the general shape and direction of those patterns in his later playing. Moreover, we have come a long way since the 1920s in the appreciation of jazz's complexity as an art form, and with this increased appreciation has come the realization that form and structure are as important as swinging.

Therein lies the dichotomy regarding Ernest Loring Nichols and his marelous bands. He was one of only four bandleaders, during the "Jazz Age," who grasped the principles of structure and design that jazz had borrowed from European classical music in the creation of its own jargon,

and knew how to apply them to "pure jazz" arrangements.
The other three were the afore-mentioned Ferdinand "Jelly
Roll" Morton (1885-1941),[4] Edward "Duke" Ellington
(1899-1974), and Hartzell Strathdene "Tiny" Parham
(1900-1943). Morton and Ellington, of course, have become lionized legends, their music studied and dissected
by scholars as much as that of Bach and Mozart; but Nichols and Parham have been ignored, begrudged or depreca-
ted. In his book *Early Jazz,* for instance, author Gunther
Schuller completely omited Parham and Nichols. The
aroused ire of classic-jazz buffs made him re-examine
Nichols's music, which he discussed briefly in his sequel,
The Swing Era, but Parham is still an enigma to most
modern collectors.

The reasons for their neglect are, ironically, opposite ones.
Parham recorded only about four dozen sides, the bulk of
his output being the thirty-eight Victor sides of 1928-30,
and his performances are often sloppy and loose even
when the musical structure is fascinating. Nichols, conversely, recorded so much that it is doubtful even at this
late date that all of his discs have been identified and
found, and his performances seem so rigidly controlled
that certain critics (e.g., Panassié) have come to reject him
completely. Indeed, most pre-1970 American jazz critics,
whose principal criterion was the heat of a jazzman's
swing, generally pigeonholed Nichols as the "poor man's
Bix Beiderbecke," a cornetist-trumpeter who absorbed the
outward characteristics of Bix's style without conveying
its emotional warmth and fire.

There is, of course, a kernel of truth in this generally
unfair judgment, and it was because of this that my own
first reaction to Red's groups was primarily negative.
This was in the late 1960s, when I first heard Nichols's

---

[4] I know that modern scholarship places Morton's birth-year as 1890, but this is based on a
later replica of his baptismal certificate. In those years, illegitimate children were seldom
christened the year of their birth, and both Morton's memories and compositions simply date
too far back, though I would concede to 1887 could further proof be found.

bands in the old 4-LP Columbia set, *Thesaurus of Classic Jazz* (C4L-18). Having discovered Beiderbecke first, and read the various disparaging comments about Nichols's "cold, unemotional playing," I automatically dismissed his work on those grounds. That I have turned around so completely as to now be offering this analysis of his life's work is in some measure due to a maturation process on my part, as well as my coming back to Nichols's performances after a long hiatus of not really thinking about him at all.

This may sound strange, but it's true. Having early on rejected Nichols as hopelessly "corny," I, like so many jazz critics, missed the forest for the trees. I reverted to my adoration of Beiderbecke, collected every record he ever made, and placed him on a pedastal next to Armstrong while Red remained on the slag-heap. But then, a curious thing happened. I began to notice—nit-picker that I am—that the playing of Armstrong's and Beiderbecke's colleagues, on their records, was generally sloppy and imprecise, sometimes as stiff as, if not stiffer than, what I remembered of Nichols. So I went back to a quick re-examination of Red's discs. And what I found, as much to my own surprise as anyone's, was that not only were all his players usually in a good groove, not only was the overall musical conception and execution of a Nichols record more aesthetically balanced and pleasing than the catch-as-catch-can atmosphere of Beiderbecke and early Armstrong, but that in many cases *the very same players* who sounded sloppy and imprecise on a Beiderbecke record—i.e., Jimmy Dorsey, Chauncey Morehouse, Arthur Schutt—were the ones who sounded cogent and creative on Nichols's dates.

This led me to explore Red's output more closely; and that was when I discovered, with shame for my former ignorance, that this man was a genius in his own right. True, he seldom swung as hard as Beiderbecke, but he understood intellectually, *even better than Bix himself,* what made that legend's solos and compositions so musically fascinating. In other words, Nichols realized, probably early on, that he could never really compete with Beiderbecke in terms of swinging ability, so he did the next best thing: he created a sound-world based on Beiderbecke's musical principles that was entirely his own. And, in so doing, he produced music as brilliant (in my opinion) as any that Beiderbecke himself might have created had he lived a full, normal life.

This, then, is the impetus of this book. Of course, Nichols continued to produce good *solo* work beyond the scope of these pages, but insofar as overall musical conception goes he said it all between 1925 and 1932. The unfair treatment his records have received, even at the hands of Schuller, has prompted me to write this fuller analysis of his work. It is sincerely hoped that it will, if nothing else, spur a renewed interest in the records, many of which deserve to be re-released; for Ernest Loring Nichols, as we shall see, was one of the founding fathers of jazz as we know and enjoy it today.

1. Prelude (1896-1924)

The diverse elements that went into the production of the jazz machinery that Red Nichols developed, and operated so well, were set in place at least a few years prior to his birth. By the late 1900s, thanks largely to the pioneering efforts of Joe "King" Oliver, Bunk Johnson, and Jack "Papa" Laine,[1] the music was slowly but surely working its way out of the ragtime mold in which it had first been cast. In the early decades of this century, in various places around the country, the dissemination of black and white jazz brought the message to audiences who were looking for a new musical fad.

The oldest of the musicians who later became part of the first "Five Pennies" group was drummer Vic Berton, born in Chicago in 7 May 1896. His father was a teacher and theater violinist; Vic, a child prodigy, was hired as the regular pit drummer for the Alhambra Theater in Milwaukee at the age of seven. At this point, of course (1903), he had heard no jazz; in fact, his first ambition was to be a classical drummer, especially since his brother Eugene—a lyric baritone—had a lively interest in the then-modern French classical music of Debussy, Ravel, and, a few years later, Stravinsky, who was French by association. While in his teens, Vic studied with Joseph Zettleman of the Chicago Symphony, who taught him the use of the tympani. This talent, which otherwise might have gone unnoticed in any other jazz drummer of the 1920s, was to become one of the hallmarks of his art. Vic Berton was the first drummer to use these difficult instruments in a jazz context, and indeed after the 1920s he was the only

---

[1] Jack Laine (1873-1959) was a drummer who led his first band in 1891; indeed, it was his "Ragtime Band" which first set the style of "Dixieland" jazz popularized twenty-six years later by the "Original" Dixieland Jazz Band. It is interesting that Laine's bands often employed clarinetist Achille Bacquet and trombonist Dave Perkins, who were both Creoles—indicating that a racially mixed group operated even at this early date!

1

drummer to do so.

Irving Milfred Mole, more popularly known as "Miff," came from even farther away from New Orleans: he was born in Roosevelt, Long Island, on 11 March 1898. He studied violin for three years as a child, but switched to trombone as soon as his arms were long enough to reach the slide positions. He, like Vic, was a "quick study"; by 1914 Mole was playing trombone in a Brooklyn theater for silent films while house-painting for his father during the day. He later expanded his technique via private lessons (it is not certain with whom).

These two men, Berton and Mole, later represented the opposite extremes of racial tolerance within the Nichols band. Berton, who grew up on Chicago's south side, became extremely comfortable around blacks once they migrated north after World War I. Mole, on the other hand, admired the jazz styles of black musicians, but because of his upper-middle-class Long Island upbringing, always felt uneasy in their presence. This dichotomy always embarrassed Mole, who had no intention of giving offense, and unfortunately branded him as a racist.

In 1919 Miff joined drummer Sam Lanin's band at the Roseland Ballroom. Lanin, whose name has all but disappeared from jazz histories except in connection with such players as Mole, Nichols, and Beiderbecke, was an energetic go-getter who recorded prolifically between 1920 and 1931—in fact, producing more dance records than any other contemporary leader with the possible exception of Ben Selvin. Most of Lanin's music was stiff, ragtimey pseudo-jazz, though he did produce recordings by the Original Memphis Five, under their own name as that of Ladd's Black Aces. Also, as time went on and he began to appreciate the difference between pseudo-jazz and the real thing, he spent a great deal of time and money promoting jazz musicians, not only in his own big band but also in small-group sessions under such names as Lanin's Famous Players, The Broadway Broadcasters, The Broadway Bellhops, and Lanin's Jazz Band.

In those early decades, most known artists tried desperately to obtain recording contracts from one of the two "giants," Victor or Columbia. This was partly because they were so well known and established, but the main reason was that they owned the patent on lateral-cut discs, the "conventional" 78s of the time, in which the playback stylus vibrated side-to-side in the groove walls. All other American companies were forced to use the vertical-cut process, in which the stylus vibrated up and down. Obviously, lateral-cut records could not be played on a machine devised for vertical-cut discs, and vice-versa; and, since salaries were low and phonographs somewhat dear to the middle classes, there was an obvious preference for lateral machines, where one could play such popular favorites as Sousa, Caruso, and Al Jolson.

Then, in 1919, the Starr Piano Company of Richmond, Indiana, who had been making records on the Starr label since 1915, began a daring experiment. They changed their label name to Gennett, and began issuing lateral-cut discs. Victor immediately brought suit against them for copyright infringement. But Starr, who was encouraged both morally and financially in their suit by General Phonograph (OKeh), Aeolian (Vocalion), and Compo (H.S. Berliner of Montreal, Canada), all of which stood to gain by a Starr victory, had superb legal counsel from Drury W. Cooper, the brilliant patent attorney of the New York law firm of Cooper, Kerr, and Duncourt. For the first time in legal history, motion pictures were admitted as evidence in a courtroom, and Cooper proved that Starr's lateral-cut method was different from Victor's. After six successive trials, the Supreme Court handed down a decision in favor of Starr in 1921.

This monumental decision, scarcely mentioned in most jazz histories,[2] was of the utmost importance in the prop-

---

[2] The only jazz or blues histories to give significant focus to this event were Robert Dixon & John Godrich's *Recording the Blues* (Stein & Day, 1970), pp. 7-8, and Rick Kennedy's *Jelly Roll, Bix, and Hoagy* (Indiana University Press, 1994), pp. 23-26.

agation of the music. Although Fred Hager of General
Phonograph began issuing lateral-cut OKeh discs by the
end of 1919 (apparently confident that Victor's patent
would be upset), it was this 1921 decision that threw open
the doors so that small, independent labels could now
more realistically compete with Victor and Columbia. By
1922 several new labels, including Arto, Ajax, Banner,
Black Swan, Cameo, Domino, Emerson, and Paramount,
arose to cover the blues and jazz fields which had,
curiously, been abandoned by Victor and Columbia after
both labels dropped the Original Dixieland Jazz Band.
But Gennett was the greatest beneficiary: being located
not too far from Chicago, and having a satellite studio in
New York, they were able to record the established jazz
bands emigrating north from New Orleans to the Windy
City in addition to new groups which were springing up in
New York and the Midwest.

Among the former groups were King Oliver's Creole Jazz
Band and the New Orleans Rhythm Kings (NORK). The
star of the Creole Band was, of course, young Louis Armstrong (1901-1971), who in terms of a powerful cornet
tone and ability to "swing" was miles aboe his competitors, followed closely by clarinetist Johnny Dodds (1892-
1940). The star of the NORK was clarinetist Leon Roppolo (1902-1943) who, though he did not swing as hard as
Armstrong, was nevertheless the most harmonically sophisticated jazz musician of his time, followed closely by
cornetist Paul Mares (1900-1949). Both bands recorded
for Gennett in Richmond, and their discs were dissemina-
ted far and wide where they influenced a great many
youngsters in their decision to pursue a jazz career. In
1923, Jelly Roll Morton also hit Chicago, and by the end
of 1924 had piled up a sizeable legacy of piano solos and
some band recordings for Gennett and Paramount.

Among the latter groups, the most famous today was The
Wolverines, an octet of young white collegians who had
never seen the South. But they were the first band to
feature, on records, Leon Bix Beiderbecke (1903-1931),

the great cornet genius who revolutionized white jazz. Bix could swing as well as any black player with the exception of Armstrong, and he too was harmonically sophisticated in his approach to the music. But Bix was one of those "vague" personalities: immature and inarticulate, sensitive and repressed, he had a magnificent ear but could not intellectualize or analyze his own playing. He also suffered an extreme inferiority complex, hammered into him by his stoic but hopelessly uncomprehending family. Eventually it was this inability to cope with his own genius, which his own father and brother not only failed to recognize but fought to suppress, which led him down the black sink-hole of alcoholism and, eventually, to an early death.

There were other groups, however, much less well-known today and originating in New York, who thought they were on the right track. One of these was the Original New Orleans Jazz Band, whose ranks included (of all people) pianist Jimmy Durante; another was the Original Memphis Five, founded by cornetist Phil Napoleon (1901-1990), whose bland tone and paucity of ideas very closely resembled that of the ODJB's Nick LaRocca. Neither band was particularly good, at least on records; but the latter also included trombonist Miff Mole, and it was his playing in this group that so profoundly affected the subject of this book.

Ernest Loring Nichols was born in Ogden, Utah on 8 May 1905, to a family of German descent whose ancestors had made the long, covered-wagon trek across the plains to Utah with Brigham Young. One would, then, reasonably expect his family to be every bit as stodgy as Beiderbecke's; but his father, also named Ernest (perhaps one reason why Red preferred to use his middle name of Loring), was a music professor at Weber College, a conductor, and the boy's first teacher. Ernest Junior, nicknamed "Red" early on as a result of his flaming hair, was a quick study. His first instrument was the violin, and by the age of six (1911) he was playing *The Carnival of*

Venice publicly on cornet. Nichols Senior obviously fore-
saw a brilliant light-classical career for his son, possibly
even as a successor to Herbert L. Clarke (1867-1945), the
internationally-renowned cornet virtuoso whose compositions included the well-known *Bride of the Waves.* But it
was not to be. At age twelve, Red was a member of his
father's concert dance band; but that was in 1917, the year
of the first ODJB records, and for the next two years Red
neglected his triple-tonguing and coloratura roulades in
order to learn *Lazy Daddy, Ostrich Walk* and *At the Jazz
Band Ball.* Another, more direct early influence on Red
was the now-obscure Louis Panico, star trumpeter of the
Isham Jones band, who taught the young cornetist his
"flutter" technique.

In order to "straighten him out" Red's father sent him to
Culver, a military academy in Indiana, in December 1919.
Red continued to pursue jazz, however, with a local combo of his own creation. He was dismissed from Culver
"for bad conduct" in September 1920, at which point his
father sent him a letter that included the house keys. "If
you want to be a musician, go ahead," he wrote; "Good
luck—but keep this handy." Oddly enough, Red not only
returned to Ogden, where he worked with Jack Bower-
ing's Orchestra, but in March and April of 1922 he again
worked with his father, in the pit band of the Ogden Theater. Glen Brandenberg heard Red there, was very impressed, and contacted Harold "Greenie" Greenamayer
who wired Nichols shortly after his seventeenth birthday
to join his band in Piqua, Ohio. Red joined the band at
$50 a week, and roomed with trumpeter "Socky" Miller,
mellophonist Dudley Fosdick, and reedman Humphrey
Horlacher.

A little later in the year Nichols joined the Syncopated
Five. His own first official recordings were made in November 1922 (*Chicago* and *Toot Toot Tootsie*) with this
band, which was now a septet (even in this early period,
Red was fond of including six or seven musicians in his
quintets), for which each musician *paid the Gennett rec-*

ord company $25! In return for this, each of the young
musicians received twenty-five privately-pressed copies of
the record. As of 1980, only two copies were known to
still be in existence. Red had gotten rid of his years
earlier.

By the summer of 1923 the Syncopated Five broke up;
Nichols spent the summer playing at Lake James in Joe
Thomas's band. In September of that year Red landed in
Atlantic City, at the Ambassador Hotel, replacing Bob
Ashford in Johnny Johnson's Orchestra. During this ten-
ure he first heard two subsequent collaborators, violinist
Joe Venuti (1898-1978) and guitarist Eddie Lang (1902-
1933), both of whom also had a then-advanced concept of
swing. But the biggest impression made on the eighteen-
year-old was by the Original Memphis Five, which was
also at the Ambassador, and especially the playing of Miff
Mole.

To understand the impact that Mole had, not only on
Nichols in particular but on jazz in general, it is imperative that one understands the function of the instrument in
New Orleans jazz. In such groups, with their polyphonic
improvisation, the trombone was primarily a counterpoint
instrument; it slid and smeared its way under the "front
line" of cornet (or trumpet) and clarinet (and/or alto or
soprano saxophone). As a result, many early jazz trombonists could "fake it" with regularity; so long as they had
some concept of keys, and a powerful (if sometimes
coarse) tone, they could employ their "sludge-pump
smears" to raucous or humorous effect behind the playing
of the others.

Mole himself played this style in the beginning, and in
fact his earliest recordings are hard to distinguish from
any other trombonist; yet his virtusic bent came to the
fore, and he became the polar opposite of this. Despite a
propensity to "stiffen up" in his swing, he played the
instrument with a staccato virtuosity unknown at the time.
His solos were beautifully and logically constructed, models of tone and intonation, and as a result he liberated the

instrument from its background role and made it an equal in the front line. Not all jazz historians are particularly happy about this development; indeed, Brian Rust once wrote that "It is open to question whether jazz has benefitted by this."[3] But liberate it he did; and young Nichols, with his razor-sharp musical mind and virtuoso training, appreciated and became influenced by Mole's trombone.

It cannot be overstressed how important this is to appreciating and understanding Nichols's musical development. Up to this point, it is doubtful that he had heard any New Orleans jazz musicians, with the exception of the ODJB on records. Though his keen intellect could grasp and reconstruct the outward characteristics of jazz performance, his lack of direct influence from any of the black masters of the music inevitably retarded his growth as a jazz musician. Mole was the first *original* white stylist that Red ever heard; the almost mathematical order and logic of his playing could not help but appeal to him; and, in addition, the Mole "staccato attack" *became an ingrained element of his style.* This, in addition to his repressed nature, is one reason why Red found it difficult in later years to "loosen up" his swing.

Red and Miff became fast friends in Atlantic City and spent many a night "woodshedding," talking about music and playing records. Afterwards the Johnson Orchestra, including Red, migrated north to New York City. Red split his time between playing with Johnson and free-lancing as a soloist for George Olsen's Music. Mole, meanwhile, began to free-lance as well, especially for leader Sam Lanin. He first recorded with Lanin's band in March 1923, and both Mole and Napoleon recorded for Lanin in April. Miff introduced Red to Sam, but since he was working two bands at once Lanin could not immediately use the cornetist.

On 26 June 1924, Nichols recorded *You'll Never Get to*

---

[3] Rust, Brian & Harris, Rex, *Recorded Jazz: A Critical Guide* (Pelican Books, 1958), p. 132.

Heaven with Those Eyes for Victor with Olsen's band. Arranger Eddie Kilfeather had given Red a full-chorus solo, which was an almost literal transcription of Bix Beiderbecke's *Jazz Me Blues* solo on Gennett—which Red had not yet heard. Fascinated, Nichols asked Kilfeather where he had come up with this chorus; when he was told, he made it a point to hear Bix and the Wolverines. A month later, while playing with Dick Bowen and his Blue Streak Orchestra in Walled Lake, Michigan, Red heard that the Wolverines were playing in Jean Goldkette's Blue Lantern Casino, about twelve miles away. He drove over to see them and sit in.[4] Not only was he so impressed by Bix that he immediately adopted some of the characteristics of *his* style, but he was knocked out by the band's new drummer, who was also their manager: Vic Berton.

Much had come and gone Berton's way since we discussed him last. He and his family had been living in Chicago since 1917; Vic had been in the Navy, where John Philip Sousa requisitioned him for his service band; and, since at least 1921, Vic had alternated gigs between the Chicago Symphony Orchestra and jazz dates. He had also invented four devices for playing the drums, none of which he owned a patent on, though three of the four were used by drummers everywhere before the end of the decade. These were the metal cymbal rod, which freed the cymbal from its rawhide thong on a metal hook and gave it a crisper, more percussive sound; wire brushes, now a mainstay of any complete drum kit; the so-called

---

4 This account of Red's first meeting with Bix, recalled by Bowen band members Gerald Finney (piano) and Fred Morrow (sax, who later played on disc with Red), contradicts the account related by Richard Sudhalter and Phil Evans in their book, *Bix: Man and Legend* (Arlington House, 1974), that Red first heard Bix at the Marquette Park Pavilion in Indiana on his way *out* to join Bowen. But as Nichols expert Stan Hester assured me, the Marquette Park Pavilion was 100 miles out of Nichols's way after he left New York on July 3; and the fact that he made it all the way to Walled Lake by July 5 practically negates the chance that Nichols would have been able to make a round trip to Indiana and still have time to reach Michigan.

"sock cymbal," a pair of medium-small "zinger" cymbals mounted on two-by-fours with a spring, which gave a marvelously funky sound to the backbeat; and the so-called "Charleston pedal," which attached to the tympani in order to change its pitch (as well as produce a unique "sliding" sound). The "sock cymbal" was improved upon, and became the hi-hat, the third innovation used by drummers everywhere. But except for a limited use by Hal MacDonald of the Paul Whiteman Orchestra, no other drummer dared to attempt using the "Charleston pedal." It was a technique born with Vic Berton and, after the 1920s, used by no other drummer.

As Vic's younger brother Ralph put it in *Remembering Bix: A Memoir of the Jazz Age,* by 1924 Vic "was a restless man. At twenty-five he had run out of worlds to conquer."[5] And so his next world was The Wolverines, and specifically their boy-genius cornetist. Berton was so taken by Beiderbecke that he offered to manage the band, even though he had no prior experience in that field. To his credit, he took over the drum chair from the energetic but rhythmically lagging Victor Moore, which gave the band a better rhythmic impetus; and, also to his credit, he did manage to book them into New York by the end of the year. But, typically of Berton, he failed to realize that Beiderbecke was too good for a small-potatoes band like the Wolverines, even with Vic Berton. All the New York engagement really did was allow music scouts to hear how great Berton and Beiderbecke were, and how pedestrian the rest of the band was. By November Bix had packed his bags for Detroit, where he joined the Jean Goldkette Orchestra, and Vic was left to free-lance in New York.

Throughout the past several pages I have been speaking of Beiderbecke, Armstrong, Dodds, Roppolo and Venuti as having an advanced concept of "swing" and an advanced harmonic concept for their time. I think this should be explained, and put into context. By 1910, when jazz was

---

5 Berton, Ralph, *Remembering Bix: A Memoir of the Jazz Age* (Harper & Row, 1974), p. 107.

still in its infancy, Western classical music was under-
going a revolution. Having gone through two centuries of
growing harmonic sophistication, it had reached a point
where audacious key-changes, layered tonality and multi-
tonalism were all quite commonplace. It was time to
reach, as it were, "on beyond zebra." And at that time,
there were three composers who were doing exactly that:
Igor Stravinsky (1882-1971), who thrived on harmonic
clashes and highly syncopated figures; Bela Bartok (1881-
1945), who incorporated the crude yet almost Asiatic
modes and scales of Hungarian folk music into a classical
base; and Arnold Schoenberg (1874-1951), the largely
self-taught composer who almost single-handedly revolutionized the face of music. Not content with mere
harmonic clashes, multi-tonal or atonal music, Schoenberg
devised the twelve-tone system, whereby music was
reduced to the component half-steps within an octave.
None of these twelve "half-tones" were more important
than any other, and each one had to be used at least once
before any one of them could be repeated in sequence.

It has been said that Schoenberg's innovation "liberated"
music, but in reality it replaced one discipline with another. It also threw music completely out of the tonal system: with no half-tone being more important than any
other, there was of course no such thing as a "key." Some
of his followers, specifically Anton Webern (1883-1945)
and Alban Berg (1885-1935), produced some music of
genius. But the twelve-tone approach was *so* complex that
it became more and more difficult, after Schoenberg's
death, to say anything original or meaningful within its
strict rules.

Jazz, on the other hand, was harmonically simple. Its first
models had been marching-band music, the blues, and
popular songs, all of which used simple AABA or ABAC
structures and a harmonic base no more complex than,
say, the popular music of a century earlier. In comparison
with classical music, even the classical music of Beethoven, Berlioz, Wagner, Mahler, and Debussy which was

already "old hat" by 1924, jazz was harmonically and structurally immature.

But that is missing an essential point. Though we may have a difficult time believing it today, jazz was a music of rebellion. Its very crudity was part of its charm and appeal; it was raucous, funky, impolite. The records of the ODJB, though they didn't swing by modern standards, were a way of thumbing one's nose at the Establishment. Their message was to get drunk, get rowdy, dance, and make as much of a racket as you could. This, of course, is yet another reason why jazz took so long to gain acceptance as an art. Its combination of brashness and simplicity lowered it, in the eyes and ears of many, to the level of musical garbage.

And yet, not all New Orleans jazz was as stiff and essentially uncreative as the ODJB. Willie "Bunk" Johnson (1879-1949), one of the greatest and most underrated of the jazz originals, had shown in the first decade of this century how one could take a pop tune, "rag it," and then add decorative touches which embellished the melody while pushing the rhythmic pulse to the breaking point. Those decorative embellishments were called improvisations; pushing the rhythmic pulse was called swinging. After Bunk came "the kid," "Dippermouth," "Satchelmouth," the man whom all critics are agreed was the single greatest jazz artist of the decade, Louis Armstrong. Armstrong's tone was so huge, so round (trumpeter Ruby Braff once described it as "that big, *orange* sound") that it left competitors literally gasping in awe; but it was Armstrong's rhythmic audacity that placed him head and shoulders above the rest. With the advent of his first recordings with Fletcher Henderson's Orchestra, in 1924, Louis single-handedly took a popular band with an energetic but unswinging beat and made it swing. He was that powerful, than influential, that great.

Harmonically, however, Armstrong confined his excursions outside the tonality of a piece to his "breaks"—two bars at the end of a sixteen-bar chorus—or to out-of-tempo intros and outros. In a way he had to, because the majority of jazz players in the 1920s, even his classically-trained pianist-wife, Lillian Hardin, could not integrate the classical harmonic concept into the pop-jazz framework. This is not, of course, because they were completely *ignorant* of classical "changes"—even the self-taught Jelly Roll Morton was familiar with the music of Bizet and Verdi from his visits to the French Opera House in New Orleans—but simply because it took players with Armstrong's genius to figure out *how they fit into the surrounding harmonic framework.* This, by the way, is not merely a problem for jazz of the 1920s, but a continuing problem even today. The only real answer is to find supporting players with ears good enough to "follow the leader" into further-out harmonic realms; if the lead soloist treads on foreign harmonic soil during his (her) solo, the supporting players in the harmonic base (piano, bass) must follow. If they don't, the result is chaos.

Roppolo did pretty much the same thing as Armstrong, except that in the NORK there were two supporting players—pianist Elmer Schoebel and bassist Steve Brown—who could occasionally follow Roppolo, for a couple of bars at least, into odd (for jazz) harmonic territory. And Beiderbecke, in 1924 the most harmonically advanced of all, was using passing tones and whole-tone scales at a time when the majority of players, Armstrong included, were still learning how to go a little out of the tonal center in their breaks. When Bix played a solo on an established jazz piece, e.g., *Ostrich Walk, Tiger Rag,* or *At the Jazz Band Ball,* he too was forced to confine his wildest excursions to intros or breaks. Once in a while, when he did throw in an odd lick while the piano was backing him, the resultant clash would make one or the other sound "wrong."

There were only two alternatives, in the mid-1920s, to the solutions posed above. One was to re-write standard tunes, using substitute harmonies and rhythms in lieu of the more "conventional" ones, but this solution seemed not to occur to the majority of jazz musicians until around 1926 or 1927. The other was to create your own compositions, utilizing whatever "odd" harmonies (for jazz) you so desired. Again, it was Jelly Roll Morton who showed the way, with his original creations *The Pearls* and *New Orleans Joys (Blues)*, both recorded in 1923 for Gennett. For the white Wolverines, their main (and only) contributor in this respect was Hoagy Carmichael (1899-1981), whose composition *Riverboat Shuffle* varied not only the "normal" harmonic patterns of popular song-forms but, especially in the introductory chorus (or "verse"), an irregular, asymmetric pulse. When the Wolverines recorded this in Richmond on 6 May 1924, it all but set the jazz world on its ear. One can be sure that it was a staple in their repertoire by August, and that young Red Nichols heard and appreciated its uniqueness.

Back in New York, in September, Nichols joined Lanin's orchestra, partly so he could be close to Miff Mole. From this point on, all of Nichols's musical activity would center around New York. Aside from the good money that Lanin paid highly-competent sidemen like Nichols and Mole, he had since worked out a system of "record contracting" that appealed greatly to Nichols's business sense. Under this system, Lanin refused to sign exclusive contracts with any one label, one reason why Victor and Columbia refused his services, but would record for several different labels at once. Since in those days most labels would not give most artists royalties on the number of copies sold, Lanin simply ran up his bids for the amount he could get for each side recorded (roughly $50). This way, he could re-record the same tune, and even the same arrangement, for two or three or four labels within, say, a week's time. He also discovered that certain companies were interrelated, which meant that he could have a single master emerge on two or three "different" labels simultaneously, and be paid for each first-time issue. Red learned many of Lanin's "contracting" techniques, and began using them to good advantage by the end of 1925.

Nichols also formed his own small band, The Red Heads, for an engagement at the Pelham Heath Inn in December 1924. Once Bix left the Wolverines, to be replaced by Jimmy McPartland for a while before they broke up for good, Berton was Red's drummer. The band also included Joe Venuti and mellophonist Dudley Fosdick, who later played for many years with Guy Lombardo. The presence of Fosdick, aside from his abilities as a jazz soloist and the fact that he was in and out of the band for the next three years, is of paramount interest. The mellophone is an odd instrument, with piston rather than rotary valves and a range similar to that of a French horn; thus it is not really an ideal "bass" instrument, like the tuba or bass saxophone, but an instrument used for "color," as the French horn is. The use of French horns in jazz dates from a much later period, specifically the Claude Thornhill band with arranger Gil Evans (1942); but its use by Nichols even at this early date indicates that he was at least thinking along similar lines. He wanted an instrument that could provide a mellow balance to the high-pitched and generally shrill sounds of trumpet, violin and clarinet.

In January 1925 Bix Beiderbecke, already in and out of the Goldkette organization (for the first time; he would rejoin in mid-1926), was looking for free-lance work. Gennett, who had already lost several of their jazz "names" through attrition or defection, was more than willing to give one of their former stars a chance to make a few sides. On January 26 Bix, in conjunction with drummer Tom Gargano and four members of the Goldkette band—clarinetist Don Murray, trombonist Tommy Dorsey, pianist Paul Mertz, and banjoist Howdy Quicksell—recorded two sides. The second of these, *Toddlin'* *Blues,* was basically a good-natured "jam" by six very drunk musicians (they had taken a jug of corn liquor to the studio with them). But the first, *Davenport Blues,* was one of only two original compositions that Beiderbecke would ever record, the second being his famous piano solo *In a Mist* (1927). Like Carmichael's *Riverboat Shuffle,* *Davenport Blues* was an original piece, utilizing whole-

tone breaks as well as a funky "bridge" passage that Bix
literally improvised into being. Also like *Riverboat Shuffle,* it was considered "revolutionary" in its day, and had a
profound effect on the white jazz scene.

Nichols bought the record. He listened. He learned. And
he made a decision. Henceforth, his small recording
groups would work, whenever he was allowed to, with
original compositions and rewritten standards. His was
the first jazz group to do so to such an extent, and it created a "pocket" outside the normal ken of what jazz bands
were doing, musically, or should be doing, commercially.

2. Into the Pocket

(1925-November 1926)

In retrospect, it is somewhat incredible that the musical experiments of Nichols, Mole, and Berton should find such ready acceptance in the record studios of their time. Granted, there was a "jazz-age" dance market "boom" on, when a great deal of material, good, bad, and indifferent, was recorded prolifically by various labels, and paying a group of eight or less musicians was certainly cheaper than a fifteen- or twenty-piece orchestra. And yet, when one surveys the Nichols output, one finds an absolute minimum of vocals, which were so often considered essential to "selling" a song (and, in turn, a record), and also a minimum of recognizable "pop" tunes with which record buyers of the time were familiar.

Even more to the point, there were few titles among the originals that Nichols recorded which are even played today by many "trad jazz" bands. Clarinetist and jazz historian Frank Powers has assured me that *some* of this repertoire is played by *some* trad bands, from time to time. But a greal deal of it remains in the grooves of these now-ancient discs, and nowhere else.

One could say that the reason for this is that the level of technique required for a replication of the Nichols-Mole performances is sometimes beyond the capabilities of many trad players. But this isn't entirely true. Granted, Nichols, Mole, Berton, Arthur Schutt, and Jimmy Dorsey represented a level of instrumental virtuosity which was unusual for its time *in jazz,* and many other players who had similar techniques (then) were not jazz musicians. But technique has gradually improved over the years, so that now one can often hear players in trad bands who would have been considered astounding in 1925. The real problem is that the majority of trad players either (1) rebel against the formal structure of Nichols's aesthetic, prefer-

ring a looser, more emotional approach to jazz, or (2)
completely fail to understand that Nichols's formal structure was the underlying impetus of his aesthetic, and as a
result use these compositions for mere "taking off" in an
improvisatory sense without retaining the overall balance
and shape.

Oddly, however, what sounds so orderly and pre-planned
on the records was not necessarily conceived that way. In
a 1937 interview with British correspondent B.M. Lytton-
Edwards, Nichols asserted that the "'tidy mind of jazz,
refining influence' stuff they attribute to me is bull. Actually, when I started, my ideas were wild and woozy... We
were sometimes sober! But rehearsed? No. The intros
and codas were set, the rest genuinely busked [faked]."
Yet, in the same interview, Red made his prejudices in
this direction quite clear. "A gin-soaked bunch, however
inspired individually, is usually so darned individual that
the general effect is smeary. My bad boys produced good
jazz because they were technically trained musicians; not
just haywire hobos with a flair for rhythm. Something in
their equipment stopped them losing balance, however
merry. Our records were good in spite of, and not
because of, liquor."[1] The mixture, then, becomes clear:
musically ordered minds, trying to do something new and
original while still having fun.

With all that in mind, it is fascinating to go back to 26
February 1925, when the Nichols saga began in earnest
with a session at Columbia's studios in New York. The
band was rather large in contrast to most of the records
that followed; Mole was not present; and, in fact, the
personnel comprised what was then the bulk of the Lanin
band. But the musical approach was subtly different, and
as we shall see it presaged a new era in jazz performance.

Before beginning the musical analyses, it should be pointed out that I have heard and evaluated more than 300

---

[1] Lytton-Edwards, B.M., *Pennies to Pounds. Rhythm Magazine,* October 1937, pp. 40, 43.

performances by the various Nichols-Mole groups; a complete listing will be found in the appendix, along with original labels and numbers of issue. I have, however, reduced the number of recordings to undergo detailed analysis to less than 200. This was done for three reasons: to save space, to eliminate discussions of dull or uninteresting performances, and to bypass those alternate takes or remakes which did not improve on the original. And yet, though each recording may not receive a thorough examination, all are at least mentioned in passing. My intent was not to alienate those who have a particular fondness for a recording I dislike, but merely to bring attention to those arrangements and performances which *are* unique in ways that illustrate Nichols's genius.

LANIN'S RED HEADS: Nichols, Hymie Farberman, ct; Herb Winfield, tb; Chuck Muller, cl/a-sx; Dick Johnson, Lucien Smith, cl/s-sx/t-sx; Bill Krenz, p; Tony Colucci, bj; Joe Tarto, tu; Vic Berton, dm. 26 February 1925.

On 15 January 1925, a huge choral group calling itself the Associated Glee Clubs of America crammed themselves into Victor's Camden studios to record *The Lost Chord.* This record is not especially valuable musically, and in fact is all but forgotten today; but what made it special, then, is that it was the first electrical recording made in America. Western Electric had been experimenting with carbon microphones, the same kind then used in radio transmission, for more than a year, and had found that by shortening the range needed for transmission it could produce a richer, more realistic sound in a controlled studio environment.

Victor had been the first major label to purchase rights to the patent, but Columbia did not follow until approximately two months later. Purchasing the rights was an expensive proposition, at least at first, and most of the minor labels could not participate for two to three years. Yet, oddly, lowly Gennett jumped into the fray shortly after Victor did, probably so as not to lose whatever ground they felt they had gained since their lateral-cut patent victory. As a result, while Red Nichols was making these acoustic recordings in New York, the Gennett studios in Richmond, Indiana were already planning their first electrics.

It should be pointed out, for the benefit of those who are not music historians, that "blues" in the 1920s did not always mean the twelve-bar format that evolved in the South from field chants and hollers. Richard M. Jones wrote an eight-bar blues, *Trouble in Mind*, in 1921, and many of the popular songs published and marketed as "blues" during the remainder of the decade were actually sixteen-bar songs that merely bore a superficial resemblance to the blues form. *Davenport Blues* was just such a tune; so was Jelly Roll Morton's *Wolverine Blues;* and so was the first song recorded by "Lanin's Red Heads," Charlie Davis's *Jimtown Blues.*

This piece is in F, and was rearranged from the stock by Einar Swan, composer of *When Your Lover Has Gone.* An out-of-tempo brass intro is followed by two bars of clarinet, uptempo, at ♩ =192, then by two separate themes. The first, played by the two cornets with soprano sax, follows the blues pattern (8+8), but does so with a jagged 2+2+4 melody. The second, a repeated reed riff with a banjo break in bar seven, is played by the two clarinets with cornet "cushion" in a syrupy, vaudeville style. Krenz's piano solo, based on the chords of the second melody, is strictly ragtime; then comes Nichols, punctuated by banjo and tuba. A short break by Winfield leads to a whole-tone ensemble passage (Example 1); the top line is played by cornet (Nichols), the bottom line (an octave higher, but *softer)* by clarinet. There are banjo breaks, then the whole-tone break again in abridged fashion, then an ensemble variation, somewhat ragtimey. Muller's alto sax solo follows in vaudeville slap-tongue style; there is a clarinet break (Johnson?) with glisses; then a good, clean trombone break by Winfield. The melody is then played

Example 1: *Jimtown Blues,* ensemble break.

somewhat straight by Nichols while a clarinet improvises around him. A final drum thud ends it.

Red often claimed that Fletcher Henderson's band was a strong influence on him, and this recording proves it. Unlike most full-band Lanin recordings, Nichols uses each instrument available to him, including the soprano, alto, and tenor saxes played by the three reedmen. Indeed, the textural diversity is quite remarkable for its time; and one must remember that, in February 1925, the Henderson band not only didn't swing any better than this but was actually less harmonically advanced. True, Henderson's crew played numbers in odd, difficult keys, a habit they continued throughout their history. But before the addition of Louis Armstrong, and for some time after, they seldom played anything like the whole-tone passage above.

The second number made at this session was, astonishingly, Morton's *King Porter Stomp.* This was astonishing for three reasons. First, except for the New Orleans Rhythm Kings, no white bands were playing Morton this early, at least on record. Second, this arrangement predates the Morton Victors by nearly two years. And thirdly, *King Porter* was one number that Morton conspicuously failed to arrange for band! Nichols's version may have come from the stock; let us see what he made of it.

The opening strains are in Ab, at a tempo of ♩=180 which is rather relaxed compared to the various "swing" versions by Henderson, Benny Goodman, Count Basie, Glenn Miller, and Teddy Hill. There is a staid four-bar intro; the first theme is played with little variation, the second features breaks for trombone (Winfield) and tuba (Tarto). The repeat is more unusual, featuring suspended chords in bars 1 and 3; the alto sax break (Example 2), with added

tenor in the last beat of bar 3 and the first beat of bar 4, is
rather astounding, utilizing octave leaps, passing tones,
and a D-diminished chord that the Morton of 1925 would
never have thought of.   Quick-burst breaks by Nichols,
Krenz, and Smith (on tenor) lead to the famous trio theme.

Example 2: *King Porter Stomp*, alto sax break.

A clarinet solo (Muller?), not really good but odd, follows; Krenz's piano is more Morton-like, though sticking
close to the melody.   Then comes some imaginative
orchestration, alternating the tuba with "stride" chords in
the other instruments, to provide a remarkable simulation
of Morton's penultimate chorus in his 1923 solo piano
recording.   The piece passes through Morton's own ending
of Db^7 to an even more remote augmented Db minor ninth.

Again, it should be pointed out to those unfamiliar with
recordings of the era that Morton's first band recordings,
made acoustically in 1924, also did not swing.   Moreover,
there is only a bit of the imaginative tone-color in them
that was to characterize the pianist's late 1926-1928 Red
Hot Peppers recordings, and certainly nothing comparable
to the alto break in Example 2 or this odd ending.   If
Morton helped inspire Nichols, this session is ample evidence that the influence worked the other way round as
well.

In the second week of March, Bix Beiderbecke blew into
New York and stayed with Red for about seven days.   Un-
like Bix, Red was not a drinker—liquor made him ill—but
Bix had a piano brought in, as well as a few jugs of bath-

tub gin. and kept Red up all hours of the night playing
things for him while they were both smashed. Because he
wasn't much of a drinker, Red's tolerance wasn't as good
as Bix's; as a result, by his own admission, he woke up
hung over on more than one occasion, laboring through
his commercial dance dates and recording sessions. As
Red himself put it, "How I got through them in that con-
dition I'll never know. There was one morning that we
hadn't been to bed and I was really afraid that I couldn't
get through the date, so I asked Bix to go along with me
and help me out. In return I'd split the money with him.
He agreed. Who this was for I'll probably never know,
cause it was a case of the blind leading the blind."[2]

Since no recording featuring both Nichols and Beiderbecke has ever come to light, one assumes that Red managed to pull through by himself. The piano came to an
even more crashing halt than Bix's stay. On his last day
with Red, Bix invited Joe Venuti, Eddie Lang, and a few
of "his boys" to Red's apartment. Venuti took five-dollar
bets on which tone or tones would predominate if all the
keys on the piano were hit at once; then he, Lang, and two
others, to Nichols's horror, picked up the piano and threw
it out the window. According to Red, all they could hear
was cracking wood and snapping strings. Joe handed
everyone's five dollars back with the line, "What the hell
are you crying about? You got your money back, didn't
you??!?"

That was the Roaring Twenties.

The next Lanin's Red Heads date, in May 1925, was electrically recorded with the same band as above. Yet though
the improved sonics help us hear the purity of Nichols's
tone, and the drive of Berton's drums, the arrangements
are pretty much standard dance-band fare of the period.
Flag That Train (To Alabam') is a little better than *I
Wouldn't Be Where I Am* in that they use a quote from

---

2 Sudhalter, Richard & Evans, Philip, *Bix: Man and Legend* (ibid), p. 134.

Dixie for the modulation to Nichols's solo, and then suddenly transpose from Db to E for the ride-out.

GOLDIE'S SYNCOPATORS: Nichols, Frank Cash, ct; Tommy
Dorsey, tb; Jimmy Dorsey, Arnold Brilhart, cl/a-sx; Freddy
Cusick, t-sx; Adrian Rollini, bs-sx; Irving Brodsky, p; Tom Felline,
bj; Stan King, dm. 4 May 1925.

The same day he made *Flag That Train (To Alabam'),*
Red slipped into the Pathé studios to join the California
Ramblers, an excellent white jazz band managed by Ed
Kirkeby (later Fats Waller's manager) that played at the
Ramblers Inn in Pelham, New York, and later toured
(sometimes with Nichols). The personnel varied widely,
though the Dorseys and Rollini (more of whom later) were
usually constants. The first title made that day, *Dustin'
the Donkey,* is a pleasant, semi-commercial romp, as most
Ramblers records were; but the second, a spirited version
of the well-known *Tiger Rag,* created such a sensation in
1925 that no less than *ten other labels* leased the master
for issue, the most common versions (Domino and Apex)
being released under the monicker of "Goldie's Syncopators." Other pseudonyms were "The New Orleans Jazz
Band" (Banner), "Missouri Jazz Band" (Regal), "Dixie
Jazz Band" (Oriole 984), and "Ted White's Collegians"
(Oriole 1544, later using the Whoopee Makers's *Tiger
Rag* on the same number record, under the same pseudonym).

This record is scarcely known today, except to period collectors, yet its profligate disbursement in 1925 indicates
that it was highly thought of, and sold well. Though it
lies somewhat outside the scope of this book, it is interesting to note that, perhaps as a reaction to the commercial
arrangement that preceded it, the band refused to soften its
approach. It is played in A, at about the same tempo as
the NORK recording. In the opening ensemble on the "A"
theme (verse), Nichols never touches the melody. Then
comes the "B" theme (bridge) with Jimmy Dorsey's clari-

net on the breaks, the second of which pays homage to Leon Roppolo. The "trio" ensemble is followed by Tommy Dorsey on trombone, sounding very much like Mole (who was his early model) for a half-chorus; then Nichols, also showing some Roppolo influence (with Bix-like whole tones in the break). There is a piano break, then a soft, syncopated ensemble with a break from Rollini's bass sax.

THE COTTON PICKERS: Nichols, ct; Mickey Bloom, ct/mlph; Miff Mole, tb; Chuck Muller, cl; Alfie Evans, C-sx; Rube Bloom, p; Harry Reser, bj; Tarto, tu; Phil Role, dm. 21 August 1925.

This is another little-known session, yet one which *does* fit into the pattern of the Red Heads/Five Pennies concept. It was Miff Mole's first jazz recording with Nichols, as well as their first recording for Brunswick, the company that would be better known for the Five Pennies discs about two years later. Like Pathé, Brunswick was a little slow in getting the rights to electrical recording, though (as we shall see) they possessed it within a half-year of this session. *If You Hadn't Gone Away,* the second number made on this date, was a standard dance tune in both orchestration and structure. None of the solos are particularly adventurous, and it was obviously a stab at commercialism.

But the other number made that day was Morton's *Milenberg Joys.* Red had already recorded it, on July 21, with a very commercial-sounding contingent from Max Terr's orchestra called the Seven Missing Links (the jazz effects spoiled by Sam Lewis's awful trombone and Jimmy Johnston's clunky, stiff-sounding bass sax); but here we have a solid jazz performance, and again it is fascinating to contrast this arrangement with the one that Morton himself recorded as a guest artist with the NORK. The tempo is faster, for one thing; for another, it begins with an original eight-bar intro, extended to twelve via a two-bar piano break. Then Jelly's "A" theme is heard, with whole-tone

chords substituted in bars 3 and 4; the rhythm is altered in
a later break. Red also uses whole-tones in the transposition (bridge). Then comes a Nichols variation on the main
chorus, with Mole in a two-bar break over tuba and banjo
punctuation. Bloom's piano transposes from Db to Bb for
Mole's solo (with piano break), then back to Db for the
ride-out, ending on Morton's suspended, unresolved chord.

Throughout the band's early period, the tuba playing of
Joe Tarto (1902-1986) is not only a continual pleasure but
immensely important to the band's concept of swing—at
least, as "swing" was understood by the majority of musicians in 1925-1927. Born Joseph Tortoriello in Newark,
New Jersey, Tarto was a late bloomer as compared to
Nichols, Berton, and Mole. He began his musical studies,
on the trombone, at the age of twelve, but like Mole he
was immensely gifted and soon became a virtuoso of the
instrument. He lied about his age in order to enlist in the
Army in 1917, where service bandleader Dick Schaff
switched him from trombone to tuba because he was short
of bass players. Like Nichols and Mole, Tarto was bitten
by the jazz bug, and on 29 June 1922 he made his first
jazz record for Paramount in the company of trombonist
Ray Stillwell, pianist Arthur Schutt (of whom more later),
and drummer Chauncey Morehouse. He was a stalwart in
the band of Paul Specht before joining Sam Lanin in late
1924, where he found like-minded partners in Red and
Miff. Like them, too, his services were constantly in
demand for white dance-band dates, and in 1927 he alternated on the string bass with equally superb results in
order to modernize his sound and keep up with the times.

Undoubtedly his former duty as a trombonist led him to
revolutionize the concept of tuba-playing. Instead of
oom-pahing remorselessly on beats one and three, as the
majority of players did in those days, Tarto rode the beat
in a light, swinging manner; his lip work was astonishingly fleet, including the ability to play rapid triplets in his
breaks while most brass bassists were still trying to break
free of marching-band style. This virtuosity tied in neatly

with Berton's light yet propulsive drumming, creating a
ground beat for the soloists to "take off" over that was
both consistent in time (a frequent fault of many white *and*
black bands of the era) and more modern in concept than
the ragtime sound then prevalent. He was also a bit of a
writer and arranger, and in fact his composition *Black
Horse Stomp* was recorded by Fletcher Henderson—another example of the black-white crossover influence that
some writers try to claim didn't exist.

The Lanin's Red Heads session of 19 October goes back
to a more commercial approach, with arrangements by
George Crozier of the Jean Goldkette band. Dick Johnson
plays a violin solo that sounds a tad like Venuti on *I'm
Gonna Hang Around My Sugar,* and there are nice variations by Nichols and Mole before the ride-out. In some
respects *Five Foot Two* is even worse, since the players
stick fairly close to the melody and the arrangement centers around a perfectly dreadful vocal by one Art Gillham;
but there is a very offbeat clarinet intro (Example 3)
which the band was to use to good effect a month later.

Example 3: *Five Foot Two,* intro.

Ten days after these Red Heads and Syncopators dates,
there was one with the Earl Carroll's Vanities Orchestra,
then conducted by reedman Ross Gorman. And, despite
the not-inconsiderable interest of the February and August
sessions, this is where the real experimentation begins.

ROSS GORMAN & HIS EARL CARROLL ORCH.: Nichols, ct;
Donald Lindley, James Kozak, tp; Mole, tb; Gorman, cl/a-sx/br-
sx/leader; Alfie Evans, cl/a-sx/vln; Harold Noble, cl/a-sx/t-sx; Billy
McGill, cl/t-sx; Barney Acquelina, bs-sx; Nick Koupoukis, fl/pic;
Jack Harris, Saul Sharrow, vln; Arthur Schutt, p; Dick

McDonough, bj; Tony Colucci, g; David Grupp, dm. 29 October 1925.

Arthur Schutt (1902-1965), an itinerant musician from the white "novelty" piano tradition, was one of the first band pianists to play extended solos in a style which merged elements of ragtime, stride, blues, and classical techniques. While not denigrating the work of Krenz, who was certainly an accomplished technician, Schutt went beyond him in a way that compared favorably to the band work of Morton, James P. Johnson and Earl Hines. He could and did expand the tonal palette that Nichols was struggling to create in a way not unlike Beiderbecke; and it is not surprising to learn that Schutt, like so many of his generation, idolized Bix.

Like Nichols, Schutt had studied with his own father, Gustav, and originally planned to be a concert pianist. He made his professional debut playing for silent movies in 1915; in 1918 he joined the Paul Specht Orchestra, and in 1921 he met Joe Venuti. Soon after that he began to play in many bands. In 1924 he heard and met Beiderbecke, who changed his life and musical conception. Schutt was one of the first jazz pianists (if not the very first) to use passing chords as other soloists used passing tones. This, of course, was an element of jazz pianism that Art Tatum (1909-1956) elevated to a high art, so indirectly Schutt, like Lee Simms, was an influence on the man many consider the greatest jazz soloist of all time. By the time this session was cut, Schutt was already making a big impression on those leaders for whom he worked; and there is little doubt that his big technique, imagination and swinging abilities made an instant impression on Red Nichols. From the point of this session, he became a semi-permanent member of Red's small bands.

The tune this band recorded was *Rhythm of the Day,* with composer credits reading Murphy-Lindley. The credit for this remarkable arrangement is not forthcoming, but I wouldn't be surprised to learn that it was a Nichols-Schutt collaboration. Rhythmically, there is still much here that reverts to a pre-Beiderbecke and Armstrong concept of swing; but harmonically, and in its subtle use of orchestral colors, this is a landmark recording in the annals of big-band jazz. Considering that the Vanities was a popular touring show that played on Broadway, a clone of the more famous Ziegfeld Follies, their band was ostensibly expected to play stock show arrangements, not avant-garde jazz, as in fact they did on the first tune of this session, *I'm Sitting on Top of the World.* On this lone recording date in 1925, however, they "got away" with one.

Despite the jerky, somewhat ragtime beat and inflection, the harmonic audacity and intelligent construction still startle the ear seventy years later. The piece begins with trumpets (and then saxes) playing a repeated motif of descending chromatic triplets; this leads directly to the principal melody, played by the saxes in thirds, with occasional comment by the trombone (Example 4). This weird theme then modulates, quite logically I might add, into a more common riff in F^7/Bb major, though vacillation with Bb minor makes the base key ambiguous. The central "bridge" sounds more conventional, yet is perfectly in keeping with the preceding and succeeding sections.

Example 4: *Rhythm of the Day,* "A" theme.

Two full choruses of Mole's trombone then ensue, his playing technically adept and harmonically daring. This, in turn, is followed by two choruses of muted trumpet. Many writers have attributed this solo to Nichols, but I disagree. For one thing, the tone—even muted—sounds unusually tentative and thin for him; even the 1922 Syncopated Five session showed more forcefulness in muted passages. For another, the solo is harmonically *un* adventurous, following safe, secure little patterns within the whole-tone maze in the first eight bars of each chorus. Red is definitely the open cornet (trumpet?) riding over the last chorus by the full band; but who is the muted trumpet who comes back for the coda? It couldn't be Red —he had no time to put a mute in his horn—and yet, it sounds exactly (in both tone and style) like the author of the two-chorus solo. Who was it? My guess is trumpeter Donald Lindley; after, he wrote the piece, so who better to get the muted solo nods?

In these and previous pieces, one notes that Red was working whole tones somewhat to death. But he was not alone; as time went on in the 1920s, the use of the whole-tone scale to denote something "weird" or "modern" became rampant. Yet, as authors like Gunther Schuller have pointed out, no other musical device sounds so dated today, or more redolent of the Jazz Age. The reason is that the whole-tone scale cannot he developed musically; all it can do is stay there, startling the ear for a bit, before it is forced to modulate into something more tonal. Yet *Rhythm of the Day* (which should, incidentally, have been more appropriately titled *Harmonics of the Day)* avoids most of the traps of such later works as James P. Johnson's *You've Got to Be Modernistic* or Morton's *Freakish* by virtue of its vacillating, broken-field melodic structure, which is more adaptable to the following (though inevitable) tonal modulations, not to mention easier to improvise on. All of which goes to show that Donald Lindley was an interesting composer, if not a particularly good improvisor, though he wrote books on how to play hot jazz.

THE HOTTENTOTS: Nichols, Mole, Bloom, Berton; Dick Johnson, cl. 11 November 1925.

With names like "The Cotton Pickers" and "The Hottentots," it would seem that the Brunswick-Vocalion group was intent on promoting Red's band under the guise of being black. "Cotton Pickers," of course, was the name that Jean Goldkette later gave to William McKinney's all-black orchestra, when they recorded for Victor under Don Redman's leadership; but it was also a name used beginning in 1922 for various manifestations of the Original Memphis Five, and in fact a name used by record companies through 1929 for various small white band sessions. "The Hottentots" (and, later, "The Six Hottentots") were Red's alone. He wasn't proud of the name, and seldom mentioned these discs in later years, yet the music is good and they fall within his evolving style.

Down and Out Blues is another eight-bar piece, this time in typical medium blues tempo. The theme is simple and attractive, leaning downwards; after the opening ensemble there are breaks by Mole, then Johnson and Nichols together. Then comes a key change, followed by a theme with an ambiguous major-minor vacillation. Nichols was not a very convincing blues player, but he "smears" his notes well for a classically-trained musician. There is another theme which is essentially sustained chords with piano breaks, then clarinet over weaving brass chords. The performance is notable for its loose yet connected swing. This is followed by a double-time chorus, then back down to the original tempo for a chorus before a rising, dramatic coda.

The Camel Walk is an angular, quickly-moving New York Dixieland tune with shifting tonalities and asymmetrical phrase-shapes. There is the standard four-bar intro; an opening ensemble, then alto sax with the *bass drum* cutting through cleanly. This was a major accomplishment for an acoustic recording! An ensemble break is followed by a Nichols-led ensemble with Mole counterpoint; then a syncopated passage alternating between B and Eb. There is a trombone break and solo, then a final ensemble.

THE RED HEADS: Nichols, Mole, Schutt, Berton; Bobby Davis,
Fred Morrow, cl/a-sx. 15 November 1925.

Perhaps spurred by the increased sophistication of *Rhythm
of the Day*, this Nichols sextet explores a much more
daring sound-world, rhythmically and harmonically. They
were beginning to break free of the shackles of pop-
schlock dancebandom, and in fact for more than a year
they rarely sullied their jazz with a singer. It is rather
astounding that Pathé, Paramount, Perfect, Edison, Brunswick, OKeh, Vocalion, and Victor left them alone to de-
velop and hone their craft; as we shall see, there was little
in these arrangements or performances that could possibly
have appealed to Charleston-crazy teenagers of the time.
Little of their repertoire were "popular" pieces; many were
rather complex originals; and, though they still had some
way to go from this point, the group's concept of swing
was improving session by session.

The reader must bear in mind that NOT all jazz of this
time, especially small-band jazz, was as meticulously pre-
planned and rehearsed as Nichols's. One case in point is
the famous series of recordings by Louis Armstrong and
his Hot Five (and Seven), where rehearsal and pre-planning were rudimentary at best. As Baby Dodds said, "We
weren't a bunch of fellows to write down anything. If
there was any writing involved, Lil (Hardin, then married
to Armstrong) would write down what the musicians were
supposed to do." Lil herself added that "We had no idea
in the beginning that jazz was going to be that important,
that someday people would want to know how we started,
what we did, what records we made, and it's amusing to
read in books people telling why we did this. I'm glad
they know, because we didn't."[3]

---

[3] Quotes from John Chilton's notes for *Louis Armstrong Hot Fives Vol. II* (CBS CK-44253).

Red Nichols was like Louis Armstrong in this respect: he
didn't think, in 1925, that someday his work would be
dissected and discussed like this. To him, this was just a
job, albeit a job from which he derived a great deal of
satisfaction and pleasure. Yet his inquisitive and inventive
mind, always open to new sounds, different voicings and
imaginative rhythms, was similar to Morton's. It was a
steel trap, in which the various influences around him
would be swallowed whole, then digested and dissemina-
ted in his band performances. There is no question but
that, as his recording career progressed, Nichols not only
took professional pride in what he did but sought to
establish his own musical character. To that extent he
succeeded handsomely. Though his band's style was to
change drastically, both the pre- and post-1928 recordings
inhabit sound-worlds as uniquely Nichols as his competitors's recordings were uniquely Morton or uniquely
Ellington. The blacks were Hot, and influenced the immediate future, while he and his white musicians were
Cool, and influenced the far future.

Fallen Arches, despite its small-band arrangement, has a
surprising swing-era feel, not only in the tune's layout and
style but in its execution: only Morrow's alto sax solo
sounds stiff and ragtimey. It is played in F, with an introduction reminiscent of *Dippermouth Blues.* Nichols and
the saxes play the melody, with breaks by Mole. An ascending whole-tone break leads to a Nichols solo with
saxes, very good; then comes Morrow's bad alto chorus.
Red saves the day, however, with a marvelously-construct-
ed solo, reminiscent of mid-1930s Max Kaminsky, full of
leaps, blue notes, and double-time figures. It is astonishing to hear Red's growth as an artist in nine short months.
An ensemble ride-out plays with the time, Nichols's staccato tonguing being particularly interesting and effective.
Nervous Charlie is a more typical 1920s piece, with its
brusque, choppy melody, stop-time phrasing, and whole-
tone chords, yet it too commands attention. It resuscitates
the *Five Foot Two* intro from October 19 (Example 3),
but this time it leads to a Nichols original with leaping

phrases, and beat-abridgements that push the pulse out of
its expected time frame. The saxophone chorus is lifted
from *Farewell Blues,* after a modulation from F to Bb.
Mole's solo is interesting and virtuosic, based on *Farewell's* changes. Few if any jazz trombonists in 1925 could
play with such dead-center accuracy of intonation as this;
indeed, Mole's lip and slide techniques are so precise that
at times, here as well as in future recordings, he sounds as
if he were playing valve trombone. But he wasn't. Is
there any question as to why he was the role model for all
white trombonists, including Tommy Dorsey, Bill Rank,
and Glenn Miller? Granted, Rank and Miller failed because of inherently weak tones and imperfect techniques,
but for nearly a decade Dorsey sounded like an extension
of Mole.

Following Miff's solo, there is a bridge in G minor, then a
chromatic transposition to Ab major. There is a splash of
the relative minor (C) for color before a whole-tone break
brings us back to Ab. A diminished break leads to a clarinet in G major, where we stay for the brief ride-out.

Headin' for Louisville is an uptempo romp in C. There is
a clarinet intro with a brass cushion, then the melody is
played in what became known as New York Dixieland
style. There are nice breaks in the bridge, then a "B"
theme which leads to Nichols's surprisingly cautious solo.
Schutt's piano, by contrast, really swings, passing through
neighboring chromatics with aplomb. Then there is a
transposition to Eb for Mole's solo; perhaps spurred by
Artie's piano, his playing here is less imaginative but
more swinging than in *Charlie.* Bell-chords introduce a
pedestrian clarinet solo (Davis?) before Nichols's light,
staccato cornet rides things out.

THE HOTTENTOTS: Nichols, Mole, D. Johnson, L. Smith,
Bloom, Colucci, Berton. 8 January 1926.

We move back into electrical recordings with this, the
band's second session for Vocalion. Red always claimed

Fletcher Henderson as an inspiration, and these recordings prove it as both titles are "covers" of Henderson discs, a pair of tunes by the popular composer Billy Rose. *Nobody's Rose* is an uptempo jam number in G, the middle section based on the *I Ain't Got Nobody* chords. A glissando clarinet break by the little-known Johnson leads to the "B" theme, which exhibits great virtuosity in its execution. Then a quick transition to Eb for Mole's trombone solo, and back up to G for ensemble. Passing chords are used for the out-of-tempo coda.

Pensacola has a piano intro with brass punctuations. The opening theme alternates between G minor, F minor, and Eb major with audacity; the "B" theme features descending chromatics with clarinet breaks. Then we land, firmly, in Eb for an ensemble romp, followed by a trombone break and a syncopated coda.

ORIGINAL MEMPHIS FIVE: Nichols, ct; Mole, tb; Jimmy Lytell, cl; Frank Signorelli, p; Jack Roth, dm. 21 January 1926. Same, but add Tarto, tu; 23 January 1926.

One would think that Miff Mole's original group, long since having broken up, would be just a memory by January 1926. Yet for some reason Brunswick insisted on reviving the name (as Phil Napoleon did in 1931) for these Nichols sessions with Roth replacing Berton on drums; and, to make matters even more confusing, the last two selections were issued not on Brunswick but on its sister-label Vocalion, and not as "The Original Memphis Five" but as "The Hottentots"!

The music, nevertheless, is superb. *Chinese Blues,* the one number recorded twice in the two sessions (for the two different labels and pseudonyms), is a Fats Waller piece featuring a quasi-oriental intro before a medium-uptempo romp in G with E minor in the bridge. There is more quasi-oriental material in the "B" theme, but played with heat. Then comes a Mole solo with Nichols commentary, an ensemble break, and a G minor stop-time

chorus with a whole-tone break. Signorelli, a pianist
whose style lay somewhere between those of Bloom and
Schutt, uses passing tones in his four-bar break, followed
by the ride-out.

'Tain't Cold, by Harry Barris of Paul Whiteman's Rhythm
Boys, is played rather slowly at ♩=160 (4/4) with an intro
based on *Dippermouth Blues*. This leads to two ensemble
choruses on the jagged "A" theme (Example 5); clarinet
and trombone play the "B" theme, with Nichols hot in the
middle.   Then comes Mole's trombone, a whole-tone
break, then the "Trio," played sub-toned by Lytell's clarinet with stop-time chords before the ensemble ride-out.

Example 5: *Tain't Cold,* "A" theme.

Bass Ale Blues is a medium-slow piece by Signorelli in
Bb minor. The extended introduction turns into an attractive twelve-bar blues theme, the ensemble with tuba
swinging nicely, followed by clarinet over ensemble in a
transposition to Bb major. The second chorus starts with a
tuba solo; them come suspended chords, a three-bar tuba
break, and Dixie ensemble.   Indeed, the diversity in the
layout of choruses is astonishing.   Nichols's cornet doub-
les the time for a half-chorus, followed by a full-chorus
tuba solo (twelve bars) with clarinet "flutters" on beats 2
and 4; then double-time again before a return to tempo,
ending with an out-of-tempo coda with chimes.

If Nichols's claim that these pieces were only lightly
rehearsed is true, then *Bass Ale Blues* must truly stand as
one of the finest pieces of improvised jazz in existence.
Every note in every chorus has the inevitability of Beiderbecke's *Ostrich Walk* and *Clarinet Marmalade* solos, and
here we do not have to put up with drunken, out-of-tune
(and rhythm) ensembles.   But by this time Nichols and his

musicians were beginning to be old hands at producing three-minute masterpieces.

*   *   *   *   *   *

In early 1926, Earl Carroll was literally caught with his pants down in a wild, drunken party celebrating his birthday. The resultant scandal set back the popularity of his Vanities, a situation which lasted for months. In order to legitimize their image again, Ross Gorman was replaced as head of the Vanities orchestra by sober, classically-trained Donald Voorhees, who had a reputation as a moral, middle-class person. As we shall see, however, Voorhees was even more interested musically in what Nichols's little band was doing on records, and as a result helped push the young cornetist's fame into a new market.

THE RED HEADS: Nichols, Mole, Berton; Jimmy Dorsey, cl/a-sx; Alfie Evans, cl/t-sx; Rube Bloom, p; Arthur Fields, voc. 4 February 1926.

Jimmy Dorsey (1904-1957) was, of course, one of the most famous musicians of the ensuing Swing Era. Though softer-spoken than his younger brother Tommy, he was just as adept at needling people with his quick wit and Irish temper; he was also a somewhat better jazz musician, his solos (especially during the 1930s and 1940s) sounding more relaxed and inventive than Tommy's sometimes did. But that was in the 1930s; in the 1920s, Jimmy's idol was Rudy Wiedoft, a technically spectacular vaudeville saxophonist. Since Wiedoft was also an idol of Coleman Hawkins, we should not disparage a non-jazz influence on an eventual jazz player, but JD took longer to break free of the vaudeville-styled shackles of ragtime rhythm in his phrasing, and in some of the more complex numbers he played during the 1920s one notices that he was uncomfortable with unusual rhythms and chord patterns. Nevertheless, he was a virtuoso reedman, and his replacement of Bobby Davis on this early Red Heads session makes an immediate impact on the band as a whole.

Just as we noted that the Nichols band rarely got stuck with a vocalist, here we are with *Poor Papa (He Ain't Got Nothing at All)*, a Dixieland-styled number centered around Arthur Fields. Fields, along with Irving Kaufman and Billy Murray, were relics of the pre-jazz era when their homely or raggy vocals were all the rage. (Victor even dropped Al Jolson in 1913 because they were convinced he would never be as big a star as Irving Kaufman.) By the middle of the "Jazz Age," however, their singing not only sounded out of place but their voices had become heavier and less resilient to the new rhythms.

In the first chorus there is good, driving Nichols cornet and Dorsey clarinet. Dorsey's solo is more notable for Berton's outstanding drum work than for his own imagination. The bridge leads to a bad Fields vocal, then Nichols leads to an ensemble chorus with great drive and imagination before the outro.

The remake of *'Tain't Cold* is a vast improvement on the original—in fact, one of the greatest recordings they ever made. There is a new, more interesting intro, featuring a suspended cornet-clarinet chord (Db and the Eb below) with a break by Mole; this leads to the melody (Example 5), played by Nichols with Mole and Dorsey counterpoint. After Bloom's piano break, a nice polyphonic bridge leads to a very hot and imaginative Nichols cornet over the ensemble; then two bars of Mole's trombone, and an ascending chromatic break. There are quick alternations of whole-bar chords, 1 bar Mole, 2 bars Dixieland ensemble; this is repeated, except that the last ensemble becomes a *descending* chromatic break! Then comes Dorsey's alto sax for a full chorus, with marvelous underpinning by Bloom. (Though not as imaginative a soloist as Schutt, Bloom could swing when he wanted to—and he certainly wants to here.) Then comes Nichols, with highly imaginative phrase-shapes (one ending on the sixth below the tonic); there is an ensemble passage with cymbal breaks by Berton, to the end.

Hangover is a more uptempo piece, also in Eb, and the
only tune composed by both Nichols and Mole. It starts
with "drunken" chords played by the ensemble (Example
6) for a chorus, with ensemble breaks; then there is a
chorus with solo breaks by Dorsey and Berton. A full-
chorus solo by Bloom proves that, though he had a good
tone and technique, he was no Artie Schutt. Then comes
Nichols—a little stiff in places, and with a little fluff
(mark the date on the calendar!)—but generally imaginative. Then a ride-out, with Berton on woodblocks.

Example 6: *Hangover,* main theme.

At this point it should be mentioned that, somehow, Nichols managed to get Berton's drums better-recorded than
any other percussionist on acoustic records. I don't know
how he managed to do this, but it certainly wasn't Berton's doing: his other acoustic recordings, e.g., the Wolverines cuts from June 1924 on and the two sides he made
with Bix and the "Broadway Bellhops" in 1927, are so
under-recorded (as was usual for drums in those days) that
his instruments seldom register as being present at all.
But Nichols, apparently, not only appreciated Berton's
outstanding playing—even on woodblocks, he sounds like
a dancer rather than a pounder, the beat light and relaxed
rather than hot and heavy—but appreciated its value in
underpinning and propelling the solos and ensemble. If
the acoustic recording still sounds dated for some modern
listeners, the balance remains none the less extraordinary.

Another interesting aspect, for die-hard collectors of the
period, is the way Nichols managed to introduce creative
elements into even the most commercial dance-band dates
of the period. Though the recordings lie outside the scope
of this survey, it is interesting to hear how Nichols used
whole tones, key changes, and tempo-shifting in the intro-

ductions and breaks of otherwise "stock" arrangements played by the bands of Ben Selvin, Harry Reser, and (of course) Don Voorhees. Such fillips, as well as the occasional jazz solo by Nichols and Mole, often lifted these recordings above the mundane and placed them in a category close to, but not exactly, jazz.

WE THREE: Nichols, Schutt, Berton; Eddie Lang, g. 24 March 1926.

Salvatore Massaro, a.k.a. Eddie Lang, must be credited as the man who popularized the guitar in jazz; or, to be more precise, the man who made the banjo obsolete. He was still playing both instruments in 1926, but as this session proves his tendency was towards the guitar even in an acoustic setting. His sense of rhythm was so buoyant, lithe, and propulsively swinging, that he certainly would have been one of the Swing Era's great rhythm players had he not died after a tonsillectomy in early 1933.

This particular configuration, the trio that is sometimes a quartet, was highly unusual in the middle 1920s; indeed, it was not until the Benny Goodman Trio and Quartet, in the mid-1930s, that chamber jazz on so small a scale became common in public performance. One doubts that this configuration actually played together on the radio, just as Jelly Roll Morton's trios were recording-only groups, though of course we should take nothing for granted. The problems inherent in a group of this size are considerable. First, it is imperative that all members have a superb sense of jazz "time," as opposed to the typical dance-music beat of the era; and second, such small groups should interact in terms of coloration and tossing ideas back and forth. The afore-mentioned Morton trios certainly met these requirements, whether the clarinetist was Johnny Dodds, Omer Simeon or Barney Bigard; but Nichols seems to have had some trouble freeing himself of the rhythmic constraints of dance music, with which he was already inextricably identified.

The first title recorded this day, *Plenty Off Center,* is actually a trio of Nichols, Schutt, and Berton. There is an excellent Nichols intro, a Schutt break, and then an ambiguous, quirky melody. All three participants are in great form in the "A" theme; the "B" theme, played by Red, combines parade-band styling with smeared, off-rhythm, and off-tonal licks. Nichols's improvisation is somewhat stiff in the swing, but wonderfully imaginative. Schutt's breaks, on the other hand, swing mightily, as do Berton's drums. Red's next chorus is the best of all; the last, muted, is more polite, more conventional.

Trumpet Sobs substitutes Lang for Schutt (through most of it, anyway). It begins with an out-of-tempo intro by the guitarist, who then backs up an inventive Nichols. Eddie's single-string solo is slow, but contains some nice bluesy "note-bending." Red's muted chorus, by contrast, is safe. Schutt comes in for a brief break; the last chorus features Nichols in stop-time with Lang backing him. Schutt reappears for four bars, then the coda and out.

We shall discuss this combination in greater depth a little later on.

THE RED HEADS: Same as February 4, but omit Evans; Schutt replaces Bloom. 7 April 1926.

With Schutt back on piano, one would expect that this Red Heads session might be even finer than the one in February, but such is unfortunately not the case. Jimmy Dorsey sounds uncomfortable from the first note of the first piece, and in fact never really relaxes until the last selection *(Dynamite);* nevertheless, there are moments of interest in the first and third pieces.

Wild and Foolish, an uptempo swinger in Bb, is more interesting for the harmonic audacity of its ensemble than for the excellence of its breaks and solos (again, Mole and Berton excepted). This is one of those "cycle of fourths" pieces, but with a twist: except for the intro, the tonic is never touched. The principal melody is played over a succession of sub-dominant (Eb), relative 3rd (D⁷), then G⁷, C⁷, F⁷; but instead of returning to Bb, we go back to C⁷, D⁷, and G⁷...before returning to Eb to start over again. And when they resolve, of course, they are no longer in Bb but in C! The break is more firmly entrenched in Eb; Dorsey's clarinet solo is squawky in places, and neither very creative nor swinging. Red also plays it somewhat safe, but Mole runs up and down the trombone with audacity for two choruses. When Red comes back in, he is swinging hard, though JD is still off form.

Hi-Diddle-Diddle is a more conventional tune and arrangement, more pop than jazz, by Carlton Coon of the popular radio orchestra, the Coon-Sanders Nighthawks. Excepting Mole and Berton, who could apparently never play badly, even the solos and breaks are punk. Fletcher Henderson's *Dynamite,* however, is somewhat more creative, in Eb though the tonality keeps shifting to D⁷. After the intro, there is a first-chorus Dorsey alto sax solo with brass cushion; then, Charleston-styled breaks and a Dixie-styled ensemble chorus. Dorsey's clarinet is more technically secure here, but not any more swinging. Mole slips around with wry humor; then a stop-time chorus with Berton breaks, ensemble, and out.

THE RED HEADS: Nichols, Mole, Dorsey, Evans, Schutt, Berton; Leo McConville, tp; Dick McDonough, bj/g. 14 Sept. 1926.

Leo McConville (1900-1968) is, for some reason, one of the unsung heros of Twenties jazz. Born in Baltimore, he played trumpet with local bands at the age of fourteen, though he made his professional debut with the Louisiana Five in 1919. In the early 1920s he joined Jean Goldkette in Detroit, then did some vaudeville tours before working with the big bands of Paul Specht and Roger Wolfe Kahn. Though not the most scintillating of soloists, McConville was one of those players, like Charlie Spivak and Conrad Gozzo during the Swing Era, who could spark a band in

ensemble with his terrific drive and swing. One notices his beneficent effect almost immediately on this, one of the Red Heads' most consistently satisfying dates.

The second new addition to the band, guitarist Dick McDonough (1904-1938), was another unsung hero of sorts. Constantly living and playing in the shadow of Eddie Lang, McDonough did not have the all-around lift and drive of his more famous colleague; but he could swing, and his single-note playing was more fleet. He too contributes some superb moments to the group, and (again) Nichols had the foresight to record him well despite the continuing acoustic sound.

Alabama Stomp is the first recording of a Nichols band staple (they did it four more times, including alternate takes). It too is in Eb, taken at a bright ♩=112 in 2/4; the band is in great form, and seems to revel in the alternating Eb major and Ab minor chords. Mole's solo is virtuosic, though not much happens musically, but Leo drives the ensemble like Bix, and Nichols's solo dances and darts around McDonough's guitar. Berton peppers the ensemble; Schutt's piano is swinging, and the final ride-out includes four bars, at the very end, which alters the time in an interesting way (Example 7), Nichols's final high D coming as a sort of musical exclamation point!

Example 7: *Alabama Stomp,* coda.

Hurricane was yet another Nichols favorite, co-written by the leader and Goldkette pianist Paul Mertz; they waxed it on five different occasions, including this one. Except for Berton, the group sounds somewhat tentative at first; perhaps the harmonic and rhythmic complexities seemed a bit daunting. After a rhythm-altering intro, they play twelve bars in regular 4, followed by twelve of muted McCon-

ville trumpet. Then comes the fun: a Berton drum break,
two bars ensemble, drum break, then a descending chromatic passage (Example 8) ending with a drum break that
extends the time by one beat; then a Schutt piano break
that distorts the time even further, before a straight-ahead
chorus in 4. There is a McDonough guitar solo, with
Nichols in the break, and a Schutt solo that swings like
mad (though Dorsey is somewhat stiff in *his* break). The
ride-out has Berton playing a suitcase,[4] with Mole for
eight in the middle.

Example 8: *Hurricane,* cornet break.

After these two consecutive masterpieces, Barris's *Brown
Sugar* sounds like a relaxed finish to a brilliant session:
though more conventional, it is nonetheless swinging.
There are solos by McDonough, Mole (with Schutt and
Berton in top form), a rare Berton solo, then Nichols at his
most driving and inventive. There is an ensemble with
Berton on woodblocks; then a bass drum break and shout
from Berton, and out.

By this point one will have noticed the sheer diversity of
orchestration and brilliance of execution in Nichols's
groups. Though our appreciation at this point is somewhat
stunted by the acoustic sound, it is evident that Red found
a way of using every instruent well; moreover, he used
every instrument that each player was capable of handling
(except for Jimmy Dorsey's rather awkward cornet work).
When he had a man who could double on clarinet and alto
(Dorsey), or banjo and guitar (McDonough), or even triple
on clarinet, soprano, and alto (Alfie Evans), he utilized

---

[4] The bass drum suitcase was often used, on early jazz records, to produce swing without
the "booming" sound that could cause the cutting stylus to jump or mistrack.

their sound-colors in the presentation of his music. This is but one reason, aside from the harmonic and rhythmic difficulties of some of his scores, why his arrangements are so seldom played by trad-jazz bands nowadays. Despite the occasional lack of swinging, his small-group records display the highest level of virtuosity then available; and, though his groups did not have the completely *distinctive* ensemble sound of the Morton or Ellington bands, they nevertheless brought their "New York style" to a level of excellence unmatched by any but the very best of larger jazz orchestras.

RED AND MIFF'S STOMPERS: Nichols, Mole, J. Dorsey, Evans, Schutt, Tarto, Berton. 13 October 1926.

Red's next date was a rarity, recorded for the Edison company. Of course, Edison was the man who "invented" the phonograph (actually, he adapted it from a machine used to record Morse code), but he unwisely stayed with the cylinder method long after Emile Berliner's flat discs had proved it archaic. The difference was not merely in the shape of the recording, but its method of reproduction. Whereas the flat disc could produce a metal "mother," or stamper, from which hundreds or thousands of copies could be struck, each cylinder had to be individually recorded. As a result, Edison sessions generally consisted of singers or players focusing their talents into a large cone, to which fifty or a hundred tubes were connected; these tubes led to fifty or a hundred separate cylinder machines, where the actual recording took place. If the company predicted a record would become a big seller, the singer or player would perform it eight or ten times over, until they got as many copies as they wanted.

By the time Edison turned to flat discs, in 1914, he was far behind the times; and, like all other companies then in business, he had to restrict himself to the vertical-cut or "hill and dale" method. But Edison went them one further: his "Diamond Discs" were a full 1/4-inch thick, and

had to be played on an Edison machine. (Thankfully, the
Edison machines could also play Pathé, Starr, and all the
other vertical-cut labels.) The plus side, as we shall see,
was that each side of his 10" discs pushed the five-minute
mark while his competitors had to go to 12" just to try and
fit about four and a quarter minutes; but he was equally
slow in switching over from vertical to lateral-cut records,
holding out until 1927. Because of this, Edison disc releases by famous artists of the 1920s, both jazz and classical,
are rather rare collector's items. The Nichols discs are no
exception.

Alabama Stomp is, of course, a remake from the Red
Heads session of a month earlier; it is much the same in
format and execution, though I personally sense the loss of
McConville and McDonough. But *Stampede* is more
interesting. This was a Henderson big-band specialty,
recorded by him on 14 May 1926, that had a tremendous
impact on contemporary big bands. Indeed, the Goldkette
forces, which from October 1926 now again included Bix
Beiderbecke and Frank Trumbauer, were so impressed that
they made their own arrangement. This was largely a
"head," with notation assistance from Bill Challis; but
when they recorded it, Eddie King, Victor's stodgy, reac-
tionary A&R man, destroyed the master. Because of this,
the Nichols version remains the only white recording of
this tune contemporaneous with Fletcher's.

Stampede is one of those major-minor tunes that were so
central to the Henderson band's repertoire in the Twenties.
Its attraction to New York jazzers of the era is readily
apparent in its alternation of simple, attractive, arranged
passages with short but telling solos, built on chord patterns (predominantly E minor and G major) and rhythmic
patterns conducive to helping the players "really go." The
Henderson recording is "hot," with two Rex Stewart solos
at the start and finish framing ensemble breaks, interjections and choruses (especially a clarinet trio in minor,
reminiscent of early Duke Ellington), as well as Joe
Smith's trumpet in black New York style and young Cole-

man Hawkins, showing off his technique on tenor though vacillating between jazz and vaudeville styles.

Not too surprisingly, where the Henderson version is "hot" the Nichols is "cool," though in my opinion some of this stems from the acoustic sound plus the fact that Leo McConville was absent. As the only cornet or trumpet on the date, Red simply had to work harder to make the ensemble swing, and repressed, white Nichols was simply no match for Rex Stewart in 1926. On the plus side, the Nichols *Stampede* is actually less of an arranged affair than Henderson's, and more a string of solos—some good, some mediocre, and some breathtaking—that build one upon the other with a delicious cumulative effect. Some of this is due to the fact that Red's version is 4 minutes and 32 seconds long, without doubt the longest one-sided commercial recording the band ever made.

In place of Henderson's piano intro in C, Nichols features a much trickier intro with cornet-trombone counterpoint and drum interjections. Red's keys are the easier-to-play F minor and Ab major (concert Bb), with a bit of Bb^7. JD's clarinet kicks things off with a cornet-trombone cushion and tuba punctuations, followed by a Berton break; then comes Mole, more harmonically advanced than *anyone* on the Henderson version! A tenor sax follows, presumably Evans, which also alternates jazziness with vaudeville licks; towards the end, though, he hammers at repeated Fs in a rhythmic pattern that foreshadows the R&B players of the 1950s. Nichols's solo is actually better compared to Joe Smith than Stewart, and in fact though he is cooler he is more inventive. A Schutt break leads to an ensemble emulating the clarinet trio of the original; then comes a Berton cymbal break, and a Dixie ride-out accompanied by woodblocks.

THE RED HEADS: Nichols, Lang, Schutt, Berton. 4 Nov. 1926.

This revisit to the "We Three" combination of March puts Lang and Schutt together to make a quartet. Oddly, how-

ever, the configuration and routine of these records are not
much different. *Get With,* a Nichols original, has a guitar
intro in D, very ruminative, but the tempo picks up for
Nichols's cornet solo. Red is both inventive and relaxed;
this is one of his finest solos on record. He continues
going after a diminished, whole-tone break, then Berton
plays a break, followed by Schutt, then more cornet. Red
really gets going here; an upward slur is nicely answered
by Lang's guitar, then out.

Get a Load of This is a slower piece, played in E. A
drum intro leads to a Nichols solo with Lang underneath;
then Eddie plays a single-note solo with a particularly inventive bridge. Red transposes to Eb for the final chorus,
though it *sounds* as if he has transposed *upward;* Lang's
guitar ends it. Red's solos here are nice, though not quite
as brilliant as on the previous cut.

Oddly enough, except for their one trio record with piano
(Plenty Off Center), Schutt contributes very little to the
"We Three" combination. This, in my view, was a
mistake on Red's part. Certainly, the empathy between
Lang and Nichols, and Lang and Berton, was considerable, but Nichols and Berton seem to have had some
problems in communication. Perhaps Vic, in his desire to
"follow" Red's excursions, was somewhat at a disadvan-
tage because his jazz "time" was so much more acute; had
he been allowed to take the lead, the results might have
been better. Yet the underplayed piano robs this music of
the richness that permeates the Morton sides. The Nichols
group is "top-heavy," with two such bright-sounding
instruments as cornet and guitar allowed to dominate, and
as a result they are not the best chamber jazz I have heard,
though they certainly have their moments, and are quite
pioneering in their own way.

RED & MIFF'S STOMPERS: Nichols, Mole, J. Dorsey, Evans,
Schutt, Tarto, Berton. 10 November 1926.

By this point, Don Voorhees was firmly entrenched as the

conductor of Earl Carroll's Vanities Orchestra, and had
become fascinated with the structurally sound and harmonically complex music that Red's small band was playing. Indeed, he was fascinated to the extent that he began
giving the small band "spots" of their own in the dance
halls and radio broadcasts (over WOR) featuring the full
orchestra, much as Tommy Dorsey later did for his Clambake Seven and Goodman for his own Trio and Quartet.
This exposure served to gain recognition for Red as a leader, as well as prompting the group to continually rehearse
both numbers they had already recorded and new tunes.
This session is a case in point, consisting as it does of a
number already recorded for Pathé in September and a
new work by one of jazz's major creators.

The remake was *Hurricane,* and the tempo is cranked up
to ♩ =120 at 2/4. The routine of intro, ensemble, breaks,
and solos is similar to the original version, but with Jimmy Dorsey's clarinet subbing for the absent McConville.
The intro sports a rather corny slide whistle—undoubtedly
to reinforce the title—followed by the full ensemble, no
longer tentative (as in the September version) but swinging like mad. Some good Dorsey clarinet follows, then
the routine of drum break-ensemble-drum break-ensemble-
Nichols break-Schutt break, as on the original, before a
full chorus of ensemble with Dorsey predominating. It is
fascinating to hear Jimmy developing as a jazz artist
before our very ears; his playing here is far better than
when he joined the band in February. Then comes another "break" period, the routine being drums-ensemble-
piano-cornet-ensemble-piano, leading to an alto sax solo
(Evans?) with Schutt and Berton, the latter on suitcase.
Then, since the tempo is so fast that the band has extra
time to play with, we get an excellent chorus by Mole,
with Tarto lightly staccato in the background and Berton
on cymbals. Nichols returns for a break; then ensemble
with Berton on woodblocks, and out.

This breathless, virtuoso performance contrasts strongly
with Jelly Roll Morton's *Black Bottom Stomp.* Morton

himself had just recorded the piece, in his very first Red Hot Peppers session for Victor, on 14 September. Considering that the record had just been released (October), it may be that Nichols based his arrangement for this date on the published stock. Since this is a first recording of a rather complex piece, the band is naturally more tentative. Instead of Morton's upbeat tempo of ♩ =130 (at 2/4), Niohols is far more relaxed, at ♩ =100. Instead of jumping right in to Morton's original eight-bar intro, Nichols (or somebody in the group) had the misconception to recast it in their typical style, four bars ensemble and four bars cornet. Then they jump to the middle strain of Morton's tune, in ensemble, with Nichols and Dorsey on the breaks, followed by a Dorsey clarinet solo. The bridge follows, then the trio theme played straight by Dorsey with Nichols obbligato and Berton on woodblocks; then the lead instruments reverse this pattern. Mole plays trombone for a chorus with Schutt and Berton; there is a piano break, then a Nichols solo, not very imaginative or swinging. Then we get more breaks, and an alto solo; whether Dorsey or Evans, it is pretty interesting. A Nichols break precedes a typically exuberant Schutt solo; then ensemble with Tarto accenting the syncopations and Berton, for the first time, playing tympani.

I listened to this ending three times before concluding that Berton *was* playing tympani, and not suitcase. There is a slightly richer, more reverberant "boom" to the sound, though Edison's acoustic recording could scarcely do the instrument justice. Of course, this is an instrument that Vic would exploit brilliantly (and to greater advantage) on his electrical recordings, but we shall save that discussion for the beginning of the next chapter.

THE RED HEADS: Nichols, McConville, Mole, Dorsey, Schutt, McDonough, Berton; Brad Gowans, ct, added on *Heebie Jeebies*. 11 November 1926.

We move back from Edison to Pathé for what would be
the group's last acoustic session for a while. Here, they
are a septet on two titles, an octet on the third, and this is
in many respects a benchmark session for the band.

That's No Bargain, credited to Nichols, is ostensibly in G,
but it has a rather ambiguous harmonic base and (later)
rhythmic pulse. The tempo is a rather slowish ♩=160 in
4/4, which translates to about ♩=80 in 2/4—even slower
than their first version of *Black Bottom Stomp.* Yet the
compositional cohesiveness of the piece, not to mention its
complexities, mark it as a masterpiece of the first rank.
The melody, the first bars of which are displayed in
Example 9, is played over the following chords: A⁷, Ab⁷,
Db, E⁷; A⁷, Ab⁷, D⁷, A⁷, D⁷, G...then a leap to Bb⁷! Note,
too, the sophistication with which the fifth of Db (Ab)
becomes the third of E⁷ (G#, the enharmonic) in bar 8
(Example 9), without changing the melodic line. This is
played by Nichols, with Mole and Dorsey "filling in" the
chords.

Example 9: *That's No Bargain,* principal theme.

Then, with the tonality firmly in Eb, Mole solos, very ef-
fectively. Dorsey transposes to Db for *his* solo, but is
more slap-tongued and corny. Schutt's break brings us
back to Eb for a different strain, one in which the rhythm
(rather than the harmony) becomes ambiguous (Example
10). This moves from solo cornet to full ensemble; an
upward chromatic break brings us back to the first strain,
then coda and out.

Example 10: *That's No Bargain,* subsidiary theme.

That's No Bargain is undoubtedly one of the landmarks of mid-1920s jazz, though this is not the group's best recording of it (see the beginning of the next chapter). Directly or indirectly, it influenced small-group performances of the future—e.g., the John Kirby Sextet and the various harmonic-rhythmic experiments of Thelonious Monk—just as surely as *Rhythm of the Day* presaged the work of Eddie Sauter for big bands. I am tempted to consider that Berton, with his acute rhythmic ear, may have had more to do with the asymmetric middle strain than Nichols; but collaboration or not, one cannot—or, at least, *should* not— underestimate its complexity.

Heebie Jeebies is the Boyd Atkins tune recorded by Louis Armstrong's Hot Five the previous February 26. Nichols plays it a bit faster; and, if his lead cornetist (Gowans) could not really emulate the power and swing of Louis, the ensemble is a good deal crisper and less rhythmically stodgy. After a trombone-ensemble-guitar break intro, the ensemble plays the melody with Gowans using Bix-like upward rips. Schutt, by contrast, plays an uncharacteristically fumbling solo, followed by Gowans and Nichols together with Red solo in the middle eight. After the bridge, Mole solos with Berton on suitcase. Then McDonough plays a single-note solo, followed by ensemble with Gowans leading and Mole in the break.

Except for Schutt, there is really nothing wrong with this performance—it still sounds pretty good after seventy years—but, conversely, there is nothing memorable or out-

standing here except the delightful intro. But the band had one more number in store, an excellent remake of *Black Bottom Stomp.* Here, wisely, Morton's original intro is restored, with an alto sax break by Dorsey, and the tempo is considerably improved to ♩=112 (2/4). There is ensemble for sixteen bars, a clarinet break, then Nichols (again with clarinet breaks). This is followed by Dorsey clarinet for sixteen, with a brass cushion; the transition, then the trio theme, altered melodically with interesting results. Nichols swings well; after a guitar break, there is solo piano for eight. Then a drum break and Dixie ensemble with Berton on woodblocks and a trombone break.

More so than the unsuccessful November 10 version, this *Black Bottom Stomp* is a wonderful example of how the Nichols band could mold and transform even the most complex material for their own use, maintain the integrity of the original, yet bring their own style across. To the best of my knowledge, no other small band in 1926 (or 1927, for that matter) even dared attempt anything as complex as *Black Bottom,* for the simple reason that they couldn't. But Nichols, if not on the cutting edge, was at least in the jazz hunt of his day, and this disc proves it.

      *   *   *   *   *   *   *

At about this time, whether due to a growing interest in their records or the exposure that Voorhees was giving them, the band landed a recording contract with the Brunswick-Balke-Collander company, at that time the No. 3 American label (behind Victor and Columbia). They also underwent a name change, due in part to Voorhees's prodding but more so to Berton's inegnuity. Vic informed Nichols that, since he was the only red head in the group, calling themselves "The Red Heads" wasn't such a good idea. "So what would you suggest?" Red asked. "Well," said Vic, "since you usually play with four or five other guys, how about Red Nichols and his Five Pennies?"

And the pun was so bad that Nichols *knew* it would sell.

3. The Five Pennies

(December 1926-1928)

"Every man in the band has the opportunity for individual expression. We play with freedom, but it's disciplined freedom, so that the result has an over-all pattern."

Those are Red Nichols's own words, spoken some thirty years after these records were made. One will note that they could just as easily have come from Gerry Mulligan, or John Lewis of the Modern Jazz Quartet; but Red meant every word of it, both in 1957 and 1927. The records made by his bands *are* collaborative efforts, but as time went on the group's founder and (for a time) spiritual leader somehow got lost in the shuffle.

This, of course, was Vic Berton, who not only came up with the name "Five Pennies" but organized the sessions. His younger brother Ralph also claimed that, at least at first, Vic picked most of the tunes and arrangements they would play. This is certainly in keeping with his complex, classically-trained musical mind; it would not surprise me in the least to learn that Vic had uncovered and/or promoted such classics as *Fallen Arches, Nervous Charlie, Wild and Foolish, 'Tain't Cold, Hangover, Alabama Stomp, Hurricane, Washboard Blues,* or even *That's No Bargain* or *Black Bottom Stomp.* Yet, as the band headed into its first full-blown electrical period, Berton added one more fillip to his already-impressive credentials.

This was the "hot tympani," a pair of tuned kettledrums to which Vic had rigged up wires which led to a couple of organ-like pedals. These stretched the skins of the tympani so that various different pitches could be played; and, if one of the drums were struck *before* the pedal, he could raise the pitch in a way that resembled a glissando. To understand just how difficult this technique was, consider that classical tympani players have to have their drums tuned before each and every rehearsal and performance;

and that, once tuned, they cannot alter the pitch one iota without another time-consuming tuning. For Vic to have found a way to keep changing pitch on kettledrums *while playing them* was akin to a dancer changing his or her shoes while in the midst of a routine. It required the utmost skill and concentration; it was impossible to do; but he did it.

Vic's brother Ralph also claimed that, when the first Five Pennies records came out in England with the "hot tympani" on them, the British critics couldn't identify the instrument. As a result (he said), *The Melody Maker,* Britain's leading "hot" magazine of the day, sent a reporter over to interview Vic and find out what it was. But the actual review of the first Five Pennies record, *Washboard Blues/That's No Bargain,* tells a slightly different tale. The reviewer (identified only by the pseudonym "Needlepoint"), working from across the Atlantic Ocean, correctly identified the "'hot' breaks taken on tympani," but erroneously attributed the drumming to Ben Pollack. Apparently they recognized the instrument, but were completely unfamiliar with the name of Vic Berton.

In any event, Berton *was* interviewed by the magazine, after they heard the tympani glisses and weren't sure how they were done. Even after he saw it with his own eyes, the reporter didn't believe it: after all, such a technique was impossible. So Vic demonstrated his device, which either he or the critic dubbed the "Charleston pedal," and the reporter returned to England, still scratching his head in amazement but at least believing what he had seen.

Within a short time, other jazz drummers craved the unique sounds that the "Charleston pedal" produced. But they found they couldn't do it. The skins kept slipping when they were stretched, creating a slightly *lower* pitch each time they snapped back into place. By the end of two numbers, they found that the difference was somewhat over a half-tone away from where they had started. Vic the virtuoso just laughed; he knew very well that this happened. He knew this because he had spent hours,

sometimes eight straight, practicing on the tymps between gigs; but his infallible ear, and knowledge of how far the pitch would slip at any given moment, allowed him to *make adjustments* to the amount of pressure he would place on the pedals to "correct" the deviation. As a result, he was the only drummer in the world who could play jazz tympani, and the technique left jazz forever after his last big-band recording sessions in 1935.[1] In addition to the small-group sessions under discussion, Berton's hot tympani can be heard on a few excellent Victor recordings with the bands of Paul Whiteman and Roger Wolfe Kahn, which are listed in the discography.

RED NICHOLS & HIS FIVE PENNIES: Nichols, Dorsey, Schutt, Lang, Berton. 8 December 1926.

With the release of their records on the laterla-cut Brunswick and Vocalion labels, which were electrically recorded to boot, closer attention began to be paid to Red's little bands—not by musicians, who already knew they were good, but by the general public (and what few jazz critics then existed). As a result, Red did not hesitate to re-record some of his favorite arrangements from the immediately preceding Pathé-Edison period, as well as new pieces that the group was rehearsing and performing.

For some reason, Miff Mole was absent from the first Five Pennies session. Their first tune was Hoagy Carmichael's famous *Washboard Blues,* written for Bix but not recorded by him until 18 November 1927, his very first session with Paul Whiteman. Hoagy was on that record, too: a pretentious, "concert" arrangement of his song, with slow tempi, syrupy strings and Hoagy's then-squeaky, high tenor, enlivened only by a "Dixieland" interlude for Bix

---

[1] It should be noted that drummer Hal MacDonald of the Paul Whiteman band *did* play tympani on Whiteman's recording of *There Ain't No Sweet Man,* but MacDonald replicated Berton's feat not via the Charleston pedal, but by having *three* tympani already tuned to the pitches he would be playing.

and the Dorsey Brothers. Hoagy's own best version of it was made twenty-nine years later, in 1956, for Whiteman's "50th Anniversary Album" on Grand Award records. The slushy strings were replaced by jazzier clarinets, Hoagy's voice was mellower and more swinging, and the overall performance came off much better.

Nichols's version, though a little tepid, is in my opinion even better than either of the Carmichael-Whiteman collaborations. It begins with an eight-bar intro (four bars ensemble, four bars of Lang's guitar), then the main theme played by ensemble with tympani breaks (alternating F and the C below). Interestingly, the middle section is played in *minor,* whereas Carmichael's own version has it in *major;* perhaps there was a change of heart between December 1926 and November 1927. Then comes the "B" theme with four bars of clarinet, followed by an exquisite Nichols-Dorsey duo-improvisation. We hear Schutt's piano for twelve bars; Lang on guitar; then Nichols in excellent form on cornet with tympani underpinning. When Dorsey comes back in, he is quite jazzy; then ensemble with tympani breaks, ensemble with cymbal breaks, and the outro.

That's No Bargain is a remake of the tune they had first recorded in November; and, though we may miss Mole's trombone in its customary solo spot, there is almost no time to miss him in ensemble, since it is taken at a blistering ♩ =130 (at 2/4; ♩ =260 at 4/4!). Dorsey plays the counterpoint to Nichols's lead in the first chorus, with piano and cymbals. Then Red takes a full chorus, in good shape, followed by JD's clarinet improvising on the "A" theme, a little technically insecure. Then comes the stoptime chorus with Berton's cymbals, and the full-band rideout. The final six bars are interesting, as they alternate loud and soft on the riffs; such dynamics were highly unusual in early jazz.

On December 30 the band was back in the studio, this time with Mole present to round out the personnel. Two more masterpieces resulted. The first, *Buddy's Habits,* is an uptempo number originally recorded by King Oliver's band in 1923. Nichols's version is in B♭, and starts with Berton on tympani behind Nichols and Dorsey playing in thirds. The "A" theme is an attractive, downward melody played over B♭, D[7], G min., B♭[7], E♭, B♭, F[7], B♭, changing every beat (at 2/4). The "B" theme is more standard Dixieland with Dorsey in superb form, flying over the ensembles with aplomb. Mole solos on the "A" changes, backed by Schutt and Berton. After a Dorsey clarinet break we get the "trio," a chorale-like theme in E♭ reminiscent of such Morton pieces as *Wolverine Blues* and *Sidewalk Blues,* with Dorsey's alto sax and a booming Lang every four bars. Then comes a good Nichols solo; a Lang break; Schutt solo, and Dixie ensemble.

Their second number of the date was in some ways even better: *Boneyard Shuffle,* a Carmichael composition which, in my opinion, is an even finer *jazz* vehicle than *Riverboat Shuffle* or the overrated *Washoard Blues.* After a cornet-trombone intro, two bars, there are two bars of Nichols with Mole joining him in the second; a Berton tympani break (F-G) before Dorsey plays the theme on alto with Schutt and Berton underpinning. Then comes a bridge for the three horns before a "B" theme in Dixie style (for which JD switches to clarinet) with Berton on cymbals and woodblocks, and Nichols on the breaks. Mole plays a stop-time chorus, Lang solos for sixteen bars, then an ensemble break leads to a Schutt solo. Berton plays a cymbal break, then ensemble with more cymbal breaks; the coda is the same as the intro, but this time Berton ends it with a tympani gliss—low F to the C above —with perfect precision!

Recounting the schematic layout of *Boneyard Shuffle* scarcely does it justice; like *Hurricane* or *That's No Bargain,* it is far more complicated than it first appears. Moreover, the organization and layout of the piece, and even the "fills" and solos, all give a pleasing overall structure to the performance that demands a more detailed investigation. So let us go a little further into Carmichael's composition, and see what we can find.

To begin with, there is the introduction (Example 1), which immediately commands attention because of its insistent rhythmic configuration. Note, too, that in bar 3 Nichols ascends *not* to the "expected" F, but to E; this type of ambiguity is enticing, not least because it "deceives" the ear. (I myself always thought it was an F until I transcribed it.) The opening theme by Dorsey incorporates the whole-tone scale, descending and ascending, in bars 7 and 8, then "blue notes" in bars 11 and 12.

Example 1: *Boneyard Shuffle,* introduction.

There is a hint of whole tones in bars 3 and 4 of the bridge, but the tension thus created is released in the "Dixieland" chorus, which contains a particularly attractive theme (Example 2). One will note that this chorus ends on an unresolved chord, and that the tension is continued in Nichols's outstanding breaks. (When I first played this record for Ken Kresge, an excellent jazz pianist who had no idea of the complexity of early jazz, he was startled to discover traces of Miles Davis in Nichols's playing.) Then, the *rhythmic* tension is increased during Mole's trombone solo, with his playing being *on* the beat while Schutt and Berton accent the *off*-beats. Some stasis is reached in Lang's guitar solo; yet, though it is somewhat tentative, it serves as the musical equivalent of the "eye" in a hurricane. Schutt complements Lang's calm *melodic* movement while being more adventurous *harmonically.* Then, the entire last chorus dances over Berton's

Example 2: *Boneyard Shuffle*, middle theme.

cymbals: we are heading out the door now, but what will
the exit be? The same as our entrance—but this time,
poked in the ribs by Berton's tympani.

After four consecutive masterpieces, it was almost inevitable that a let-down would occur, and such is the case in
their first recording session of 1927 (January 12). This
presented remakes of *Alabama Stomp* and *Hurricane*
which, though energetic and presenting Berton's tympani
in well-recorded performances, are somehow less swinging and less satisfying than their acoustic predecessors.
Dorsey sounds particularly stiff, both on clarinet and alto;
Nichols is uninventive; and only Schutt and Berton really
sound "into" the music.

THE CHARLESTON CHASERS: Nichols, Mole, Dorsey, Schutt,
McDonough, Tarto, Berton. 17 January 1927.

The first record on this date, *Someday Sweetheart*, has
more the "feel" of a Molers performance (see next page).
It is also one of the most original of all Nichols discs,
highly creative if somewhat unswinging. Red and company bring the tempo way down, to ♩=58 at 2/4 or ♩=116
at 4/4. Again, after the ensemble opening, the "string-of-
solos" concept is exploited; but this time, the melody is
never touched until the final chorus! Nichols's first solo
shows that it was he, and not Beiderbecke, who more
greatly influenced Bobby Hackett, his phrase-endings having the same unexpected twists of melody that go deep

into the heart of the harmonic changes. Mole is typically brilliant in his chorus, followed by exceptionally good JD clarinet. McDonough plays with Tarto underpinning, then ensemble (with Nichols finally bringing out the melody on cornet), and a coda mirroring the intro.

After four straight somewhat relaxed sides, *After You've Gone* is like a wake-up call with a bucket of cold water in the face. It is taken way up (o =135 at 2/4); after an alto sax intro by Dorsey, Nichols and Mole improvise on the main melody. The ensemble plays the verse with terrific verve, followed by Dorsey on alto with Tarto pumping double-time figures like mad; a McDonough break (on ukelele!), ensemble peppered with drum breaks, and an insidious, slurring outro.

A day later they were back at Pathé for a "Red Heads" session, this time acting as accompanists for the rather wretched singing of one Frank Gould. In a way, the band's growing fame was starting to defeat their purpose of straight-ahead instrumental jazz, for during this year they were also forced to accompany other singers, such as the old-fashioned Irving Kaufman and an unswinging Kate Smith, in addition to the superb Annette Hanshaw.

On January 28 they entered the OKeh studios for the first in a long line of records under the name of Miff Mole's Molers (sometimes Little Molers). The diversity of names that the band recorded under may seem confusing to the layman, but each had its own purpose and function. The Red Heads were for Pathé, The Charleston Chasers were Columbia, The Hottentots were Banner-Bradway-Oriole, the Molers were OKeh, and "Red and Miff's Stompers" were transferred from Edison to Victor. Only for Brunswick were they to remain "The Five Pennies."

At this point, too, one should mention the recordings made for the Harmony label under the monicker of "The Arkansas (a.k.a. Arkansaw) Travelers." Though they are far better from a jazz standpoint than many of Nichols's later, more commercial dates, in comparison to the other record-

ings from this era they are decidedly inconsistent in quality. The first "Travelers" date actually took place in December 1924, a commercial Lanin session with Nichols
but without Mole, and the results were (like the May "Red
Heads" session) pretty pedestrian.

The "Arkansas Travelers" of 1927 were much more jazz-
oriented, but Harmony's dreadful acoustic sound was even
boxier than parent-label Columbia, Pathé, or Edison, and
the performances are generally tossed off more casually,
without their usual attention to detail. Typical of this is
the session of 4 January 1927, when the band made inferior remakes of *Washboard Blues, That's No Bargain,* and
Boneyard Shuffle (the latter being faster, but less cohesive
and without the hot tympani). Nevertheless, since some of
the Travelers sides were interesting, we shall discuss the
best of them as they emerge chronologically.

MIFF MOLE'S MOLERS: Nichols, Mole, Schutt, McDonough,
Berton. 26 January 1927.

The first "Molers" disc made was Irving Berlin's *Alexander's Ragtime Band.* Berlin preferred hearing his melo-
dies played "straight," and did not like changes or improvisations except in small doses. No swinger he! Considering that, he must have hated this treatment of one of his
most popular songs.   Like *Someday Sweetheart,* it is
brought down in tempo from the usual, circa ♩ =208 (at
2/4) to ♩ =174. After an out-of-tempo guitar intro, the
theme is played insidiously by muted cornet and trombone
with blue-note slurs in bars 3 and 7; after a guitar break,
Nichols plays a variation on the verse, followed by Mole
improvising on the chorus. Berton is subdued throughout,
confined mainly to light cymbal work.   McDonough's
single-note solo is pretty good, then open cornet and trombone for the ride-out.

After such an interesting record, the session continued as
essentially a relaxed sequence of solos with interspersed
arranged passages. This is as true of *Some Sweet Day* as

it is of a completely reworked version of *Hurricane;* the tempo is much more relaxed than on January 12, and follows the general pattern of intro, Mole solo, Nichols break, McDonough solo, Nichols muted, Schutt solo, Nichols break, and Mole again with Nichols and Berton in the breaks. Yet, in an odd way, this is a more interesting alternative to the superb Edison version than the hot but heavy Brunswick.

This brings up an interesting point, one often missed by those who listen more casually or less in depth to the Nichols-Mole records of this period. Many fans and critics tend to look upon this era as being all of a piece, but from this point forward there was a subtle but marked stylistic division between some of the band's pseudonyms. The Five Pennies and Red & Miff's Stompers sessions concentrated on tighter, more complex arrangements, while the Molers and Charleston Chasers presented generally relaxed tempi (with exceptions, of course) and more of a string-of-solos approach. Moreover, the Charleston Chasers, with or without vocalists, were a little more aggressive in their jazz approach than the light, subtle, almost delicate Molers sessions.

I'm not certain why the latter style evolved, but it seems to me that the other styles reflected the proclivities of the session leaders. Mole, who was a more subtly inventive jazz musician than Nichols (though no less a virtuoso), obviously preferred looser, more wide-open blowing dates, while Nichols's penchant for jazz *compositions* found its expression in the Stompers and Five Pennies discs. This distinction is important; for, as we shall see, the passage of time eventually led to rifts between Nichols and his sidemen, with the result that by 1929 neither Mole nor Berton were found with any regularity on Nichols dates.

*   *   *   *   *   *

In February 1927, four of the small band's members—Nichols, Dorsey, Lang, and Berton—joined Paul Whiteman's gargantuan popular orchestra. Whiteman, who

styled himself "The King of Jazz," had in fact not had a
bona-fide jazz musician in his ranks since clarinetist Gus
Mueller had quit in 1921. But with the advent of radio,
and the increasing popularity of such "hot" bands as Fletcher Henderson, Jelly Roll Morton, Tiny Parham, and Jean
Goldkette, Whiteman wanted some of the real stuff "to
go" in his own troops. His first move, naturally, had been
to try and lure Goldkette's biggest stars away from the
Motor City; but Bix, Frank Trumbauer, trombonist Bill
Rank, and bassist Steve Brown all decided to stay put,
though all of them would eventually be foot-soldiers in
Whiteman's musical army.

Having failed (for the time being) to get the names he
wanted, Whiteman "settled" for the Five Pennies—or at
least four-fifths, as Miff Mole declined to come aboard at
the last moment. Nichols's solos for Whiteman were like
a breath of fresh air in an otherwise stale, stagnant atmosphere; like Bix's later work for the same band, they lifted
the records out of their doldrums of vaudeville-styled
saxes, syrupy strings and bombastic "concert" arrangements of mediocre popular songs, and gave life to the
proceedings.   The best Nichols-Berton-Whiteman collaborations were *I'm Comin, Virginia* and *Side By Side*,
both of which also contained Bing Crosby vocals (uncred-
ited as a soloist on the original labels), and Lang's guitar.

During his short stay with Whiteman, Nichols met and
married a chorus girl named Willa Stutsman. Paul acted
as best man at the wedding, but the marriage lasted longer
than the job. Red was frustrated by the small amount of
real jazz he was allowed to play—more so than his own
idol, Beiderbecke, who reveled in the outdated "concert
jazz" of Whiteman's approach because he felt it gave him
"legitimacy," just as Louis Armstrong reveled in the white
Guy Lombardo sound for *his* own band of the early 1930s.
Nichols, however, came from a well-schooled background;
he knew the difference between good big-band jazz and
the saccharine, pretentious, pseudo-classical approach of
Whiteman, even if critics (then and now) didn't.

Thomas de Long, author of *Pops* (New Century Publishers, 1983), also suggests that Nichols was angry with Whiteman's restriction on his players continuing their independent recording contracts, but this argument doesn't hold water. Nichols made twenty-two sides for Columbia, Victor (Whiteman's label), Brunswick-Vocalion, OKeh, Banner, Broadway, Domino, Pathé, Oriole, and Apex between February and May, and later on Trumbauer, Bix, Dorsey, Lang, and Venuti continued their fruitful association with OKeh and other labels while with Whiteman.

According to Nichols himself, "Miff was expected to join the band also, but when he declined (at that time) I quit because I was unhappy without Miff. Furthermore, Paul, flush with his success at the time, was not devoting his full attention to the band. Many times he didn't show up on a job. On such occasions Henry Busse would front the band. I would have to take over Henry's book and sit there while Henry played his muted solos."[2] Whatever the reasons, however, Nichols was gone by June, Schutt felt out of his element and begged off, Lang went off with his old mate Venuti, and Berton left shortly after a fist-fight with Whiteman in a men's room. According to Ralph Berton, Paul was getting jealous of Vic's flashy drumming, which had the tendency to steal the show, and this erupted in an ugly if mercifully brief encounter.

RED & MIFF'S STOMPERS: Nichols, Mole, Dorsey, Schutt, Colucci, Berton. 11 February 1927.

The group's first recording session for Victor was an especially happy one. That label had never had a particularly liberal jazz policy, but in February 1927 Victor's notorious A&R man, Eddie King, was temporarily replaced in New York by the more jazz-appreciative Nathaniel Shilkret. The results were these recordings, as well as one of the finest of all Goldkette sides *(My Pretty Girl)* featuring

---

2 Shapiro, Nat & Hentoff, Nat, *Hear Me Talkin' to Ya* (Holt-Rinehart, 1955), p. 276.

Bix, Venuti, Lang, and Steve Brown. In addition, Victor
had by far the finest sonics of any record company at that
time, being warm and spacious in addition to having a lot
of "presence." When these sides were digitally remastered
in 1991, collectors flipped over the superb ambience and
careful balance of the various instruments.

Delirium is a Schutt original in Db, though the intro passes
through Eb, F and G, with the 3rd of each being the top
note of the chord, while Nichols plays a high repeated Db
throughout (Example 3). This almost seems to be a showcase for Berton: after the trombone break, it is the tymp-
anist who plays the first chorus, alternating Db, Eb, and
the Ab below with the ensemble in the breaks. Nichols
plays over a cushion with woodblocks, then comes a transposition to F for a very high-pitched, almost shrill Dixie
chorus with trombone breaks. Mole solos with woodblocks and banjo; then another bridge, followed by Dorsey
clarinet with Nichols in the breaks, Berton peppering like
crazy on cymbals. Then back down we go, in a chromatic
break, to Db for Schutt's swinging and harmonically ambiguous solo, with Berton on suitcase; there is another
ensemble break, then Dorsey on alto. The outro is similar
to the intro, but much softer and with a diminuendo; as on
Boneyard Shuffle, Berton ends it with a tympani gliss
(low Ab to the Db above).

Example 3: *Delirium,* introduction.

Davenport Blues is, of course, Bix's famous tune of 1925.
Nichols plays a very pretty, Hackett-like intro, with Berton on tympani; then a break containing one of Bix's licks
before the chorus by full band. There is a whole-tone
break by Dorsey on alto and Berton (on celeste), then the

verse, with Berton really swinging on cymbals. Mole lays down a chorus with Berton back on tympani; an ensemble break, then back to the chorus, embellished, with JD on clarinet in the middle eight sounding eerily like Trumbauer. Berton plays a short tympani solo, then comes an ensemble ride-out. These two masterpieces were followed by a Charleston Chasers session, three days later, where the band accompanied singer Kate Smith (for Columbia); these sides are best left undiscussed, except to mention that Smith doesn't sound quite as awful on *I'm Gonna Meet My Sweetie Now* as she does on *One Sweet Letter from You.*

THE CHARLESTON CHASERS: Same personnel as January 17. 25 February 1927.

Eleven days after the Kate Smith session, the band was back at Columbia for a straight-ahead jazz date. But either some of the band members were hung over, or tired from lack of sleep, because the first two sides—*Farewell Blues* and an unsuccessful remake of *Davenport*—are disappointing. Jimmy Dorsey is stiff and unimaginative, especially on *Farewell;* McDonough ditto; and Nichols, surprisingly, is also not in the best of shape, somewhat fumbling for ideas. As usual, it is Mole and Berton who save the day on these first two tracks—what utterly dependable, consistently interesting jazzmen they were!— though the final ride-outs on each have a little more heat than the preceding choruses.

Perhaps the band took a break (or, better yet, a nap) after *Davenport,* but in any event the third track of this session, *Wabash Blues,* is decidedly the winner. The opening Dixieland chorus features some blistering-hot Nichols cornet; Dorsey has one little fluff in his clarinet chorus, but is otherwise creative and swinging. Nichols tears off one of his best solo choruses, and then comes a real rarity: a solo by tuba-player Joe Tarto. Indeed, Tarto's playing in general came as a pleasant surprise; since I normally detest

the sound of the instrument, mostly because of its association with bad traditional and pseudo-"Dixieland" bands, I
had badly overlooked Tarto in my haste to proclaim string
bassist Steve Brown the undisputed white rhythm-maker
of the day. But now, having heard so much more of him
than before, I recognize that he was—along with Fletcher
Henderson's John Kirby—the greatest virtuoso on the
instrument of that time. What a swinger he was! And
what chops!! He is followed by McDonough on banjo,
Mole is superb on trombone, then comes a good ride-out
for all concerned.

During this same month and year, on February 4 to be
exact, Frank Trumbauer began his famous series of recordings for OKeh featuring sidemen from the Goldkette
and, later, Whiteman bands. Yet, curiously, even when
the same musicians were used—Jimmy Dorsey and Mole
on the first session, Lang and Schutt later on, not to mention Chauncey Morehouse, who later played drums for
Nichols—their playing is neither as relaxed nor as technically precise as it was for Red. This situation puzzled me
for many years, until I learned that Red was practically a
teetotaler, not to mention a martinet when it came to
rehearsing and technical perfection. This is one reason, I
think, why the reputations of Schutt, Morehouse, and even
Jimmy Dorsey in this period, have suffered through the
decades. Since critics and fans paid (and pay) consistently
more attention to the Beiderbecke sides than to Nichols's,
they assumed (wrongly) that Bix's sidemen were not in
the same league, whereas in fact they were probably just
drinking so hard and worrying so little that they simply
produced sloppy playing.

Moreover, the whole Beiderbecke-Nichols influence, and
even Armstrong-Nichols and Armstrong-Beiderbecke, actually worked two ways rather than just one. Louis, in
later years, recalled those "wonderful" jam sessions in
which he and Bix were not out to cut each other but to
learn from one another. This type of cross-pollination in
jazz is one reason why critics and scholars should not be

so hasty to make snap decisions about some player's style. Insofar as Nichols-Beiderbecke goes, just as Red adopted an entirely new vernacular after hearing Bix in 1924, so too did Bix learn things about technical security and phrase-shaping from Red. Not until 1927 did Bix's playing exhibit those thrilling upward "rips" that were a trademark of Louis (and Red via Louis) in 1925 and 1926; and some of those Nichols-like double-time figures, for instance near the end of his *Goose Pimples* solo, had been a part of Nichols's style from as far back as 1924.

The Nichols-Armstrong connection has always been considered more tentative, but there is proof that it did exist. In 1926, Louis's "Hot Five" recorded a tightly-structured, Nichols-like arrangement (by his wife at the time, pianist Lil Hardin) called *Jazz Lips.* And Nichols himself recalled that, while Armstrong was with Fletcher Henderson at the Roseland Ballroom, "Louis and I used to play for each other in the musicians' room downstairs. We were happy to exchange ideas. He was very interested in the false-fingering ideas I was working on and I showed him how it was done. The jazz musicians of that day were a kind of fraternity—all working together to promote and advance the music and each other. It's quite different now."[3]

RED NICHOLS & HIS FIVE PENNIES: Nichols, Mole, Dorsey, Schutt, Lang, Berton, Joe Venuti, vln. 3 March 1927.

The band's next session, their first-ever with the mercurial Venuti, has been hailed as one of their finest. The first selection made that day was *Bugle Call Rag,* with a typical "reveille" intro; Nichols lead with JD and Mole; a Venuti break, ensemble with tympani, Lang break, ensemble with cymbals, and Venuti sixteen bars. Dorsey's sixteen-bar alto solo is somewhat staid and unadventurous, but there is good Mole trombone. This is followed by ensemble break, Nichols break, ensemble and a Schutt solo;

---

3 Shapiro & Hentoff, *ibid,* p. 275.

then, a triple chase-chorus between Nichols, Venuti, and JD before the ride-out ensemble and a fade-out ending.

Back Beats, written by an ex-bandmate of Schutt's named Frank Guarante, starts with a Venuti-Lang intro that they would later slow down and recycle for their 21 June 1928 Victor recording of *Doing Things.* The simple melody is played by ensemble, then JD's alto sounding much better (if still a little stiff); Venuti and Lang, then ensemble on the "B" theme. A bridge leads to Mole's trombone, then ensemble with Venuti breaks, and a Venuti-Berton coda.

Bugle Call Rag has been reissued a number of times, and in *The Swing Era* (Oxford Univ. Press, 1989), author-musicologist Gunther Schuller lists both it and *Back Beats* among the group's outstanding performances. Yet, somehow, I get the feeling that this session failed to gel. One would assume that the effervescent Venuti would have charged into his music with more enthusiasm than he actually displays; in a way, it sounds as if the subtle, cerebral qualities of the "New York style" imbued Venuti's normally infectious playing, rather than the other way round. Joe would eventually make several more sides with Nichols's bands, and in my opinion those later collaborations are far superior to these. This is not to say that they are not *good* records—they certainly are—but they just miss the mark of greatness. Maybe I'm just too used to more enthusiastic and less constrained versions of the first tune.

MIFF MOLE'S MOLERS: Nichols, Mole, Dorsey, Schutt, Tarto, McDonough; Ray Bauduc, dm. 7 March 1927.

Four days later, the band—with New Orleans drummer Ray Bauduc (1906-1988) substituting for Berton—was in the OKeh studios for a Molers session. Here, too, the Nichols-Mole subtlety worked to subdue a normally exuberant player (Bauduc would later gain fame as the sparkplug of the Bob Crosby Orchestra), but perhaps because of the intelligence and creativity of the session's nominal leader I find the results more satisfying.

This remake of *Davenport Blues* dispenses entirely with an intro, jumping into the chorus with JD clarinet breaks. Mole solos on the verse, followed by a superb Dorsey alto solo (far different from the previous session!) of beautiful and logical construction with Tarto underpinning. Schutt solos, followed by the ride-out with Bauduc on cymbals. *Darktown Strutters' Ball* removes all taints of stated or implied racism by virtue of its exultant concentration on the musical aspects. It is a nice, loose, uptempo jam, the opening ensemble featuring JD's clarinet breaks which are a little squeaky but inventive. Schutt solos for a chorus, a capella, followed by ensemble, Mole's solo, Tarto (staying close to the melody), and ensemble. According to Tarto, both Red and Miff asked the OKeh executives to reject this title because Schutt left out a few measures during his solo. Unless one counts, the mistake passes unnoticed, but it proves how meticulous Red and Miff were about their jazz—despite later comments from Red that "we goofed around" and "we got away with murder."

A Hot Time in the Old Town Tonight starts with a spoken introduction—by who? It is a slowed-down treatment, à la *Alexander's Ragtime Band,* with an opening ensemble, a Schutt piano break, Mole solo with woodblocks, and JD back on alto, again excellent and airy. Tarto again stays close to the melody in his solo; after McDonough's guitar, there is an ensemble ride-out and a slowed-down coda.

Following these superb jazz sides, the "Six Hottentots" session of March 23 is very commercial-sounding and corny, centering as it does on the dated vocals of Irving Kaufman. The most interesting feature of this session, as with the one previous, is to discover how Jimmy Dorsey's alto was beginning to assume the liquid improvising properties of Frank Trumbauer's C-melody sax. This was a kick he was to stay on for a while.

THE SIX HOTTENTOTS: Nichols, Mole, Dorsey, Schutt, Tarto, Berton. 2 May 1927.

The lone title made on this date was *Memphis Blues*, and it is indeed good enough to make us forget the insult of the Kaufman series. It is medium-slow in tempo, with a Nichols intro and first ensemble chorus; though the performance is not overly slow, it has a wonderful slow-motion effect that I found unique in Nichols's *ouvre*. The melody and chords owe much to Jelly Roll Morton's *Tom Cat Blues*. There is a Mole solo, breathtakingly inventive, and Nichols is superbly wry and underhanded. Dorsey's clarinet picks up on the others pretty well. Then there is an ensemble with clarinet break, a transposition, and more ensemble with clarinet; the last chorus is highly syncopated, with JD's break being particularly outstanding. This is easily one of the band's finest moments. What a record!!

THE ARKANSAS TRAVELERS: Nichols, Mole, Dorsey, Morrow, Schutt, Berton. 10 May 1927.

The next Travelers date turned out two good performances of *Ja-Da* and *Sensation*, both old numbers even at this time. The latter is especially notable for the second chorus of JD's clarinet solo, in which the rhythm is altered slightly by a fraction of a beat. *Stompin' Fool* is even better, a medium-slow piece reminiscent of the Johnny Mercer song *Small Fry*. The intro leads to Morrow's alto sax, then Nichols cornet in an insinuating mood for a half-chorus. Mole swings nicely, followed by Dorsey in a relaxed vein. After Schutt's break and solo, there is an ensemble ride-out in which Red is particularly good.

THE SIX HOTTENTOTS: Same as May 2. 16 May 1927.

A week later, the band was back in the studio to record two more titles. *Melanchoily Charlie* is an ambiguous melody by Frank Crum with whole-tone implications; note how, this time at least, the cell-motive of the four-bar intro becomes the cell motive of the "A" theme (Example

4). After the ensemble (played twice), there is a "B" theme that jumps into the key of D; it too is repeated. Then we have Mole's trombone with Tarto and tympani; we slip back down to B for the trio, then up again to D for Nichols's solo (with tuba and cymbals). JD's alto is still on a Trumbauer kick, but good, followed by an improvised ride-out with cymbal breaks. This final version of *Hurricane* is also quite good, certainly better than the stiff and nervous-sounding January 12 recording.

Example 4: *Melancholy Charlie*, intro and beginning of "A" theme.

THE CHARLESTON CHASERS: Nichols, Mole, Dorsey, Schutt, McDonough, Tarto, Berton. 18 May 1927.

Though the preceding three titles (as well as the sub-par Kaufman session) are all electrics, one would scarcely know this from the sound alone. This is because most of the "cheapie" labels of the time that recorded electrically used cheaper, inferior systems. Here we are back at Columbia, and the sound quality is far superior—as are the arrangements, both by Schutt.

My Gal Sal is played in Gb at a very relaxed ♩=138 (4/4). There is a slurred intro, ensemble with Nichols on lead and in the break, while Mole plays the second chorus. Then Dorsey on alto with guitar, tuba and cymbals for a full chorus. A chorded McDonough break leads to another ensemble, led by Nichols and Dorsey (now on clarinet, in superb form), then coda and out. *Delirium* omits the stunning intro of the Victor version; the theme is played in stop-time chords with celeste (or vibes) with

Schutt breaks, JD alto in the middle eight. The bridge transposes from D to G for the alto solo; then Nichols, explorative and relaxed. A Mole trombone break leads to his solo in D, then a whole-tone break before Schutt piano, much the same as on the Victor. Another break leads to a Dixie chorus with a duo-improvisation between Nichols and JD clarinet, with the latter predominating.

RED NICHOLS & HIS FIVE PENNIES: Nichols, Mole, JD, Schutt, Lang, Berton; Adrian Rollini, bs-sx. 20 June 1927.

This session introduces to Nichols's records bass saxist Adrian Rollini (1904-1956), the finest jazz exponent of that cumbersome instrument. Rollini could play counterpoint like a brass bass, or slide around the instrument with the audacity of a trombonist; he is also one of the few musicians to sound as good on Beiderbecke records as on those with Nichols. One might say that Rollini, like Berton, was one of a kind, but his younger contemporary Spencer Clark was nearly as good.

On *Cornfed* a Berton tympani glissando introduces the newcomer on the intro, followed by Dixie ensemble on the simple "A" theme (with Mole breaks). Berton's dancing drums have a beneficent effect on the middle section, having a light but swinging beat. JD's alto break introduces the next theme, essentially sustained chords with Rollini and Berton breaks. A Lang break leads to Dorsey's alto, this time (curiously) taking on the qualities of Nichols's cornet rather than Trumbauer's C-sax. Red himself follows, playing nicely. There is an ensemble with Rollini predominating, then a bass sax outro with guitar.

Five Pennies was the band's theme, a not particularly attractive or memorable melody by Red. It is taken at a possibly too-relaxed tempo; Nichols states the melody with a chord cushion, Schutt on the middle eight. After Lang's break, Mole solos with slurred, upward chords and cymbal accents accompanying him; then comes Rollini with Lang, JD's clarinet on the middle eight. Nichols finishes the chorus, plays a coda, then Berton plays a double tympani gliss to end it.

Five days later the same band waxed *Mean Dog Blues.* The intro is reminiscent of *Delirium;* then Rollini plays with Nichols and Berton punctuating. This is followed by a Lang solo, simple but effective. Mole, not terribly inventive (for once) but lightly swinging, is heard next, then Berton's tympani with ensemble breaks, Nichols on the last four of each chorus. There is some excellent Schutt piano; then an ensemble chorus, with Red in top form, Rollini on the first break. The repeat has Nichols and Dorsey (alto sax) on the break.

RED NICHOLS & HIS FIVE PENNIES: Nichols, McConville, Mole, Rollini, McDonough, Berton; Pee Wee Russell, cl; Fud Livingston, t-sx/arr; Lennie Hayton, p/cel/arr; Manny Klein, tp (on *Riverboat Shuffle* only). 15 August 1927.

This rather large edition of the Five Pennies (nine men, ten on *Riverboat Shuffle)* indicates to me that already, by August of 1927, Nichols was looking for new directions in which to take the band. To this end there was not only a larger-than-normal ensemble, but the infusion of new blood in the persons of Russell, Hayton, and Livingston.

Charles Ellsworth "Pee Wee" Russell (1906-1969) was, of course, one of the greatest white jazzmen of his time, a musician who refused to stand still in his exploration of evolving styles. Here we hear him at age twenty-one, relatively fresh from Herbert Berger's band in St. Louis where he had achieved some local prestige. If his playing is somewhat tentative, occasionally squawky, and includes some wrong notes, he nevertheless shortly developed into one of the music's true greats. The one obstacle that many listeners cannot overcome with Pee Wee was his raspy, "fugitive" tone, an anti-virtuosic approach to clarinet playing that puzzles historians as to its origin. Chicagoan Frank Teschemacher also developed such a style, but contemporary with Russell rather than as a predecessor.

Pianist Lennie Hayton (1908-1971) is much less well-
known today, though in the 1920s he was considered to be
one of the best and most "modern" of arrangers. His work
has, sadly, dated with the passage of time; what was considered novel and striking then sounds rather predictable
and uninventive now. Not so, however, the third new
member. Joseph Anthony "Fud" Livingston (1906-1957),
a multi-talented performer, had studied piano, clarinet and
saxophone. At the time of this recording he was the
principal "hot" arranger for the Ben Pollack band, which
in essence meant that few if any of his arrangements were
getting recorded.

It is a sad fact that, though jazz was a music of revolt and
though there were several hot bands (both black and
white) playing it by 1927, the record companies had come
to divide white and black jazz into annoying stereotypes.
Black musicians were allowed to be as "hot" and "crazy"
as they wanted, though of course the underlying image of
the black "Zulu man" was all-purveying. White bands, by
contrast, were not only discouraged but often banned from
recording their best jazz numbers, the A&R men at Victor
and Columbia assuming that such bands should appeal to
the stuffed-shirt upper middle class. This separatism ac-
counts for much in our assessment of early white jazz
orchestras, since their best charts often went by the
boards; and the greatest irony of all is that, in their personal appearances, these bands generally attracted *not* the
staid middle class but their young, college-going offspring.

As a result, the only good Livingston arrangement that the
Pollack band recorded was *Waitin' for Katie,* an uptempo
romp spotlighting Benny Goodman's clarinet and a Jimmy
McPartland-led trumpet trio reminiscent of Bix Beiderbecke's work with Goldkette. Otherwise, the bulk of his
reputation today rests on *Humpty Dumpty,* a harmonically
adventurous score that the Trumbauer band (with Bix)
recorded in 1928, and several inspired compositions and
arrangements for Nichols.

Riverboat Shuffle is one such Livingston arrangement;

though not as "hot" as the Trumbauer-Beiderbecke version on OKeh (a stripped-down version of Bill Challis's arrangement for the Goldkette band), is nonetheless tighter and more unified. Nichols's version is also more relaxed in tempo, with loud-soft dynamic contrasts in the opening. Rollini solos for four bars, followed by ensemble; Russell's clarinet (on E24225) is sour and tentative, not as good as his later form. This is followed by McDonough's guitar, nice but unswinging. Mole picks things up; Nichols is lyrical, but somewhat predictable. Then comes the ride-out and ending, the latter with ascending and descending chromatics.

An even better arrangement by Livingston (and a better performance) is *Eccentric*. After a four-bar Russell intro, squawky and out of tune, we hear the simple, melodic, and swinging principal melody, the two trumpets in especially good form. This is followed by more two-trumpet work with clarinet breaks; a Rollini solo, swinging and inventive; then yet another duo-trumpet chorus, this one reminiscent of such Goldkette discs as *Sunday* and *My Pretty Girl*, which is in fact not *Eccentric* at all but a forward-looking arrangement of the then-popular song, *You Don't Like It—Not Much*. Mole's trombone is wonderful, but Hayton tries to be Artie Schutt and fails; then a Dixie ride-out. One indication of how hard the band worked on perfecting the felicities of these arrangements may be seen in the fact that it took them three hours to record these two titles!

Ida, Sweet as Apple Cider is the old Benny Leonard vaudeville tune. Hayton's arrangement does little to lift it above that level though the opening chorus, featuring Rollini on lead in a variation of the melody, with the two clarinets (Russell and Livingston) soft in the background, had a strong impact on the young Gil Evans. Then comes a Nichols solo, fairly nice, with a double-time break at the end. This is followed by Mole trombone, then Russell clarinet, the latter stronger and more relaxed if still a little tentative, before an ensemble ride-out.

Feelin' No Pain is a Livingston original that presaged the
Swing Era by eight years, though oddly no one played it
then. Nichols really loved this tune; this is the first of
four versions (all different) made within three months. It
is also the weakest, though only by comparison with the
remakes. Played in E♭ at ♩ =218 (4/4), it opens with a
solo chorus by Russell, now fully confident of his powers,
which is more or less the "A" theme—but note how he
typically ends his asymmetrical phrases on unexpected
notes (Example 5)! He likes this groove so much that he
continues for another chorus; then Rollini follows with

Example 5: *Feelin' No Pain,* Brunswick version, opening chorus (solo clarinet).

McDonough on the middle eight. Nichols, very Bix-like,
is next, then Mole with Rollini on a keyboard harmonica
called a "goofus" that sounds like an accordion! This
artistic misfire almost ruins the recording, and Hayton's
piano is scarcely better than before; but this is salvaged by
a nice ensemble ride-out, with the coda slowing down and
transposing to E.

Though probably little noted by listeners at the time, this
was a watershed session for the Five Pennies. For the first
time, Red imported a player (Russell) and an arranger
(Livingston) whose ideas were outside the realm of their
"normal" style; he found both to his liking, and used both

of them more and more as time went on. On the other hand, one bit of fallout to result was that Hayton's stodgy arrangement of *Ida* sold a million copies. This began a rift in the Nichols style, perpetrated by Brunswick, that was to lead seven months down the road to a more "commercial" approach in some of the band's records. On the positive side, the "hot" qualities of Russell's clarinet and Livingston's arrangements were to lift Red out of the delicate chamber-jazz style which he, Mole and Berton had created into an entirely new and equally exciting phase of operations. Part of this changeover, in fact, may be noted in the little-known Harry Reser and his Syncopators session of August 29, where Red's lead work on *Shaking the Blues Away* and solo on *Ooh! Maybe It's You* indicate a new, fierier direction. It might also be noted that Reser's drummer, the practically unknown Tom Stacks, plays some mighty impressive rim shots on *Shaking.*

MIFF MOLE'S MOLERS: Nichols, Mole, Russell, Livingston, Rollini, Schutt, McDonough, Lang, Berton. 30 August 1927.

One indication that my statement in the above paragraph is true is this session, made some fifteen days later, where Red brought the Russell-Livingston combination into a Miff Mole's Molers session. Red, apparently, could not wait to try out more Livingston material and remake the good but slightly tepid August 15 version of *Feelin' No Pain,* even if it meant disrupting the normally light, airy style that Miff preferred in sessions under his own name. The times were certainly a-changin'; slowly, perhaps, at first, but definitely changing.

Imagination is a Livingston original, and one of the few apparently built around Mole's inventive yet delicate trombone style. It is played, I think, in Eb; the transfer I heard was pitched oddly, making the notes fall a quarter-tone "between the cracks." This is partly due to a feature of 1920s recordings only too familiar to collectors of classical recordings, but apparently little known or recognized by most jazz buffs: that the so-called "78 rpm" speed did *not* become an industry standard until 1935! Indeed, many discs from the 1920s (not too many, but enough to be bothersome) play at a little under or over the 78-rpm speed. One particularly famous disc which has always annoyed me, because it is always transferred wrong, is the Goldkette band's version of *Clementine (From New Orleans)*. When transferred at 78, in the key of A, the resultant sound is choppy, mechanical, and unswinging; but bring it down to Ab, at approximately 76.5 rpm, and the saxes sound warmer, Beiderbecke's cornet and Venuti's violin less shrill, and the overall performance achieves a slight relaxation that makes it swing. As I said, this version of *Imagination* falls between the cracks, which made it difficult to pitch and transcribe properly. Of course, I could have gone upwards a quarter-tone as easily as downwards, but I selected what I thought was the proper key.

Assuming it's in Eb, there is a six-bar intro, very slow, before Mole states the melody. The bridge is harmonically daring, passing through B and G-diminished. Nichols takes the next break, followed by Rollini and Schutt; the middle theme, played by Nichols, keeps changing key

Example 6: *Imagination,* trumpet theme.

(Example 6) before landing in F. Then we transpose to C for a rumination with Rollini underpinning; then to G for the next theme, with chromatic chords on the breaks.

This version of *Feelin' No Pain* is *very* uptempo, at ♩ = 126 (2/4). There is a wonderful trumpet-clarinet intro, five bars, then the A theme played ensemble before Russell takes a chorus (sounding more in tune and quite inventive). Then comes Rollini, with tenor sax in the middle (Russell), before McDonough solos with Lang underneath (this, and a date two days later, were the only sessions to feature *both* of Nichols's guitarists, though McDonough is on banjo).   There is an ensemble on the B theme, Schutt piano, then a fiery final ensemble with a "bell-chord" break and a slow-down coda.   This is, by far, the best "New York Dixieland" version of Livingston's tune.

The Original Dixieland One-Step is also an uptempo romp, virtuosic to the extreme.   The A theme is played by ensemble with Russell on the breaks, then Pee Wee improvises on the main chorus which is actually Joe Jordan's *That Teasin' Rag.*   Mole solos brilliantly, with two bars of "pregnant pause" at the end.   Then Nichols, competent if somewhat unimaginative; Rollini for eight; and a final ensemble built on a slow crescendo.

On September 1, the same band was back to continue their newfound intricacies.   *My Gal Sal* is another medium-slow treatment of an old tune, starting with an ensemble improvisation on the melody, each phrase ending on an unexpected note (usually the second of each chord). There is a Rollini break and solo, with Lang underpinning, then Russell clarinet with McDonough.   Mole also plays a break and solo.   Nichols cracks on the high B in his break, but the solo is good, the ensemble coming in behind him for the finale.

Honolulu Blues has a duo-guitar opening, four bars, with Lang in the first and third and McDonough in the second and fourth.   Nichols plays the attractive theme with a two-clarinet chord cushion and Rollini counterpoint (with bass sax in the break).   Then comes Russell tenor sax, swinging if limited in range and imagination.   Nichols's two-bar break is sparkling, showing off the triple-tonguing that he undoubtedly used in his *Carnival of Venice* performances as a child; his solo is a little stiff, but driving. Then follows a most remarkable passage: Russell on clarinet, surprisingly virtuosic in the break, soloing while Mole and Rollini play out-of-key figures behind him in rising chromatics and parallel 10ths (obviously Livingston's touch) with Schutt on the break.   Then comes Mole with McDonough chording, and a Nichols-led ensemble. The remarkable chromatic passage returns as a coda.

On 1 April 1927, Lang recorded *Eddie's Twister* for OKeh, a guitar solo with Schutt on piano. Exactly what he was "twisting" is unclear, since the piece is taken at a funereal (for jazz) tempo of ♩ =112 (4/4), and sounds even slower than that. Here, the follow-up composition *The New Twister,* by Lillard and Krise, is a much more attractive piece, taken at a better clip of ♩ =144 (4/4). Mole's trombone starts things off for a chorus; then ensemble with Rollini breaks. Lang's four bars lead to Russell clarinet, somewhat stiff. Nichols's trumpet is quite beautiful and shapely. There is a Rollini break and solo, then ensemble with Rollini breaks and an out-of-tempo coda.

The band's next two sessions in September were nice but rather unexceptional, including remakes (for Columbia) of *Five Pennies, Imagination,* and *Feelin' No Pain. Sugar Foot Strut* contains another awful vocal, this time by Craig Leitch, though Russell's clarinet is excellent, and the mediocre Jack Hansen replaces the superb Joe Tarto on tuba.

Hansen, of course, was an intimate of Red's from the Voorhees band; and, curiously, after a year and a half of being on a fairly "straight" commercial kick, the Voorhees band suddenly unbuttoned its musical collar in September 1927 and allowed Nichols, McConville, Mole, Lang[4], and Berton to shine. *When the Morning Glories Wake Up in the Morning* (September 7) sports some outstanding duo-trumpet work by Red and Leo, as well as a first-class Mole solo chorus; *My Blue Heaven* (September 9) gives us more Mole, plus some crackling Berton drums; and the session of September 10 produced not one but two masterpieces, *Clementine (From New Orleans)* and *Baby's Blue,* on the latter of which Lang's guitar and Nichols's muted trumpet combine for some tasty duet work reminiscent of the "We Three" combination.

---

[4] Though discographies list McDonough, Nichols himself claimed Lang on this date.

THE ARKANSAS TRAVELERS: Nichols, Mole, Livingston, Morrow, Bloom, Berton. 14 September 1927.

This Travelers session began brilliantly and ended dully. The opening number is, of all things, Duke Ellington's *Birmingham Breakdown,* and it is a good performance despite the boxy sound. As opposed to Duke's full-section writing, it is of necessity more Dixieland in style, though Nichols's cornet solo is quite imaginative. Livingston's clarinet is not very good, but Mole is excellent and Bloom is in a nice stride groove, with rolling triplets. There is a Dixie ensemble with a Mole break, before returning to the theme for the finale.

Red Head Blues was written for, and not by, Nichols. It is an uptempo number, with a cornet intro and off-rhythm chords on piano. An ensemble follows, then Livingston clarinet (a little better) and Red, this time more clever than truly inventive. Mole and Nichols, however, trade breaks, and do so brilliantly, followed by Bloom back in the New York style. Mole solos, followed by an ensemble ride-out with excellent cymbal breaks and a clarinet coda. After two such impressive numbers, however, the ensuing *I Ain't Got Nobody* ain't got nothing.

MEYER'S DANCE ORCHESTRA: Nichols, Schutt, Morrow, McDonough, Berton; Jimmy Lytell, cl. 10 October 1927.

This is one of those rare "commercial" dance dates that almost has to be included, as so much of the ensemble and solo work is considerably hotter than normal. As mentioned in the Preface, this survey is not overmuch concerned with Nichols's or Mole's commercial dance sides, regardless of how hot they play (and some of those Voorhees sides with Berton on drums are quite hot indeed), primarily because they were not *conceived* as jazz recordings. But *Everybody Loves My Girl,* the one title from this session that *is* quite jazzy, was never originally released in the United States! The LP transfer I heard came from a British 78 source. Possibly this disc was

considered too "hot" for the white American middle-class
dance market.

Even from the outset, a whole-tone chord opening, we are
aware that this track is out of the norm. There is a stock
first chorus with cornet lead, clarinet, and alto sax playing
together in thirds during the middle eight. Then follows a
superb break, punctuated by Berton's bass drum. The band
again plays somewhat straight for two choruses, verse and
chorus of the tune; but then Nichols comes flying in with
an inspired break and solo with Schutt underpinning. Artie takes the first eight of the last sixteen bars, with Morrow's alto finishing the chorus. Then comes an entirely
re-composed section with substitute chords, which moves
away from the stock considerably, McDonough's banjo
heard on the middle eight before the ultimate ride-out.

As mentioned previously, Nichols often brought his somewhat advanced arranging ideas into studio jobs with such
bands as Voorhees and Reser, but *Everybody Loves My
Girl* is a prime example of how—left to their own devices
—Red, Artie, and Vic could reanimate even a dated
"stock" arrangement like this. Indeed, the use of stocks
by early jazz bands is another one of those situations
rarely discussed by critics, possibly because it seems to
detract from the "creativity" of certain jazz idols, but in
fact even the great bands of Bennie Moten, Henderson and
Ellington played them in order to fill out their books. It
was not really until Casa Loma that the "era of the
arranger" took over with a vengeance, and not until the
Swing Era that bands began utilizing more often the
services of top-notch arrangers. In fact, almost ninety per-
cent of Fletcher Henderson's "Dixie Stompers" arrangements were stocks, and this version of *Everybody Loves
My Girl* is certainly hotter than some of those records.

RED & MIFF'S STOMPERS: Nichols, Mole, Russell, Livingston,
Hayton, Hansen; Berton, dm & harpophone; Carl Kress, g. 12
October 1927.

The band's next session, for Victor, was a considerable success, though displaying in microcosm the stylistic divergence which was beginning to affect the group. *Slippin' Around* is a self-composed Mole showcase in strict "New York style." Though the melody is not particularly attractive or memorable, it should have been more appropriately named "Staccato-ing Around." Then comes the last version of *Feelin' No Pain,* played in a nice, relaxed, middle-up-tempo and proto-Swing style. After an unusual six-bar intro, Nichols solos with a sax cushion. There is a Russell solo with brass punctuations, Kress underpinning. Hayton's piano is not too good but solid in the bridge; then Mole, insinuating and imaginative. The ensemble ride-out comprises two choruses, the first light and swinging and the second hard and driving. Max Kaminsky told me that Bix claimed "Red stole it from him," though when Bix might have played this piece remains a mystery.

For Red's next session, also for Victor on October 26, an abrupt about-face in style and approach is heard. Here Mole is conspicuously absent, and the band includes members of the recently-disbanded Goldkette orchestra (Trumbauer, trombonist Bill Rank, drummer Chauncey Morehouse), a pair of weak, fluttery vocalists (Jim Miller and Charlie Farrell), and a slick, very commercial arrangement by the group's second trombonist, Glenn Miller. At the time, Miller played and arranged for Ben Pollack's band; his effect on the later Nichols groups was to be both interesting and profound; but we shall reserve those comments for later. Suffice it to say that *Make My Cot Where the Cot-Cot-Cotton Grows* is an awful piece, and this *Sugar* is an uninteresting tune by Red, NOT the song of the same name by Maceo Pinkard made famous by Ethel Waters.

Such a blatantly commercial session by a band which had been firmly committed to explorative, small-group jazz (albeit with large-band overtones in their scoring and pacing) was not only a new tack but a harbinger of evils to come. As the band swung into 1928 they were facing a number of commitments, imposed on them by the record

companies, that only marginally had Red's blessing. The
players, too, were changing in both name and style, with
the result that there were now several different styles to
contend with: strictly jazz, strictly commercial, and that
insidious 1920s hybrid, the largely commercial framework
with jazz interludes and overtones. Let us see what they
made of them.

THE BLUEBIRDS: Nichols, tp; Sam Lewis, tb; Larry Abbott, cl/a-
sx/kazoo; Norman Yorke, t-sx; Jimmy Johnson, bs-sx; unknown
vln; Harry Reser, bj/g; Bill Wirges, p; Tom Stacks, dm/voc. 25
January 1928.

Harry Reser, a name known today only by archivists, was
a virtuoso banjo and guitar player who rode to popularity
in the 1920s on the "Cliquot Club Eskimos" radio program. He was a superb, swinging rhythm player, but (like
McConville) somewhat less valid as a jazz soloist. But he
loved jazz, and stocked his radio and recording bands with
as many jazzmen as had not already signed with Goldkette
or Whiteman. Red was a frequent guest, and his presence
on this nonet session is confirmed by pianist Bill Wirges,
who stated bluntly that Tom Gott (credited in most discographies) "couldn't swing that hard."

Let's Misbehave, the early Cole Porter classic, is played
somewhat straight except for a strong Nichols lead and
fine breaks. The real gem from this session was *Mine, All
Mine,* a simple riff tune in C with a repeated G-A-C-A-G
melody played around the chord pattern of C, F^7, C, A^7,
D^7, G^7, C. Red and the gang throw a D-major switch into
the intro before swinging hard through the first chorus, the
violin playing rhythmic variations on the melody and the
bass sax playing counterpoint. After a B theme bridge,
played on alto, Stacks has a vocal, with Reser switching
from banjo to guitar and the unknown violinist doing a
Venuti imitation (though he sounds more like a country
fiddler than a jazzman). Tenor and trumpet dominate the
Dixie-styled ensemble before the violin, now double-

stringed, plays the melody fairly straight, with Nichols
(muted) on the break.   The final ride-out is tremendous,
with a Reser guitar solo spot and clarinetist Larry Abbott
—another one of those names that has fallen through the
cracks—sounding, amazingly, like Frank Teschemacher
over the ensemble. Well, almost like Tesch: his technical
command is better, though his brightness and drive are
similar.

RED NICHOLS & HIS FIVE PENNIES: Nichols, McConville,
Mole, Livingston, Russell, Hayton, Kress, Berton; Dudley Fosdick, mellophone. 27 February 1928.

Despite a few more sessions under the monickers of the
Molers and Charleston Chasers, and December 1927
broadcasts over CBS radio by an unrecorded group called
"Red Nichols and his Student Band," by 1928 Red was
pushing the "Five Pennies" name for all it was worth.   In
a way, it is reminiscent of that scene in Woody Allen's
film *Annie Hall* where we meet his uncle, Joey Nichols,
an obsequious bore who impressed his name on the
youngster by licking nickels and slapping them on his eyes
and forehead. "See? Nickels (slap)—Nichols (slap)—just
think of Joey Five Cents!" Red wasn't *quite* that bad, but
it was close. The band's personal appearances now included monstrous cardboard pennies propped up in front
of and around the bass drum, as if patrons would
somehow forget who they were without a constant visual
reminder. And Brunswick, one of whose owners was
singer Al Jolson, was pushing the band for all it was
worth—with occasionally odd and incongruous results.

Avalon is a nice, swinging chart, with an absolutely
superb two-trumpet intro and first chorus.   Then comes
Russell clarinet (I'm pretty sure it's him, this time), more
in tune and inventive, followed by Mole trombone with
low two-trumpet cushion and guitar.   Hayton solos on
celeste, quite pretty; then an excellent Berton break, a
mellophone solo, and ride-out.

Japanese Sandman is the scarcest number from this session. It is a medium-slow arrangement, much in the same vein as *Ida,* and obviously trying to cash in on the former's popularity. Aside from a good Russell break, the most one can say of it is that it sold fairly well.

RED NICHOLS & HIS FIVE PENNIES: Same. 1 March 1928.

For some bizarre reason, this session was incorrectly listed for more than a half-century as having been made on February 25, even though the matrix numbers *follow* those of the February 27 session. I am indebted to Nichols collector Stan Hester (and, in turn, to Phil Evans) for the session sheet reproduced herein, which proves that these discs were made on March 1.

Nobody's Sweetheart is an attractive arrangement, starting with a trumpet-clarinet improvisation on the melody with trombone-mellophone cushion, Mole in the breaks. Russell's clarinet (or Livingston, as Dan Morgenstern suggests? Their sounds were so similar that I sometimes find it difficult to differentiate between them) is a little out-of-tune, but imaginative. There is a Nichols break, then ensemble with guitar breaks, Mole on the middle eight. The ensemble ride-out features Berton's woodblocks and cymbals. The trombone-mellophone break towards the end points to the future; the alternate take, issued in the 1980s on an MCA LP, is not appreciably different.

RED NICHOLS & HIS FIVE PENNIES: Nichols, McConville, Mole, Fosdick, Schutt, Livingston, Kress, Berton; Manny Klein, tp; Murray Kellner (Kel Murray), vln; Art Miller, bs; Scrappy Lambert, voc. 2 March 1928.

If there was any previous doubt that the Five Pennies were heading in new directions, this session was bound to dispel them. This was the band's first session released on 12-inch 78s, instead of the more standard 10-inch, and in those days 12-inch records spelled trouble rather than relief for jazzmen. The major labels were all crazy for "concert arrangements," undoubtedly fueled by the success of such Paul Whiteman records as *Washboard Blues, When Day Is Done,* and *High Water.* They had in common pretentious, high-flown arrangements, alternating "hot" or "quasi-hot" passages with quite turgid ones.

By this time, of course, Vic Berton had probably come to expect just about anything. Since late 1927 he had been employed by Roger Wolfe Kahn, the wealthy son of banker (and Metropolitan Opera board member) Otto Kahn. Roger wanted a society-type jazz band, so daddy bankrolled his folly. Much to everyone's surprise, the group attracted a large following on the East Coast, especially in hotels where they liked their jazz soft 'n' sweet. Kahn employed a few strings, not nearly as many as Whiteman but enough to lift the group out of the pure-jazz context no matter how good the arrangements got (or how good Berton was on drums). Indeed, his band was *so* popular that Ben Pollack made Glenn Miller ape their style for his own orchestra (witness *Buy Buy for Baby, Out Where the Blues Begin, Futuristic Rhythm).* This boosted the Pollack band's commercial status, and eventually landed them in the Park Central Hotel, but considerably diluted their jazz quotient.

The one divergence between Brunswick's policy on 12-inchers, and the policies of Victor and Columbia, was that the company always recorded alternate versions of each tune, one with vocals and one without. According to jazz historian and clarinetist Frank Powers, this was done so that the non-vocal versions could be marketed in non-English-speaking countries, e.g., Germany and Austria. Yet the non-vocal versions followed exactly the same sequence, merely substituting a lead trombone or mellophone in place of the singer's chorus. The two titles recorded that day, *Poor Butterfly* and *Can't You Hear Me Calling, Caroline,* were no exception. Scrappy Lambert was an omnipresent high tenor for both Brunswick and OKeh, and for some unknown reason extremely popular.

In fact, the whole phenomenon of light, high, saccharine and thoroughly emasculated male vocalists in that era (and well into the 1930s) is the result of their being popular with women and—oddly—black audiences. (It drives other critics, such as Gunther Schuller, equally crazy.) In addition to Lambert, and of course the even more popular Rudy Vallee, there were Gene Austin, whose 1927 Victor recording of *My Blue Heaven* sold a million copies; Vernon Dalhart, who before the advent of Jimmie Rodgers was practically the only country or "hillbilly" artist of note (and who combined a high squeaky voice with a nasal twang and Tennessee accent); and Jack Fulton, a trombonist in the Whiteman band, who went even further, singing in a puerile, nasal falsetto. (I omit criticism of Cliff Edwards, "Ukelele Ike," because he swung, sang on key, and never simpered.) Yet on too many jazz or pseudo-jazz records to mention (including the Trumbauer-Beiderbecke versions of *Lila, Borneo,* and *My Bungalow of Dreams),* Lambert was the man of the hour (or, more precisely, the man of three or four minutes), and Lambert who all but spoils whatever good effects the Nichols band of this period could create.

The arranging chores were turned over to William Grant Still (of whom more in the next chapter); to his credit, he made the most of this execrable situation, almost turning these lemons into lemonade. *Poor Butterfly,* played in C, has a normal first chorus in which the band sounds like a typical hotel orchestra, but on the repeat of the melody Still whips up some substitute chords that would even make a bopper squirm (Example 7). Then a quick change to uptempo, a sax chorus with Nichols on the break, somewhat stiff and corny. After this we drop down—*way* down—for Lambert's saccharine vocal (the non-vocal version, of course, merely plays the melody softly and straight). Mole's break leads to a good jazz chorus with sax cushion, for two choruses, followed by a clarinet solo with guitar, bass and drums. Then comes the trumpet trio, ripping it up à la Bix with the Goldkette band, with some whole-tone chords on the way out.

Example 7: *Poor Butterfly,* second chorus.

Can't You Hear Me Calling, Caroline follows a similar pattern: straight first chorus with substitute chords the second time around, though these are not quite as weird as the ones in *Butterfly.* Mole, Nichols, and Livingston play the melody of the verse; Lambert sings the chorus. Red picks things up with some hot trumpet, then Schutt out of tempo, followed by Mole and Fosdick (sounding like two trombones), mellow and relaxed, to the end.

A commercial slant also infected the next Charleston Chasers session, on March 7. *My Melancholy Baby* and *Mississippi Mud* are both saddled with stock arrangements and Lambert vocals, neither being even as good as the Trumbauer versions (for OKeh) with Beiderbecke. The next session, fortunately, returned the band to form with good material and performances.

RED NICHOLS & HIS FIVE PENNIES: Nichols, McConville, Klein, Mole, JD, Schutt, Kress, Berton. 29 May 1928.

During this period when the musically restless Nichols was trying out different styles, he seems to have briefly latched onto the idea of integrating a trumpet trio, like those that Beiderbecke (via Challis) used to energize the big bands of Goldkette and Whiteman, into his own smaller units. The effect was rather startling, moving as it did between the intimate string-of-solos style of the Molers and a full-blooded, rip-roaring ensemble that pretended it was a big band. If Red had utilized this instrumentation on his 1926 Edison recording of *Stampede,* it would undoubtedly have been a more successful performance.

The two tunes recorded here—*Panama* and *There'll Come a Time*—were big favorites with New York and Chicago musicians. The former, which had been acoustically recorded by the NORK, begins with a sustained clarinet C while the trumpet trio plays around it for eight bars, using the first four notes of the principal melody as a cell motive. Then comes ensemble for eight bars, followed by Mole on trombone; then piano for a chorus, followed by the brass trio in splendid form. Jimmy Dorsey enters swinging; then Livingston, interesting but technically struggling. The trumpet trio returns, followed by a low-voltage but nice Nichols solo; then a duo-clarinet passage, really swinging, to the end.

There'll Come a Time, written by Mole and trumpeter Joe "Wingy" Manone, was new for this session. It has an a capella trumpet-clarinet intro, four bars, moving from G minor to Bb major; a hot trumpet (I speculate Klein) states the melody with Dixie ensemble, with JD on alto in the break. Muted trumpet and clarinet play the B theme in G minor, with trombone counterpoint; then Mole's solo with interjections from the two clarinets, with Livingston on the middle eight and a half bars.

Throughout this book we have been discussing the phrase-shapes of Nichols's and Mole's playing, and Miff's solo here is a perfect example of what I mean (Example 8). Note, for instance, that the beginning of his solo is not harmonically adventurous, working very much within the

chords and essentially playing arpeggios; and yet, he
makes these phrases intellectually fascinating by means of
his almost classical symmetry and superb intonation. In
bar 2, for instance, he drops down a ninth, from G to the
F below, and follows this up with an ascending arpeggio;
then in bar 3, he inverts this somewhat by playing a rising
fourth followed by a descending arpeggio. In bar 6, he

Example 8: *There'll Come a Time*, trombone solo.

waver

begins his phrase by means of a triplet in thirds which is
phrased almost as a smear, while in bar 8 he *ends* his
phrase by means of a slide-smear on the "blue" note (notated here as Db, but actually a microtone beneath that),
utilizing the C below to produce a wavering sound. Such
devices lifted Mole's work out of the norm, and placed
him head and shoulders above all contemporary trombonists except Jimmy Harrison and Jack Teagarden.

McConville, Klein, and JD play the bridge, with Nichols
on the two-bar break, then JD over augmented chords, and
a particularly outstanding Nichols solo that phrases over
the bar-lines in a manner that foreshadows Lester Young.
Schutt solos for eight, followed by a full-band ride-out.

**RED NICHOLS & HIS FIVE PENNIES: Same as March 2, but
Lang (g) repl. Kress; Venuti (vln) repl. Kellner. 31 May 1928.**

Here we are, back to the 12-inch kick, with more commercial slop interfering with the jazz; and this time, Still

was apparently barred from "distorting" these tunes with his imaginative harmonic substitutions. Scrappy Lambert again vocalizes on the domestic releases, replaced by muted trumpet (straight) on the foreign issues. Red must have been feeling somewhat schizophrenic about these stylistic shifts in his band's recordings, though these two selections at least have some very good jazz to cauterize the wounds.

Dear Old Southland, which is basically *Deep River* with new lyrics, has a very sappy opening, then a tango verse in minor based on *Sometimes I Feel Like a Motherless Child.* Rewritten and phony spirituals were all the rage in the late 1920s, possibly to validate the "noble savage" concept, and in fact this distasteful and insidious form of racism carried over to the early 1930s in such recordings as Lawrence Tibbett's *De Glory Road.* The vocal (muted trumpet on the "G" takes) comes next, but all is not lost: a Lang break introduces some Livingston clarinet, followed by a hot ensemble with Nichols leading and Mole trombone interjections, then a Mole solo. Hayton's out-of-tempo piano solo sounds more like Liberace than Artie Schutt, but the medium-tempo ride-out isn't too bad.

Limehouse Blues has a somewhat reverse format, starting off in wonderful shape with Mole and the rhythm section; Nichols plays it straight, but Venuti sounds good with Lang in back. A Hayton break leads to a quasi-oriental passage (it sounds like an oboe is in there), then the tempo comes way down for the vocal (muted trumpet). Livingston's clarinet again picks things up, then the ride-out.

It must have been frustrating for Nichols, who thought that his newfound success as a leader put *him* in control, to suddenly realize that he was as much a manipulated employee as a joyful employer. He could still pick the men for his dates, but it was becoming increasingly difficult for him to insist on the straight-ahead jazz he so obviously preferred. But Red was scarcely alone in his frustration. The heavy hands of song-pluggers, white impresarios, hotel managers, and A&R men at the record companies were commercializing white jazz in a particularly weird and restricting manner; and, all things considered, Nichols at least managed to sneak in a jazz date now and then to balance things out. Still, this split musical personality, combined with more and more commercial dance and theater dates, was beginning to wear the musicians' inspiration very thin.

Their following session (May 31) is a perfect example. *Whispering* has a corny intro, followed by rather straight Nichols; even the trumpet duo (Klein was absent) is rather straight, and only an outstanding Mole solo—one of his few that shows the influence of Jack Teagarden—livens things up. *I Can't Give You Anything But Love* is considerably worse, no one particularly inspired or swinging.

Klein returned on June 1, but only *Margie* has life and drive (though some of that may be caused by the transfer I heard, which was considerably sharp—at least a half-tone, possibly a full tone). The remake of *Imagination* lacks the easy lilt of the Molers, and *Original Dixieland One-Step* is a mess, with Nichols cracking and Livingston out of tune. Things were starting to go badly for the band.

RED NICHOLS & HIS ORCHESTRA: Nichols, McConville, Mole, Fosdick, Livingston, Schutt, Kress, Morehouse. 21 June 1928.

A return to Victor seemed to bode well, especially in the Livingston original *Harlem Twist.* The arrangement, however, is by Glenn Miller, who would later be so important to the "second phase" of the Pennies, and it begins with suspended brass chords, sub-toned clarinet, and vibes in the opening; the first chorus is by Livingston and the ensemble. There is Mole trombone and Livingston on the bridge, then a rather pathetic Morehouse scat vocal. The ensemble plays the Trio theme, with Livingston tenor sax over nice chord changes, The trombone-clarinet bridge repeats, followed by muted trumpet (McConville?), clarinet, and ensemble ride-out with Morehouse on cymbals.

Despite the fine composition and arrangement, the band still sounds somewhat flat, though there is more lilt in the more common take -2 than the newly-issued take -1. Indeed, Red himself was in dispute over which was really the best take; after -2 came out on 78, he requested that take -3 replace it. Yet this is nothing as compared to the turgid, unswinging performance of *Five Pennies* that followed, possibly the most consistently uninteresting Nichols record made under his own name before 1932. Someone, either Schutt or Livingston, had the bright idea to "spice up" this already unattractive piece (see comments on 20 June 1927) with a moribund, complex arrangement; the whole thing gets so bogged down that, literally, nothing happens.

In March 1928, the brilliant Texas trombonist Weldon Leo "Jack" Teagarden (1905-1964) came East, replacing (of all people) Miff Mole on a Roger Wolfe Kahn record date. His full-chorus solo on *She's a Great, Great Girl,* his first on disc, created a stir in the jazz community unprecedented since Mole himself arrived with the Red Heads. For Teagarden had not only Mole's command of staccato and crackling triplets, but a looser, swingier, more *relaxed* sound that rode the beat gracefully rather than accenting it. Moreover, there were genuine blues overtones in his playing that Mole normally lacked. Along with Fletcher Henderson's new trombone find, Jimmy Harrison, Teagarden helped revolutionize the art of jazz trombone playing.

That same year, too, many of the Chicago jazzmen also migrated East, looking for work: tenor saxist Lawrence "Bud" Freeman, clarinetist Frank Teschemacher, pianist Joe Sullivan, banjoist-singer Eddie Condon, and drummer Gene Krupa. (Cornetist Jimmy McPartland and clarinetist Benny Goodman, peripherally also part of this group, already had work aplenty in the Pollack band.) Red and Miff, always gracious with their time when genuine talent was concerned, brought all of these but Freeman into the OKeh studios for a session that would make history.

MIFF MOLE'S MOLERS: Nichols, tp; Mole, tb; Fosdick, mel; Frank Teschemacher, cl; Joe Sullivan, p; Eddie Condon, bj; Gene Krupa, dm. 6 July 1928.

Red must have been ambivalent about bringing such uncompromising jazzmen into the studios at this particular juncture in his career. They certainly produced a brand of jazz more high-voltage and less caring of detail; they were scarcely up to the virtuoso level of Dorsey-Schutt-Lang-Berton, Teschemacher in fact being a particularly raw and unfinished clarinetist; yet, at the same time, they had a congealed style of their own and certainly knew what they wanted (even if they didn't always get it, then). Nichols's uncertainty as to how the forces-that-be at OKeh would react led him to split the date, squarely down the middle, between the tepid pop-jazz that Brunswick and Victor preferred, and the hell-bent-for-leather style that characterized their own playing. Curiously, this time the real jazz won out.

One Step to Heaven was a placid piece, played under wraps in the manner designed to relax the socialites who wanted their "jazz" soft 'n' sweet. It was not released until 1940. On the other hand, *Shim-Me-Sha-Wabble* tore up the floorboards with rollicking Joe Sullivan barrelhouse piano, blistering-hot Teschemacher clarinet (more in tune during his first solo than in his second), and a rhythm section which, though somewhat underrecorded, had a looser and more swinging feel than any previous Nichols date. Indeed, the Chicagoans even influenced the playing of Nichols, who by his own admission had trouble loosening up and really swinging, and Mole, whose own solo is almost as blistering as Tesch's. Much to Nichols's surprise, OKeh not only issued it immediately, but leased the master to Clarion, Velvet Tone, Harmony, Parlophone, and Odeon. The socialites may have been scandalized, but jazz fans were delighted. *Shim-Me-Sha-Wabble* was the hottest thing the Molers had ever done.

The record's success began to give Red ideas, but it would be months before they crystallized into a cogent new style, one that satisfied Nichols as much as the musicians he hired. Three weeks later, in fact, the Molers were back in action with more of the "regular gang"—Fosdick, Livingston, Schutt, Kress, Tarto, and drummer Stan King—and the results were as turgid as the June 1 date. *Crazy Rhythm* was neither crazy nor swinging, with a stiff intro and basically uninspired solos; and, though Livingston tried to liven things up with substitute chords in the intro to *You Took Advantage of Me,* the performance is so dismal that one wonders if Schutt was making a sarcastic comment in his cocktail-styled piano solo.

RED NICHOLS & HIS FIVE PENNIES: Nichols, Klein, Fosdick, Livingston, JD, Schutt, Kress, Berton. 2 Oct. 1928.

The group's last date of 1928 was a somewhat nicer performance of *A Pretty Girl Is Like a Melody,* a rare Nichols arrangement with interesting substitute chords (showing an obvious Livingston influence) in the ensemble chorus, a clarinet solo with alto sax-trumpet cushion, then alto solo with clarinet-trombone cushion. But the handwriting was on the wall.

It was time to move on.

4. Chicago Meets New York
(1929-Aug. 1930)

The critical fraternity is sharply divided on Nichols's next period. Some writers prefer the looser, more swinging Chicago-influenced sides, often stating baldly that Nichols's promotion of these musicians on his records constitutes his *only* contribution to jazz. Others, especially Britons, lament the passing of the subtle, sophisticated "New York" style of which his groups were the primary exponents.

The real question, of course, is not whether Nichols's later style is more or less interesting than the earlier: this is like comparing apples and oranges. The real question is whether or not Nichols had said everything there was to say within his earlier style before he switched gears. And, since the New York style had its primary base in the musical explorations of Bix Beiderbecke, this in turn leads to the question, Did the New Yorkers explore and exploit everything inherent in Bix Beiderbecke's style?

The answer to this question, ironically, has always been a loud and insistent No. Bix's staunchest supporters, among them Eddie Condon and Charles Edward Smith, insisted that had their boy lived a normal life-span he would have become the white equivalent of Duke Ellington. They point to Duke's early records, the 1926-31 sides that are firmly entrenched in the "Jungle Style," and argue (with some justification) that they scarcely indicate the type of music that his band would be playing in 1935, or 1939, or 1942, or 1963.

What they fail to realize, however, was that even from his earliest days Ellington maintained a looser, more relaxed, almost passive stance towards music, seeing it as a vast canvas upon which he and the outstanding jazzmen in his bands would contribute lines, dashes, splashes, and accents. His early grasp of harmony and orchestration were

rudimentary at best, learned on the job and without the sophistication of his later self. Beiderbecke, too, may have
taken time off to explore more academically the music
that inspired him to his greatest flights of lyric imagination; but he viewed music as a means of individual, personal expression, and in fact showed little taste or discretion
in what he viewed as "great arrangements." He was just
as likely to be enamored of Ferde Grofé's monstrosity
Metropolis or the Whiteman-era "concert arrangements" of
High Water and *Sweet Sue* as he was of such truly inno-
vative arrangements as Bill Challis's *Three Blind Mice* or
Willard Robison's *Jubilee,* on the grounds that all of these
were played by "legitimate musicians" whose training and
knowledge far exceeded his.   In other words, Bix was
often overawed by mechanics, even to the point of depre-
cating his own work. Despite his white, German heritage,
he was much more of an instinctive musical primitive than
Ellington, who—"Jungle Style" or not—was much more
rational, less impulsive, more disposed to pre-plan his
musical directions.

This is not to denigrate either musician. Though Ellington, too, later became more enamored of what he
perceived as "legitimate" classical elements in his own
music than was healthy, he contributed a lexicon of jazz
that has never been surpassed; and Beiderbecke, despite
his prediliction for musical junk, was one of those truly
rare individuals who always improvised new and exciting
ideas, rather than falling back on established patterns.
Bix's harmonic relationship to the bop and cool musicians
of the late 1940s and early 1950s has been well established, but in my opinion he might never have eclipsed the
work of those who followed in his musical footsteps, such
as Red Norvo, Eddie Sauter, Gil Evans, and Miles Davis.

As for the Nichols bands, they were of course limited by
their knowledge of *what Beiderbecke was doing at that
time.* They could not reach into the future and predict that
the musical revolution of Dizzy Gillespie, Thelonious
Monk, and Charlie Parker would occur; and, in fact, there

is every indication that Red Nichols himself did not grasp the obvious or implied connections between the two eras. By the time bop and cool were firmly established in 1952, Nichols was still alive and active, yet he chose to pursue the largely dead-ended "Dixieland" style which had become almost a parody of the music he was playing twenty-five years earlier. Perhaps this had as much to do with his age as with his musical sensibilities; yet his recordings showed no proclivity towards even a superficial grasp of the harmonic-melodic relationships of bop and cool, which his bands had done more than their share to foster.

The truth was that Nichols and Mole *had* exhausted the Beiderbeckian lexicon, taken it to its ultimate degree and investigated every nook and cranny that then existed in it. I hope I have made this clear by my exhaustive description of Nichols's 1925-28 work; and, as none but the hardiest of fans realize, there were many more Nichols records made during this period than by any contemporary jazz musician, black or white. There is certainly the chance that, had Nichols not been so prolific a recording artist, he might have stretched the New York style out an additional two or three years. But by telescoping any average artist's output so drastically, he had obviously reached a stylistic dead end.

This can be seen more clearly, I think, if one compares Nichols's bands to those led on Victor by Jelly Roll Morton between 1926 and 1930. True, the Victor officials pushed him more and more into a commercial corner by the end, and the supposedly "outmoded" style of his music had much to do with the fact that he had trouble finding adequate musicians to play his charts. And yet, when Victor welcomed him back with open arms in 1939 (on a limited basis, of course), and even allowed him to pick the band he wanted, the results were pleasant jazz in the New Orleans idiom that completely lacked the charm, charisma or cohesion of those 1926-28 discs with much less stellar personnel. Jelly, in other words, had run the gamut of his own style, and if he lived to be eighty he probably would not have duplicated or surpassed those early efforts.

And yet, Nichols's adoption of this new style was not as immediate and "overnight" as some critics (particularly the British) have claimed. His dropping of the "hot tympani" was gradual, and scarcely noticed for a while; the transmutation of his arrangements took a while to accomplish, and went (as we have seen) through some odd and not altogether successful phases; and even the addition of Chicago-style musicians did not immediately bring about a new style, or energize the old one.

Curiously, in the rare interview with B.M. Lytton-Edwards for the British magazine *Rhythm* (op. cit, 1937), Red himself had something to say about the switch in gears; and, according to him, it was necessitated as much by circumstance as by his newfound love of the Chicago jazzers. He denied that he considered the work of the earlier groups outmoded, but his earlier cohorts (Mole, Lang, Berton, Schutt) were simply too busy with other projects to continue. Indeed, Nichols verifies my "apples vs. oranges" theory by stating, "Jack T. couldn't play like Miff—why should he? His own stuff was great. Same with Sullivan and Schutt; Krupa and Berton. My new group turned out records as financially and rhythmically satisfying as the first. Jazz was becoming Swing."

And so it was.

RED NICHOLS & HIS FIVE PENNIES: Nichols, Klein, Fosdick, Livingston, Schutt, Kress, Morehouse; Glenn Miller, tb; Benny Goodman, cl/a-sx. 1 February 1929.

Red's first session of what would turn out to be the year of the Great Depression added Glenn Miller (of whom more later) and Benny Goodman to his usual mix of New York players. But Red was, at this point, still trying to combine the hot playing of musicians like Goodman into the arranged style he preferred; and, what is more, this session still clung to the somewhat commercial aspects that dominated his last two of 1928. As a result, *I Never Knew* has a trombone-mellophone statement of the melody, Nichols playing stiff and unswinging variations, a guitar break, and ensemble with Miller on the middle eight. *Who's Sorry Now?*, despite a little brisker tempo and the oddity of hearing Goodman solo on alto sax, is notable only for an outstanding Fosdick solo.

Four days later, with Hayton replacing Schutt and Berton back on drums, he yielded better results in an outstanding arrangement and performance of *Chinatown My Chinatown*. Though the opening is a little raggy and stiff, we at least have a bright, peppy tempo for the two-trumpet chorus, Miller playing the verse with "Chinese" effects. Then Goodman comes in on his more familiar instrument, clarinet, playing in his best early form. Livingston swings mightily on tenor, backed by guitar and woodblocks. Hayton's piano is bland for a chorus, but there is an impressive and swinging two-trumpet ride-out improvisation with clarinet and trombone countermelodies.

RED NICHOLS & HIS FIVE PENNIES: Nichols, Klein, Miller, Fosdick, Livingston, J. Dorsey, Rollini, Schutt, Kress, Berton. 16 Feb. 1929.

This session, though returning entirely to the New Yorkers, continues to pick things up a notch. *Alice Blue Gown* starts with a Dixie ensemble chorus, with Miller more or less playing the melody straight; then Dorsey alto, showing continued growth as an improviser. An ensemble break precedes muted Nichols cornet with woodblocks, guitar, and a clarinet-alto sax cushion (very soft). Rollini takes a break and solo, then an ensemble ride-out.

Rudolf Friml's little-known *Allah's Holiday* is taken in medium-slow tempo, Rollini stating the melody with trombone and two-clarinet interjections; he is quite bluesy towards the end. Miller's trombone is heard next, in a particularly swinging groove, but Schutt's piano is a little flowery. There is a Klein break, Livingston tenor sax, and a nice ride-out, Dorsey's alto mixing it up with the trumpets. After such a relaxed "breather," the band swings hard on *Roses of Picardy* in a medium-up tempo. Again, we have a duo-trumpet statement of melody with clarinet-trombone commentary; Rollini plays the break, then a Miller solo, followed by JD alto swinging much like he did in the 1930s. Then comes a clarinet break by Livingston, who switches to alto for an excellent improvisation behind Fosdick playing it straight. Schutt is also back in a good groove, relaxed and imaginative, before the end.

LOUISIANA RHYTHM KINGS: Nichols, Mole, Fosdick, Livingston, Schutt, Berton. 20 February 1929.

This bittersweet session was to be, as it turned out, the last Red would do with his "old" Five Pennies combination in many years, not to mention the last jazz session until 1931 to feature Vic Berton. It was also the first recorded under a new pseudonym, The Louisiana Rhythm Kings, which he apparently felt should be the repository hereafter for those "hot," freewheeling jazz performances that had once characterized most of his bands. Nichols was developing a very split musical personality, and for a time tried to keep the three different kinds of music he played segregated under different recording names.

As it turned out, these recordings—except for the last title —were only a pale echo of his former Five Pennies style. *Futuristic Rhythm* was a very popular tune in late 1928 and early '29, though there was nothing particularly futuristic about it, rhythmically or harmonically. It was a catchy tune, however, so much so that the Pollack band recorded it under the pseudonym of Mills's Hotsy-Totsy Gang in October 1928, and the Trumbauer-Beiderbecke combo waxed it for OKeh on 8 March 1929. Red's version does not contain anything so marvelous as the inverted-melody improvisation that Bix would contribute in March, but it is not as stodgy as the Pollack recording, falling in between these two. Nichols leads the Dixie

Fig. 1: The Red Heads. L to R: Nichols, Jimmy Dorsey, Bill Haid, Fred Morrow, Vic Berton, Dick McDonough, Miff Mole.

Fig. 2: Don Voorhees and his Orchestra. L to R: Jack Hansen, Nichols, Mole, Leo McConville, Arthur Schutt, Voorhees, McDonough, Berton, Paul Cartwright, Fred Morrow.

Fig. 4: Miff Mole.

Fig. 3: Leo McConville.

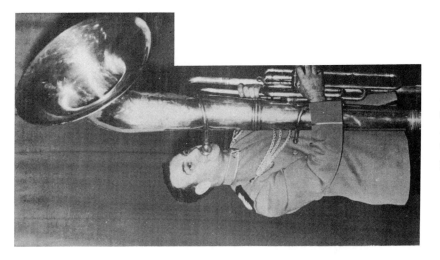

Fig. 6: Joe Tarto.

Fig. 5: Eddie Lang.

Fig. 7: Original labels of Nichols discs.

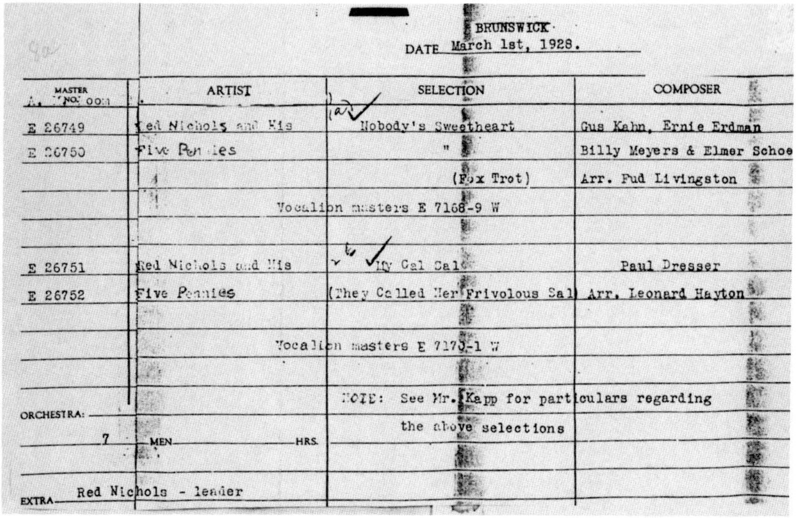

BRUNSWICK

DATE March 1st, 1928.

MASTER NO.	ARTIST	SELECTION	COMPOSER
E 26749	Red Nichols and His	Nobody's Sweetheart	Gus Kahn, Ernie Erdman
E 26750	Five Pennies	"	Billy Meyers & Elmer Schoe
		(Fox Trot)	Arr. Fud Livingston
	Vocalion masters E 7168-9 W		
E 26751	Red Nichols and His	My Gal Sal	Paul Dresser
E 26752	Five Pennies	(They Called Her Frivolous Sal)	Arr. Leonard Hayton
	Vocalion masters E 7170-1 W		
		NOTE: See Mr. Kapp for particulars regarding the above selections	

ORCHESTRA: 7 MEN HRS.

EXTRA Red Nichols - leader

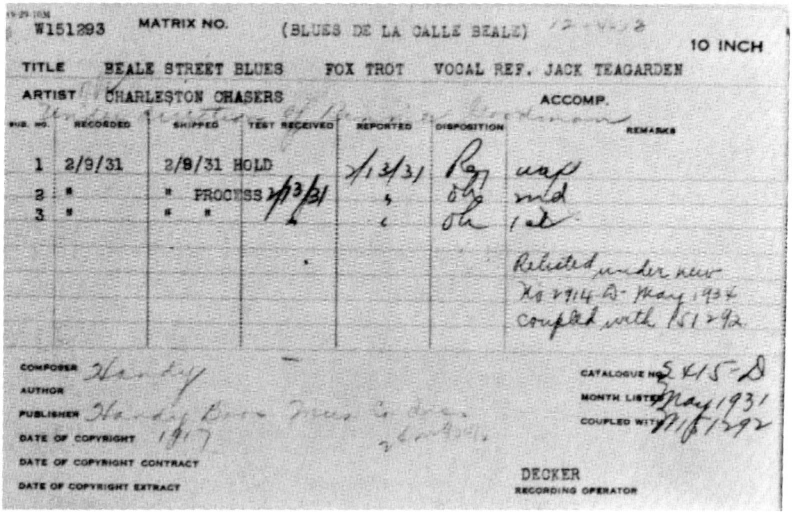

W151293 MATRIX NO. (BLUES DE LA CALLE BEALE) 12-4-3 10 INCH

TITLE BEALE STREET BLUES FOX TROT VOCAL REF. JACK TEAGARDEN

ARTIST CHARLESTON CHASERS ACCOMP.

Under direction of Benny Goodman

SUB. NO.	RECORDED	SHIPPED	TEST RECEIVED	REPORTED	DISPOSITION	REMARKS
1	2/9/31	2/9/31 HOLD		2/13/31	Rej	unap
2	"	" PROCESS	2/13/31	"	OK	2nd
3	"	" "		"	OK	1st
						Relisted under new No 2914-D - May 1934 coupled with 151292

COMPOSER Handy

AUTHOR

PUBLISHER Handy Bros Music Co Inc.

DATE OF COPYRIGHT 1917

DATE OF COPYRIGHT CONTRACT

DATE OF COPYRIGHT EXTRACT

CATALOGUE NO. 2415-D

MONTH LISTED May 1931

COUPLED WITH W151292

DECKER

RECORDING OPERATOR

Fig. 8: Recording log sheets of Five Pennies, Charleston Chasers discs.

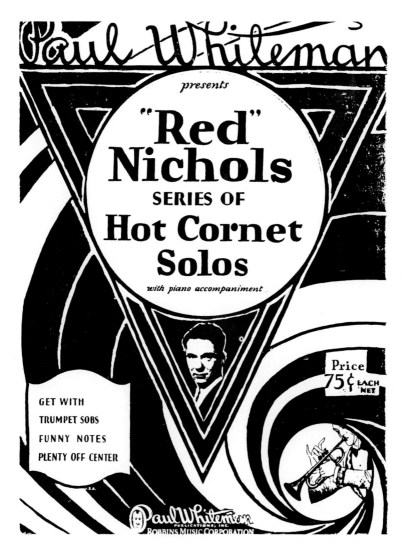

Fig. 9: Front cover of Red Nichols sheet music folio.

ensemble, followed by the verse; then solos by Fosdick (excellent), Livingston clarinet (good), and Nichols (mediocre) before the ride-out.

Out Where the Blues Begin is more spirited, though not outstanding. The real gem of this session was Lew Pollack's *That's A-Plenty,* which has much of the old verve. There is a staccato opening on the verse, with Livingston clarinet in the middle, followed by Nichols and Mole playing duo-counterpoint on the chorus. Then comes some excellent Mole trombone, a nice Dixie-styled ensemble, and a Fosdick chorus. The bridge leads to some outstanding Schutt piano, then two ensemble choruses to the end. It may be noted that Nichols arranged all three numbers.

Exactly a month later, on March 20, Red brought a ten-piece band (plus the omnipresent Scrappy Lambert) into the Brunswick studios for a very commercial session. This was made under the name of "The Captivators directed by Red Nichols," though similar, later sessions would be released simply as The Captivators. Here, Red was obviously trying to separate his more commercial assignments in a way that would not reflect negatively on the Five Pennies, for which he had high hopes of resuscitation under a new style. Tellingly, the trombonist and arranger on this session was the man who would become his "new Fud Livingston," Alton Glenn Miller (1904-1944).

Miller, the son of itinerant farmers, had miraculously graduated from Colorado University with high marks in every subject—except music. No one, not even the members of his own family, thought Glenn would ever amount to much in the music world. His trombone playing was rough and unfinished in tone, technically spotty and overall rather average; indeed, even an infatuation with Mole's style that dated back to 1924 could not help disguise Miller's problematic technique. A decade hence, of course, he was to become the most famous and legendary of all white swing band leaders, his clarinet-led sax scoring becoming an icon in popular music history. But that was in 1939; in 1929 he was just another struggling, unknown musician, though his being hired by Ben Pollack in late 1926 encouraged him considerably.

Miller, who was very much a jazz buff, saw his ascension to the trombone and arranger's chair with Pollack as a stepping-stone of considerable importance. But Livingston was Pollack's "hot" arranger, so Glenn was assigned the "sweet" spots. He developed his craft by studying the Roger Wolfe Kahn band, for several nights in a row, making notes and analyzing their style almost chorus-for-chorus. As a result, he was soon turning out such "semi-sweet" Pollack charts as *Buy Buy for Baby, Singapore Sorrows,* and *Futuristic Rhythm* while Fud garnered the spots he would have killed to do. Then, in mid-1928, Pollack band members heard Jack Teagarden play and sing; they dragged the "boss" along; and before long Pollack had two trombonists, one of whom was becoming eminently expendable.

This was a crushing blow to the sensitive Miller, but his propensity of bottling his frustrations up came to the fore. When the Pollack band was scheduled to play an extended gig at Atlantic City, Miller came up with the excuse that commercial bandleader Paul Ash had made him a better offer in order to leave Pollack. The excuse was, in fact, true; but it is doubtful that Miller, who adored the playing of Pollack, Jimmy McPartland, Larry Binyon, and Benny Goodman, would ever have left in such a hurry if Teagarden hadn't come along. Indeed, in later years Goodman himself stated that he was certain that Miller's move to the Ash band was merely a way of "marking time."

Glenn must have felt little more than courteous thanks when Nichols asked him to play on the Captivators session, and handle the rather commercial arranging chores (he had, remember, been present in October 1927 for the Stompers' Victor date). But Nichols, still looking for new directions, persuaded Miller to show him some of those "hot" scores that Pollack had bypassed; and what he saw impressed him so much that, henceforth, the "new" Nichols Five Pennies style would essentially be the Glenn Miller style.

For those who have never heard these records, and/or are only familiar with Miller's post-1938 work, these arrangements must come as a revelation. In addition to completely avoiding the repetition of the "reed-sound" band, Glenn's work of this period used several stylistic devices which, though simple in themselves, had a curiously profound effect on the ensemble as a whole. His rhythms, for instance, alternated between repetitive simplicity and breathtaking sophistication; his use of harmony was just as advanced as Livingston's, but by dropping in those whole tones and substitute chords deftly, like pebbles instead of boulders, he was able to facilitate swinging while still maintaining interest. Although he too liked Beiderbecke's work, and admired many of the earlier Five Pennies efforts, he realized that the rhythm of jazz was changing; in fact, it may come as a surprise to many that though he liked Bix he preferred Louis Armstrong, once calling him (in 1942) "the greatest thing that ever happened to music." And Armstrong's music, like that of the white Chicagoans who worshipped him, was more concerned with rhythmic than harmonic alteration, more with loosely-swinging ensembles than staccato trumpet trios, more with a bluesy-funky bent than sophisticated and pre-planned effects.

Miller's arrangements, of course, *were* pre-planned—very much so—yet he managed to capture, as no one else ever has, the "feeling" of Chicago jazz in an arranged mode. As we shall see, his cleverness (at least in *this* period) never bordered on the precious; his was a smart, adult solution to a sticky problem. Moreover, he varied his approach so much that it is difficult to pin him down, though certain aspects of these arrangements are not only similar to each other but to some of the work he was to turn in for his own band, ten years later.

As for his much-maligned trombone playing, though it was certainly not in a class with the top-notch white (or black) trombonists of his time it was not as bad as many have claimed. Miller's problem, not only in 1929 but until the day he died in a plane crash over the English Channel, was that he was always some years behind the *best* trombonists of each era. We have no record of his playing before 1927, but one must assume that it was even rawer and rougher than that of the much-overrated Kid Ory or Bill Rank, and in 1927 it was certainly not in a league with Mole or another Mole admirer, Tommy Dorsey. By 1930 it had improved somewhat in tone and technique, thanks primarily to his playing for over a year alongside Jack Teagarden, but again he could not compete with Teagarden or Jimmy Harrison. By the time he started his own band in 1937 he had improved some more; but so had Tommy Dorsey, whose smoothness and slide technique were always far superior, and of course Teagarden was still around (not to mention Lawrence Brown, Dicky Wells and valve trombonist Juan Tizol). As he entered the 1940s, the roughness in the tone was almost gone and he could perform his muted work with the stylishness of a Dorsey, but then along came Bill Harris and a host of other trombonists who could (again) play rings around him.

And yet, quite aside from his constant, relentless pursuit of technical perfection, Glenn Miller was actually one of the most *inventive* players of his time. His execution always seemed to betray his intent, both in the Jazz and Swing Eras, but the notes he played (or, at least, tried to play) were actually far more interesting than many people gave him credit for. As we shall see, he could conjure up solos, counterpoint, even commentary to blues vocals, that were easily the equal of anything Tommy Dorsey could accomplish, sometimes even more interesting than Dorsey. The technical blemishes never completely evaporated, and oftimes intruded in the act of creation, but in my estimation Miller was not a hack but a creative player who simply didn't have great chops.

RED NICHOLS & HIS FIVE PENNIES: Nichols, McConville, Klein, tp; Miller, Teagarden, tb; Goodman, cl/a-sx/br-sx; Babe

Russin, t-sx; Schutt, p; Kress, g; Art Miller, bs; Gene Krupa, dm;
Lambert, voc. 18 April 1929.

Glenn Miller's much-touted penchant for mathematically-
balanced scores was not merely a late development,
designed for his own band after studies with Joseph Schillinger, as some have claimed. In actuality, Miller's studies with Schillinger merely reinforced and gave legitimacy
to theories he had had, and put into practice, since the
Five Pennies days. Yet like modern theorist George Russell, Miller's mathematical bent seemed never to interfere
with genuine creation or inspiration, but merely enhanced
it. One can find the mathematical balance in transcribing
a Miller score to paper, but in the process of merely *listening* to it there never seems to be any strain or
artificiality.

This session begins with one of his most exciting and least
hackneyed charts, *Indiana,* which kicks off with a bright,
punchy intro (Example 1) like an exclamation point at the
beginning of a sentence. What cannot be notated, how-

Example 1: *Indiana,* intro and opening theme.

ever, is the way Nichols attacks those two opening B-flats
—pushing so much air into the horn that they virtually
explode on the ear.[1] Note how Miller's mathematical penchant is at work here, balancing the opening octave-drop
that begins the melody proper (bar 4), and transforming

---

[1] Take -B only; on the newly-reissued Take -A, Red does not attack these notes as strongly.

the descending whole-tone chords in bar 5 into a natural harmonic progression, rather than merely producing out-of-synch chords that just "sound weird."

The first chorus continues the punchy trumpet sound, yet complements it with ascending saxophone triplet figures and trombone bell-chords. What taste, what balance is evident in this seemingly "simple" arrangement! A little chord substitution in the "Banks of the Wabash" section gives it tang without upsetting the listener's equilibrium. Then we transpose, suddenly and without fuss, to G for a superb Goodman clarinet solo, followed by muted Nichols using Armstrong-type rips and Beiderbeckian balance in his phrase-shapes. A guitar break brings us back to Bb for Teagarden's solo, then the finale.

What makes this record and arrangement so effective, in my view, is the fact that Nichols's trumpet solo is used as a resting-place, or fulcrum, for what precedes and follows it. Red was only too aware that he was *not* the "hot" player that Goodman, Teagarden, and Russin were, and probably had some misgivings about fitting into their company. But Miller proved himself, even from this very first session, a master at offsetting different or negative aspects in an otherwise positive arrangement. These were tricks he was to mature, rework and re-use years later in enhancing the childish vocals of Marion Hutton or the average yet inoffensive tenor sax of Tex Beneke in his own band.

Good as *Indiana* is, however, it seems like a mere warm-up for *Dinah.* Though this tune is taken at a slower tempo, $\rfloor$ =132 (as opposed to *Indiana's* $\rfloor$ =218), it doesn't *sound* slow. What a difference between this and some of those 1928 recordings, for instance *Five Pennies,* where the medium-slow tempos actually sounded *slower* than they were! The difference, aside from superior swinging players, is Miller's catchy use of rhythmic devices. In the four-bar intro, for instance (Example 2), note how he combines a rim shot from Krupa with the staccato chords of the trumpets in the first two bars; then, also, how his own second trombone fools the ear into thinking it is in

Example 2: *Dinah,* intro and beginning of melody.

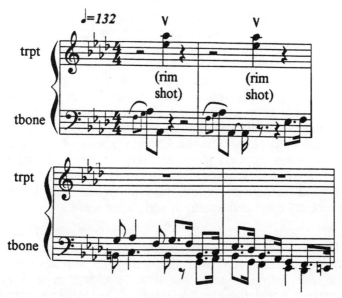

perfect synch with Teagarden, while in fact it alternates between harmonizing 3rds and 4ths and counterpoint (bars 3 and 4). Again, the actual performance contains felicities that cannot be notated; for instance, that Miller's trombone is considerably softer than Teagarden's, and that he offsets Jack's full but blunt tone with mellow, legato playing, using the slide to climb up to and fall back from notes.

After this, the melody is played by the two trombones with trumpet interjections, one of them a rising chromatic figure in thirds. Then the trumpets and trombones reverse their roles on the bridge, again giving a nice balance to the arrangement. The rhythm changes from a straight four (with accents on one and three) to a shuffle-beat behind Goodman's clarinet. We go back to 4 for Russin's tenor sax in the middle eight, then to shuffle-beat again; a trumpet break leads to a remarkable Teagarden solo, which daunted competitors for years, then a clarinet-trombone ride-out with the trumpets playing a repeated riff as punctuation.

The subtle artlessness of Miller's arrangements contrast themselves with the throat-grabbing sophistication of Fud Livingston. Both were, to a point, unique in their time, but inevitably Livingston's work found more successors because its components could be analyzed, torn apart, and reassembled. By contrast, the Miller scores were almost delicate, perfectly-constructed flowers that bloomed on their own; they seemed indigenous to the specific performances at hand, and though the interior devices could be copied or at least simulated, they appeared to make no sense when applied to other tunes. They too had to be torn apart and reassembled, but only Glenn Miller knew how to reassemble them into a logical and integrated structure, time and again, in song after song.

Unfortunately, Fred van Eps's arrangement of *On the Alamo* is not in the same league with these arrangements, mostly because Red was attempting yet another return to the *Ida* formula—and this time, sticking in a Scrappy Lambert vocal (on the "A" take). But Miller's contributions were as much a commercial as an artistic success, as the *Indiana-Dinah* combination, on Brunswick and Vocalion, also sold a million copies.

MIFF MOLE'S MOLERS: McConville, Klein, Mole, J. Dorsey, Schutt, Lang, King. 19 April 1929.

Miff Mole's last "Molers" session reverted to the New York style that he helped create, and which had characterized the 1927 band, but he did so without Red Nichols. With the arrival of Miller and Teagarden, it was evident that a rift between the two musicians was imminent; after all, Big T's solos had an extra dimension that Mole lacked, and Miller's arranging prowess—not to mention his assets as a surrogate Mole—made Miff's presence all but superfluous. Yet the rift was purely musical, and did not affect their personal relationship. Or did it? It is interesting that the two men only recorded together one more time after this session, despite the fact that both lived into the 1960s and performed regularly through the end of the 1940s.

I've Got a Feeling I'm Falling starts with a two-trumpet intro, quite nice, then ensemble theme with Dorsey's alto sax in the middle eight. Mole's trombone is heard, with King riding the cymbals and delicate Lang guitar. Schutt's piano is next, then JD's clarinet, sub-toned in the opening à la Goodman or Jimmie Noone. Klein plays for eight bars, then the finish.

In a way, this Nichols-less remake of *That's A-Plenty* is even more interesting than the original. After the ensemble opening we hear Schutt piano with good Stan King drums, then ensemble on the chorus. JD is heard next on clarinet with guitar and drums, then a wonderfully inventive passage for the two trumpets, muted. Mole is in superb staccato form; Klein solos with a sax-trombone cushion; then we transpose up a half-tone for a soft bit, followed by an alternating loud-soft-loud ending.

LOUISIANA RHYTHM KINGS: Nichols, Miller, Goodman, Schutt; Dave Tough, dm. 23 April 1929.

Four days after one of Mole's best jazz sessions came a good one by Red. Notable in the line-up is yet another Chicagoan, Dave Tough (1908-1948). Tough was a subtle but superb drummer who managed to keep up with every change in jazz through the Bebop era; he was equally adept at driving Tommy Dorsey's Clambake Seven, the big bands of Benny Goodman and Woody Herman, and various small groups playing in a somewhat modern vein. But Tough was always beset by a tremendous inferiority complex, which drove him to drink almost as heavily as Bix, and in the end his demons—exacerbated by the superiority of such bop drummers as Kenny Clarke and Max Roach—drove him into a drinking bout from which he never returned. He fell on a Newark street and fractured his skull at the age of forty.

Here, however, he was at the beginning of what seemed to
be a promising career, and the performances are light-
hearted and spirited. *Ballin' the Jack* starts with a Chi-
cago-Dixieland intro, followed by Miller and Goodman
(clarinet) solos. The ensemble plays the verse, then Nichols trumpet, Schutt piano and an ensemble ride-out with
Red smearing some blue notes. *I'm Walking Through
Clover* also has a Dixie intro, then Goodman with Schutt
and Tough giving an eerie presentiment of the mid-1930s
Benny Goodman Trio. This is followed by Schutt with
Tough on brushes, very nice; Nichols takes the break, then
leads the ensemble to the end, Miller on the middle eight.

This curious combination of New York and Chicago musicians provided a fond farewell, for Red, to the New York
style that had made his name. From here on out, he
would be committed to the looser Chicago format and the
Chicago-cum-Miller style, interspersed with whatever
commercial numbers Brunswick decreed that he record.
Mole got a studio job with NBC radio, where he stayed
for most of the next decade.

As I said before, it was time to move on.

*   *   *   *   *

The next two Nichols dates were far more commercial--
those hybrid 12-inchers combining schmaltz with jazz.
The second of these was marred by Lambert vocals on
three old chestnuts, though the May 20 recording of *Sally,
Won't You Come Back* was salvaged by a Teagarden
vocal (following Lambert's), with Miller's trombone playing a bluesy accompaniment that some critics compared
favorably to Louis Armstrong's work with Bessie Smith.
(Yes, it *is* almost that good.) Nichols must have begun to
be discouraged by the accelerating commercial pressures
Brunswick was placing on him. Though he was certainly
no stranger to commercial sessions, making most of his
money there, at least part of his worldwide fame was
based on his ability to play and create good jazz. He had
thought that increased fame would put him *more* in con-

trol of the artistic aspects of his recordings than before; instead, he learned that he was becoming more controlled. He could pick the musicians, but not necessarily the tunes or arrangements; and, as the Depression came on and deepened, the problem became worse instead of better.

Woody Backensto, the annotator on the Broadway LP *Don Voorhees and his Orchestra* (BR-121), claims that black composer and arranger William Grant Still (1895-1978) arranged several of Nichols's "symphonic syncopation" recordings. From the 1920s to the 1940s, Still had an almost legendary reputation as a pedagogue—which was well-deserved—and one for being a creative, forward-looking "symphonic jazz" arranger, which was undeserved. His work attracted the attention of both Whiteman and Voorhees, who recorded Still arrangements (e.g., Voorhees's March 1927 disc of *Fantasy on St. Louis Blues),* and in the early 1940s Artie Shaw used him for a number of pieces including his big seller *Frenesi.* But except for *Poor Butterfly,* Still's work has dated badly; it is full of mawkish sentimentalities and pseudo-jazz "licks" which sound both pedantic and pathetic alongside the contemporary work of such true jazz arrangers as Don Redman, Horace Henderson, Jimmy Mundy, Billy May, and Eddie Sauter. Since it is now difficult to identify all specific arrangements, one wonders which of the ensuing Nichols monstrosities are his. Fortunately, there were times when Red could still kick back and let the creative juices flow; and after two consecutive commercial dates, he was rewarded with two consecutive jazz sessions.

LOUISIANA RHYTHM KINGS: Nichols, Teagarden, Russell, Sullivan, Tough; Bud Freeman, t-sx. 11 June 1929.

Still more Chicagoans were coming into the Nichols jazz sessions; this one introduced Bud Freeman, a twenty-two-year-old tenor saxist whose rough, earthy but violently swinging style was to white musicians what Coleman Hawkins was becoming to blacks. Gunther Schuller has gone so far as to say that these two tenors, Freeman and Hawkins, were in fact the most original players on their instrument during the 1920s and 1930s, a statement borne out in their many records. With no guitar, banjo, or bass, the rhythm section sounds a little thin, but Sullivan and Tough manage to move things fairly well nonetheless.

That Da-Da Strain is immediately looser, more swinging than the April 23 session, Nichols allowing his players to substitute the Chicago style of Dixieland for the New York brand. It should be noted, at this point, that the concept of "Dixieland" has unfortunately changed over the years, moving away from the inventive, New Orleans-influenced polyphony of the 1920s to a slicker, shinier, more predictable style after World War II. Some have pointed, with reason, to Glenn Miller's scores for the Dorsey Brothers Orchestra in the early 1930s, and the Deane Kincaide-Bob Haggart scores for the Bob Crosby Orchestra later in that decade, as the instigators of this later, more "streamlined" style. But the slickness was intentional on Tommy Dorsey's part, in an effort to commercialize the "old jazz" for swing-era audiences, and anyway does not entirely explain how this phenomenon transferred itself to small-group performances in the 1950s and 1960s. In part, this might also have stemmed from those Beiderbecke trumpet trios with Goldkette and Whiteman, which sounded so "vintage" during the hi-fi era; but by and large, it was a desire to provide "good-time jazz" without the complexity that characterized the New York and Chicago styles of the 1920s that provided such fertile ground for corny "Dixieland" groups to grow in.

In this performance, the difference is made obvious by some excellent Nichols variating on the second go-round. This is followed by Russell's clarinet, a little off-key in the middle but swinging; then the newcomer, Freeman, on tenor, Tough good on drums in his second chorus before the ride-out.

In later years, Jack Teagarden only seemed to remember the 1931 Charleston Chasers version of *Basin Street Blues,* the tune that became his unofficial theme song. This 1929 read-through is not quite as memorable or exciting, beginning with Sullivan piano but leading into a somewhat lethargic ensemble on the theme. Jack plays a trombone solo, very bluesy, and then takes the vocal. But the words here are not the familiar ones, written for him in 1931 by Glenn Miller, but a standard blues chorus that I suspect was improvised on the spot. The lyrics are, "I'm going way down to Basin Street, baby, but I can't take you (repeated); And way down yonder, an ugly gal can't do." There are brass chords under Sullivan's piano; Russell's solo starts way down low, then builds with irregular, asymmetrical phrases before a Nichols-led chorus to the end. Gene Austin's underrated *Last Cent* proves a nice, bluesy end to a fine session; all of the solos are outstanding, and Tough's drums really kick.

RED NICHOLS & HIS FIVE PENNIES: Nichols, Klein, Tommy Thunen, tp; J. Teagarden, G. Miller, Herb Taylor, tb; Russell, cl; Freeman, t-sx; Sullivan, p; Tommy Felline, bj; A. Miller, bs; Tough, dm; Red McKenzie, voc. 12 June 1929.

Red McKenzie (1899-1948) was a St. Louis jockey-turned -jazz-musician who had stormed his way through the mid-1920s with a series of records featuring his "Mound City Blues Blowers." Red's "instruments" were the only ones he could handle—his voice, which by the standards of the day wasn't bad, and a comb-and-tissue-paper kazoo. He could really swing on the comb and tissue paper, and in fact led two dates for Victor in 1929 that are still considered classics: one with Teagarden and Eddie Condon, and the other featuring Russell, Glenn Miller, and Coleman Hawkins. With Nichols he was simply a featured guest singer, but his contributions are highly laudable compared to the Scrappy Lamberts of the world.

This rather massive "Five Pennies," practically a big band in the Swing Era sense of the word, reverts somewhat to New York style in the first number. *Who Cares?* sports

muted trumpet figures behind Teagarden's theme statement, with Russell on the last eight with ensemble and
again in the break. McKenzie sings next, followed by a
nice but unimaginative Nichols solo. The final ensemble
has Russell on top to the coda.

Much better—a classic, in fact—is this little-known version of *Rose of Washington Square.* This Miller chart rep-
resents big-band swing of a very high order for 1929. It
begins uptempo with a three-trumpet statement and sax
obbligato figures, the latter later changed a bit and re-used
by Edgar Sampson for *Stompin' At the Savoy;* the roles
are reversed in the middle. Big T is superb with banjo
and drums; then comes a three-trumpet break that will
reappear before each new solo—Russell, Freeman, Sullivan, with Pee Wee sounding especially superb over the
big-band cushion (a pleasure that was denied us during the
Swing Era)—before the ride-out.

The band's next four dates were far more commercial in
concept and execution, one of them in fact being a 12-inch
session, and all featuring vocals by Lambert and a newcomer, Dick Robertson (who, though also a tenor, was a
somewhat more musical singer). The August 20 version
of *The New Yorkers* is saved by McKenzie's reappear-
ance, and sprinkled throughout the arrangements are little
Miller touches, such as those marvelous duo-trombone
passages that he and Teagarden had worked out, as well as
some fine Russell clarinet.

RED NICHOLS & HIS FIVE PENNIES: Nichols, Thunen, John
Egan, tp; Herb Taylor, tb; Russell, cl; Eddie Condon, bj/g/voc;
Bob White, dm. July or August 1929, exact date unknown.

Around the time of these generally commercial recordings,
Red was invited to make a seven-minute short for Warner
Brothers' "Vitaphone" series. Vitaphones, introduced in
1926, were early sound shorts for which the soundtracks
were recorded on monstrous 16-inch 78s, and meant to be
synchronized with the presentation of the film. This one

was thought lost for nearly fifty years; but the film footage was discovered in the late 1970s, and a few years ago jazz archivist Frank Powers acquired the soundtrack from the widow of Cincinnati collector Charles Kindt, allowing the film to be restored for the current owner, Ted Turner.

Though there is no dialogue, this short is fascinating in that it shows how Red worked with a band in this period. There is a huge cardboard penny set up in front of the bandstand, on the left, and Red does a lot of side-to-side head-shaking, I suppose in an attempt to appear "hot." The film opens with a brief version of the band's big hit, *Ida,* trombonist Taylor playing lead in place of Rollini's bass sax, and Russell taking a brief but tasty solo. Then the other two trumpeters appear from behind a curtain, and join Red for an a capella, muted version of *Whispering,* played straight.

From this point on the jazz quotient begins to rise. Condon leaves his place on the bandstand to come down by Red and sing *Nobody's Sweetheart.* Red signals for a change in tempo, the band plays *Who Cares?,* and Condon comes back down for a second vocal. Many critics, and even some admirers, have long since forgotten that Condon was trying to make a living at this time as a singer. He displays a good beat (which should come as no surprise), but his voice is thin and shrill. Bing Crosby had nothing to worry about from the competition.

As Eddie makes his way back to the bandstand for the second time, White's drums kick into high gear and Nichols starts off *China Boy* with a scintillating, punchy solo that aptly demonstrates his ability to create beautiful musical shapes. The biggest surprise, however, comes in the last chorus, when the since-departed extra trumpeters invisibly join Red for one of those marvelous Bix-like trios-with-small-group that had become a Nichols trademark. The whole performance, in fact, puts one in mind of Glenn Miller's sardonic comment about the "Five Pennies," e.g., "If you don't count the extra seven or so we had hidden behind the curtain!" Nevertheless, the music is marvelous, some of the best jazz that Nichols was allowed to record around this period of time.

LOUISIANA RHYTHM KINGS: Nichols, Thunen, G. Miller, J.
Dorsey, Tough; Irving Brodsky, p. 10 September 1929.

Some jazz balance was restored on this date, when the
"Louisiana Rhythm Kings" reappeared for a trio of tunes
with Irving Brodsky replacing Sullivan on piano; but the
session reveals a musical schizophrenia that would never
have occurred a year earlier. *Waiting At the End of the
Road,* unlike the Whiteman recording with Beiderbecke, is
an uptempo Dixie jam with Nichols and Dorsey (on clarinet) predominating in the opening ensemble. There are
superb solos by JD, Nichols, and Glenn Miller, the latter
combining bluesiness with Mole-like staccato. But *Little
By Little* is more of a pop tune and arrangement, with the
solos so straight that one is tempted to identify the muted
trumpet as Thunen (especially since that sounds like Red
who comes in, on open horn, to lead the ensuing ensemble); and the closer, *Marianne,* lies somewhere between
the two, Jimmy Dorsey's alto sax being good if unexceptional and the lone moment of creativity belonging to Miller's trombone. The next two sessions, like the three preceding this one, returned to fairly stodgy charts with only
an occasional solo by Goodman or the Dorsey Brothers to
liven things up.

What was happening? Well, for one thing, Nichols was
getting more and more pit-band dates during this period,
at the Times Square and Alvin Theatres in New York, and
had to have some commercial stocks to fill up his sets.
And, for another, by the end of 1929 the Depression had
arrived and "the panic was on." Nichols had no intention
of passing up chances of lucrative employment, but his
newer, more "commercial" bent was beginning to annoy
the hard-core jazzmen. Beginning, but not quite there yet;
for Nichols, despite his greed, appreciated the talents of
the musicians he had in tow, and most of them joined him

at the theaters for extra money at a time when they really needed it.

Miller benefitted particularly from Nichols's protection, and in fact learned from Red what Red had learned from Sam Lanin—the trick of double- or triple-dipping with several bands and recording dates at the same time. Because of his arranging skills, Nichols also paid Miller $125 a week, as opposed to $50 for the other musicians. By 1930, the first full year of the Depression, Miller made an astounding $6,700 under Red's management, making him the highest-paid jazz trombonist in America.

But something was turning sour between the two by then. George Simon, in his biography of Miller, gives no clue as to what the cause of the dissention was, merely quoting both men with fairly nasty cracks about the other. Since Miller, like Nichols, was basically in the music business for money, I doubt very much that Glenn resented Red's omnipresence on the music and recording scene, as other musicians did. Legendary trumpeter Max Kaminsky (1908-1994) told me that, although Nichols didn't drink, he was a heavy gambler at cards and "a strange man with the finances."[2] If this was so, and Red had to put Glenn off on his paydays, I can understand his frustration. Even when his own bands were stranded in three-foot snowbanks, Miller made sure than every musician working for him got his or her fair share of whatever money he got. Holding an employee at arm's length because he had a bad day at the poker table wouldn't sit well with Glenn.

Another possible bone of contention was that Miller's deeply-rooted inferiority complex, which always made him resentful and restless when he was not completely in charge (*pace* Simon), simply came to the fore. As with his later rift with British bandleader Ray Noble, which led to his leaving to form the first of his own big bands, Glenn might have been upset about the Nichols bands'

---

2 From a telephone conversation with the author, 6 November 1992.

split musical personality. Pollack he could understand,
since Ben's orchestra had a well-defined policy about the
separation of pop and jazz charts; but Red's vacillation,
even within the same session and sometimes even on the
same record, was getting to be too schizophrenic even for
the commercially-minded Miller—who, after all, appreciated the jazz he was called upon to play.

This attitude was very much in evidence on the Five Pennies session of 24 January 1930, where charts so bad that
they sounded like cement being poured were applied to
Sometimes I'm Happy and *Hallelujah*—yet both were
enlivened by "jazz interludes" that had little or nothing to
do with the surrounding material. Yet just when things
seemed to be quite dark indeed, there came a marvelous
pair of sessions, little known except to the most devoted
period collectors today, which put Red Nichols back on
the jazz map.

LOUISIANA RHYTHM KINGS: Nichols, Thunen, G. Miller, J.
Dorsey, B. Russin, Rollini; Wes Vaughan, bj; Jack Russin, p;
Krupa, dm. 20 January 1930.

This was to be one of the Rhythm Kings' better sessions,
even though some of the tracks start out a bit sluggish and
some of the tempo-choices strike modern listeners as too
relaxed. For some reason, Big T couldn't make the date
and Mole was already ensconced at NBC, so Miller ended
up being the only trombonist. To say that he acquitted
himself well would be an understatement. I am convinced
that it is only because of the relative rarity of these sides,
since the early 1930s, that his improvising skills have been
dismissed or at least disparaged. True, the tone is still a
bit muffled and coarse, not like the more polished Miller
of 1939-42; but the musical ideas...well, they're something
else again. And they're entirely original.

Swanee gets off to a slow start, the opening ensemble
stodgy and Nichols cracking. The bridge has Dorsey's
clarinet over ensemble, doing a Pee Wee Russell imitation

(but, yes, it's JD). Jack Russin, Babe's brother, is on piano here, and he was certainly a good surrogate for Sullivan, whom he sounds much like. Then comes Miller, quite inventive and swinging if infirm of tone. Krupa's tom-toms and snares produce a sound not unlike that which he used to drive the Goodman band some six years down the road; here they power the full ensemble, which motors quite nicely with both Dorsey and Babe Russin in superb form.

Squeeze Me is taken at a medium-slow tempo, much like Chick Webb's famous big band version. It starts with a good Babe Russin tenor chorus, then Nichols in surprisingly bluesy form with Rollini on the verse, also quite funky. There ensues two choruses of Nichols-led ensemble with Dorsey on top, Krupa playing press rolls and cowbells in the second. *Oh, Lady Be Good* and *Sweet Sue* are taken at a somewhat better clip, and are notable for superb solos by Babe and Jack Russin, Nichols, Dorsey, and—lest we forget—Miller. *The Meanest Kind of Blues* is the loosest number in the session, swinging and relaxed from the first note.

One week later—after the hybrid Five Pennies date alluded to earlier—the band was back to wax six more outstanding cuts in the same vein. It should be mentioned that Jimmy Dorsey's playing on this session is *so* hot, and *so* much in a Russell groove, that even I first thought that all the discographers must be wrong. This stems from the fact that here he not only emulates Pee Wee's tone, even on alto (which he rarely did), but even some of Pee Wee's note-choices. What eventually convinced me that it was indeed Dorsey was the characteristically fast vibrato of his Albert system clarinet. JD, like so many of the New Orleans clarinetists (Dodds, Noone, Simeon, Bigard), never switched to a more modern instrument, preferring the Albert's "woodier" tone to more convenient fingering.

O'er the Billowy Sea is one of those Miller Dixieland parodies, like the later *Shirt Tail Stomp,* but the others produce swinging of varied degrees. *Lazy Daddy,* like

Swanee, gets off to a rather stiff start, and even after a fine Jack Russin solo with Krupa all over the place (on woodblocks, tom-toms, and cowbells) the ensemble is still stiff. Then comes Dorsey, very hot, with Rollini underpinning, and the final ensemble catches fire.

The least well-known tune here is *Karavan* with a K, which turns out to be a surprisingly attractive melody in F (Example 3) by vaudeville saxist Rudy Wiedoft: in fact, it is one of the finest "unknown" tunes in the entire Nichols ouvre! After the Chicago ensemble opening we hear Rollini solo, somewhat straight for eight bars before opening

Example 3: *Karavan,* opening chorus.

up in an improvisation. Then Dorsey on alto, swinging like mad if somewhat limited in range (this was the passage that originally made me think this was Russell). Nichols ooh-wahs his way into a particularly great muted solo, with Krupa's cymbals riding him like mad. Then an ensemble finish, led by JD's clarinet wailing like a banshee on high F. What a record!

Pretty Baby and *Tell Me* are a little less exciting, the former starting and ending in relaxed tempo, though containing good solos; but *There's Egypt in Your Dreamy Eyes,* despite its unpromising title, turns out to be one of the hottest numbers in this session, and a fine wrap-up piece.

RED NICHOLS & HIS FIVE PENNIES: Nichols, Thunen, Klein, J. Teagarden, G. Miller, J. Dorsey, B. & J. Russin, Rollini, Vaughan,

Krupa. 3 February 1930.

The Five Pennies session that followed a week later had its commercial aspects, but not as many as the several which preceded it. *I'm Just Wild About Harry* has a typically stiff, show-band opening, then the Russin brothers and Krupa try desperately to liven things up. Jack T takes a splendid solo, but the effect is spoiled by JD's alto in double time, showing off his triple-tonguing: very virtuosic, but *not* jazzy. There is a nice ride-out, however.

Just as collectors tend to forget the earlier Teagarden-Nichols *Basin Street Blues,* they also often overlook this early version of *After You've Gone* which he encored a year later with the Venuti-Lang All-Star Orchestra. While not quite as good, it has its moments. A snappy opening degenerates into a sluggish theme statement, doubling the time at the end of each half-chorus. Big T takes the vocal, followed by a JD clarinet solo which is both virtuosic *and* jazzy. Then Teagarden returns on trombone, in stunning form, with crackling triplets in the middle; the ensemble goes back to the original slower tempo.

RED NICHOLS & HIS FIVE PENNIES: Same. 14 February 1930.

The band's next session is particularly frustrating in its musical schizophrenia. *Tea for Two* is a truly sluggish arrangement and performance, back in the *Ida* mold; despite a nice transposition from Eb to Ab for Dorsey's solo, and Jack Russin doubling and halving the tempo on piano, it just doesn't go anywhere. Conversely, *I Want to Be Happy* is a Miller arrangement so swinging and advanced for its time that, had Nichols pursued this vein, he might have created the Swing Era two years before those marvelous Ellington and Bennie Moten records came along.

Happy is taken way up, in C, at $\downarrow$ =120 (2/4); the intro (Example 4) is mad and slashing, accenting Teagarden's trombone with three-trumpet chords which are all attacked (up to bar 7) with upward rips. The theme is played by

Example 4: *I Want to Be Happy,* introduction.

Nichols with soft clarinet obbligato; Miller's trademark
two trombones enter in the middle with trumpet improvisation behind them. Then Teagarden comes back to solo,
with drums and a soft sax cushion. Jimmy Dorsey does a
superb Goodman imitation on clarinet, starting sub-toned,
adding trills, and then building the tension with jazzy triplets and raw-edged blue notes. Red follows, quite hot,
then Babe Russin with soft piano and Krupa tom-toms.
Toward the end of his chorus, the trumpets play a repeated atonal blast that sounds like G-F#-F, then the coda
repeats somewhat the pattern of the intro.

RED NICHOLS & HIS FIVE PENNIES: Nichols, Ruby Weinstein,
Charlie Teagarden, tp; J. Teagarden, G. Miller, tb; Goodman, cl;
Sid Stoneburn, a-sx; B. Russin, t-sx; Rollini, bs-sx; Sullivan, p;
Teg Brown, bj; A. Miller, bs; Krupa, dm. 2 July 1930.

This 13-piece "Five Pennies" outfit might have boded
badly, in 1930, for any consistent jazz content; but for

some reason, Nichols was able to give Miller his head and allow him to come up with three rather nice arrangements. *Peg O' My Heart* is the least well-known of the three, and in a sense it is probably the most conventional (despite some good solos). *China Boy* features an out-of-tempo intro and coda by Jack Teagarden, more good solos (particularly by Goodman), and some nice touches such as the brass crescendo in the opening theme which is quintessential Miller.

Sweet Georgia Brown is perhaps the most inventive; after a conventional, somewhat choppy but spirited intro, we hear the trumpets with clarinet and trombone interjections. Then Sullivan's piano with drums, followed by clarinet (BG) with trumpet-section interjections, very hot. Russin's tenor shows considerable Freeman influence, followed by trumpet chords with clarinet. Then comes a surprising shift to minor with a growl trombone.

This latter section exhibits a feature of Teagarden's art which set him apart from all other trombonists as much as Vic Berton's hot tympani set him apart from other drummers. Jack would take the bell off his horn, and substitute instead an ordinary drinking glass which acted as a rather peculiar mute. This trick was never overused by Big T, but proved rather effective on several recordings (most notably *Tailspin Blues* with the Mound City Blue Blowers, and *St. James Infirmary* at a 1947 Louis Armstrong concert). What made it so difficult was that most trombonists use the position of the bell to judge the position of the slide; Jack was no exception, and in fact by his own admission it took him two years to perfect this technique. He was inspired by a report he had heard of an older trombonist who supposedly played "with a water glass." It wasn't until after he had mastered this that he finally saw the man who had inspired him, in absentia; and all *he* did was use a water glass like a regular mute, over the end of the bell!

A day later, the same band returned to Brunswick's studios to record a Miller-Teagarden masterpiece, *The Sheik*

of Araby. Though Jack's then-"hip" lyrics sound rather
silly today, the recording holds up well as an example of
how Miller could write economical as well as intricate
arrangements. After a sax-chord and trumpet intro, Teg
Brown starts singing the lyrics in typical Twenties fashion,
interrupted by Jack shouting, "Wait a minute, man! Don't
you *know* that song's out'a date?" Teg asks, "Why, who
are you?", to which Jack sings, to a new bluesy melody,
"I'm the sheik-y man, that's who I be, and all the gals
they fall for me...You've sung this song for years, it
seems, but there's better ways to catch a queen. I choose
this way, it suits my means; here's what won the gals in
New Orleans."

A trumpet and rim shot break, which will repeat itself between solos, introduces Miller playing the melody straight
while Jack improvises above him. Then the break again,
followed by Goodman with Russin's tenor playing the
melody; break, then Nichols with trombone and Krupa in
quasi-shuffle-rhythm. The three trumpets finish the chorus, then a piano break, and Jack returns for his final message: "These sheiks from Araby won't do; I know that
you can see it too. You've heard my song, and now I'm
through—I'll leave the verdict up to you!'

After this campy but charming masterpiece, *Shim-Me-
Sha-Wabble* sounds, at first, like a disappointment. The
opening choruses are in typical show-band style, and the
tempo is down considerably from the exciting July 1928
version. Russin solos, decently, followed by Goodman
hot but somewhat out of tune; then Big T, Sullivan, and
Nichols with Goodman trills and trombone counterpoint.
The ride-out is wonderful, and vintage Miller, based on a
simple yet catchy riff which is not part of the regular tune.

RED NICHOLS & HIS FIVE PENNIES: Same. 2-3 August 1930.

A month later the band reassembled for a true rarity—12-
inch transcriptions, made by Brunswick for the National
Radio Transcription Company, that were pure jazz and *not*

Example 5: *Call of the Freaks*, piano comp.

progression was later inverted, slowed down and also
played repetitiously by Artie Shaw in his theme song,
Nightmare. Sullivan plays trills for the first four bars,
then a soft solo above the chords. Goodman is next, digging and growling; then Big T, followed by his less famous brother Charlie, who happened to be an outstanding
player who nobody really noticed. The tension is relieved
by a trumpet-section break, followed by a rather nice second theme played by the saxes (Example 6) that does not
appear in the Oliver recording. Sullivan's piano follows,
then Nichols with plunger and straight mute; Rollini, a
trumpet break, then back to the chromatic chords with
piano.

Example 6: *Call of the Freaks*, saxophone theme.

Apparently, neither Nichols nor Miller could decide how
to end *Freaks,* since the repeated chord pattern just comes
to a stop. But what a hypnotic record it is! In three minutes and fifty-eight seconds (not counting the spoken
intro), we are taken on a somewhat bluesy journey to the
darkest reaches that this band was capable of. Not too
surprisingly, the "medley" of *Sweet Georgia Brown/I
Ain't Got Nobody,* made the next day, couldn't hold a
candle to it. The band starts off hot in *Georgia,* with good
Russin tenor and Sullivan in quite exceptional form.
Rollini's bass sax follows, light and swinging, but the

infected with commercial show-band hokum. Unfortu
ately, Brunswick never issued these sides commercial
and even now *Call of the Freaks* is scarcely known by a
but the most die-hard Nichols collectors (see Discogi
phy). Indeed, in his two-volume jazz discography, Bri
Rust lists it (and *Ballin' the Jack/Walkin' the Dog,* ma
the following day) at the end of his Nichols list, with ma
rix numbers but absolutely no information as to personn
and/or probable issue information.

The Sheik of Araby is, frankly, a failure. Since there
no vocal, this version starts with Nichols playing the blu
melody that Jack Teagarden sang previously, followed b
Miller playing the melody *without* Big T over him.[3] Mi
ler cracks in the first bar, and sounds ragged towards th
end of the chorus; Nichols, who follows muted with trom
bone background, also fluffs. Goodman and Russin fol
low, then the trumpets playing straight with a surprisingl
annoying "nanny-goat" vibrato, quite uncharacteristic o
them; piano break, then Nichols on the coda.

Fortunately, we have *Call of the Freaks.* Just as *Karava*
is the most attractive of the unknown pops the band
played, this is the gem of the little-known jazz arrangements. It was written by New Orleans drummer Paul Barbarin, arranged by Luis Russell (who recorded it first in
January 1929) and recorded by King Oliver's Orchestra
for Victor in February 1929, one of those Oliver records
on which the King doesn't even play. Oliver's tempo is
very slow, almost funereal; Nichols's picks things up a bit.
As in the Oliver, the trumpets (and violin?) slide up to a
suspended-chord intro, for eight bars, before Nichols's
trumpet kicks off a repeated chromatic chord pattern (Example 5) played by the piano in the bass stave. This same

[3] The absence of Teagarden's solo on this tune obviously suggests that the trombonist was not present at all; moreover, I detect a violin in the ensemble at times, which was *not* present a month earlier. I have, however, stuck with the July personnel because there seems to be no solid information on these sessions, and most of the players are obviously the same.

brakes are suddenly applied for a soggy show version of *Nobody* that even Goodman's clarinet cannot resuscitate. Then the tempo inexplicably comes back up for a *Georgia Brown* ride-out.

The band returned on August 25 for another radio transcription. Jack Teagarden was absent, and both Goodman and Babe Russin were replaced by Russell and Bud Freeman; the result is pure Chicago-styled jazz that even Eddie Condon would have been proud of. The "arrangement" here of *Ballin' the Jack* is so loose and disorganized, in fact, that I doubt if it was even written down, but the solos are wonderful—especially Freeman's, which leads directly into *Walkin' the Dog*. It is obvious that such sloppy, unrehearsed records were *not* the sort that staid Jack Kapp wanted for the Brunswick label; even more so when, after what seems to be a final cymbal crash, the band goes raggedly back to the beginning of *Ballin' the Jack* to start all over again! Apparently, there was some time left that had to be filled, and Glenn Miller's solo is superb before the ensemble comes back (once again) to end it.

RED NICHOLS & HIS FIVE PENNIES: Nichols, C. Teagarden, tp; G. Miller, Charlie Butterfield, tb; Goodman, cl; Freeman, t-sx; Rollini, bs-sx; Sullivan, p; Krupa, dm. 27 August 1930.

In 1930, boogie-woogie was a minor fad that passed quickly through the night air of New York—certainly, nothing like it would be a decade hence. It was an eight-to-the-bar "barrelhouse" piano style that had migrated from the South, primarily Texas, to Chicago in 1927; there Meade "Lux" Lewis (1905-1964) made what is considered the first boogie recording, *Honky-Tonk Train Blues*. But Paramount thought so little of Meade's efforts that they withheld release until 1929, when a slightly younger contemporary named Clarence "Pine Top" Smith made waves with his even more stylish recordings of *Pine Top's Boogie Woogie* and *Jump Steady Blues*. Smith was accidentally killed, by a stray bullet in a bar brawl, that same year (he was only 25); but his Vocalion records were receiving some circulation, and notice, so it was only natural that Red Nichols should take a stab at this fad.

Actually, of course, it was Glenn Miller who "took a stab" at it, and the result was (to my knowledge) the first example of big-band boogie—the very style that catapulted arranger Deane Kincaide *(Boogie Woogie Maxixe, Pine Top's Boogie)*, and the Will Bradley-Ray McKinley band, to popular success some years down the road. Had Miller and/or Nichols continued in this vein, the boogie craze might have hit earlier than it did, giving employment to Lewis and Jimmy Yancey during this lean period. But they didn't, and it didn't, and that (as they say) is history.

The piece in question begins with one of Glenn's most remarkable intros: four bars of *mezzo-piano* fluttering clarinet, with *piano* trombone (and bass sax in the last two bars, a fifth down), followed by four bars of *fortissimo* trombone (Teagarden) with clarinet and two muted trumpets in the first two (Example 7). Then we get *mezzo-*

Example 7: *Carolina in the Morning,* intro.

piano bass sax and clarinet in Bach-like counterpoint, four bars repeated to make eight; back to the beginning, this time a little louder with one of the trumpets replacing the trombone (and an octave higher in pitch, of course), and bass sax in the lower 5th from the start. But this time, instead of the clarinet-bass sax passage, we get the melody — *Carolina in the Morning*—boogie style.

Open trumpets play the middle eight in straight four, and the chorus finish. Then comes Nichols with the tenor in descending harmony, very pretty, Red sounding much like Bix at the end. Goodman plays very dirty with the rhythm section; then the clarinet flutters return, only this time they go into the boogie counterpoint first, followed by Teagarden's trombone on the *prestissimo* figure to end it.

This treatment is so wonderfully effective that it surprises me to note that none of the Swing Era "boogie bands" ever revived this tune. Perhaps they were unfamiliar with the record, which did not sell particularly well. Not too surprisingly, *Who?* is not nearly as creative, being merely a surprise opening—bluesy clarinet and muted trumpet before Rollini picks the tempo up for the opening ensemble—followed by good solos (Rollini, Goodman, Freeman) before the coda mimics the intro. But this would have been a pleasant finish to the session had they not bothered with *By the Shalimar,* a lugubrious tune and arrangement. It sounds like Miller playing long, long held notes (at least it helped his breath control!) with Krupa on drums; even a ruminative Goodman couldn't save this one.

The next period division may seem more arbitrary and personal, but in my opinion the easy swing of *Who?* and the creativity of *Carolina* marked the end of Nichols's second experimental phase. From here on out the dates were to become increasingly more vanilla and uninteresting, only occasionally breaking through with the kind of jazz that had made his name.

5. Out of the Pocket
(Sept. 1930-Feb. 1932)

On 13 September 1929, Bix Beiderbecke suffered a particularly serious collapse at a Whiteman recording date in New York's Liederkranz Hall. Paul sent him back home to Davenport, to dry up and hopefully return to the fold; but when Bix returned to New York eight months later, he was in no shape to resume the grind of radio, records, theater dates, and those grueling one-nighters. He jobbed around for a while, even trying out for Glen Gray's Casa Loma Orchestra, but the killer chops needed to cut arranger Gene Gifford's scores were beyond his failing powers.

By September 1930, it was obvious that even making and organizing record dates was getting beyond him. His last session with a band of his own took place at the Victor studios on September 8; a week later, he was due to play on an all-star date organized by his old friend Hoagy Carmichael. When the band assembled in the studio, however, Beiderbecke was nowhere to be seen; after a half-hour of waiting, Jack Teagarden found him hiding behind a curtain, mumbling to his cornet under his breath. He played briefly and badly on the two numbers made. They would prove to be his last records.

When news of Beiderbecke's collapse reached Nichols, he was almost shattered. More so than even those others who worshipped Bix, Red knew how much of his style and success was owed to the young man from Davenport. Of course, Red was having his own problems: between the theater dates, college gigs, and increasingly commercial demands of the Brunswick sessions, it was all he could do to pick up where Bix and Trumbauer (now firmly in the Whiteman camp, his OKeh contract cancelled due to sagging sales in September 1930) had left off, providing work and recording sessions for his fellow jazzmen.

During the summer of 1930, Nichols made a career decision that was eventually to deteriorate the jazz quality of his records altogether. He agreed to George Gershwin's request that he lead the pit band in his new musical, *Girl Crazy,* and followed up the next year with *Strike Up the Band.* Playing in a Broadway pit, in those days, normally meant complete domination to the written score; it required grueling hours of practice and performance, including two shows on Saturday; and it ostensibly left no room at all for improvisation. Red knew it was a big undertaking, but at the same time he and his musicians had to have food and shelter. And, of course, Gershwin wasn't your typical theater composer of the 1920s. Unlike Irving Berlin, who detested continuous improvisation on his wonderful tunes, Gershwin was very much a jazz buff. He knew that Red would contract the best musicians then in New York, and he gave them their head in some of the uptempo numbers, especially *I Got Rhythm.*

I Got Rhythm, in fact, became one of the greatest "jam" tunes in jazz, and inspired any number of jazz compositions based on its changes. Miller was especially in his element; despite their growing personal animosity, Nichols later admitted that Gershwin relied heavily on Glenn for the ride-outs in these two shows. With a pit band that included (at various times) Weinstein, Klein, Jack and Charlie Teagarden, Miller, George Stoll, Goodman, Binyon, the Dorsey brothers, the Russin brothers, Venuti, Lang, Art Miller and Krupa, and a new singing sensation in Ethel Merman (whose sixteen-bar held high C in *Rhythm* galvanized the New York public and critics), *Girl Crazy* couldn't help but be a smashing success. Indeed, it was not so much the first real success of the 1930s as the grand farewell to the 1920s. It celebrated the Jazz Age as never before, and closed its book on one of the most interesting and remarkable periods in American music.

Without realizing it, however, Nichols was overextending himself, and suffered a collapse of sorts in the spring of 1931. The strain of years of overwork, compounded by the newfound stress of the Depression, landed him in the

hospital with pleurisy. Had he been an older man at the
time, it might have been career-threatening; but fortunately he was still young, having not yet turned twenty-six
(we tend to forget how young he was at the time he made
all of this marvelous music!), and after having his lungs
drained (with long needles, a horrible cure that was almost
worse than the illness) he returned to the music scene
without a regular band. In those money-scarce days, his
regular players had all jumped ship with Benny Goodman
to play in another pit for another show!

Nichols needed money fast, and accepted a May 1931 tour
of New England. Red McKenzie put together a band of
Chicagoans for him—some of whom Nichols had worked
with before (Freeman, Condon, Russell, and Tough), and
several new faces (Max Kaminsky, Mezz Mezzrow, Tommy Coonin, Pete Peterson). But there were problems.
Nichols was simultaneously jealous of the Chicago players' ability to swing harder than he, and annoyed by their
atrocious reading ability. Russell, moved from his regular
clarinet chair to third alto, particularly frustrated Red who
had thought he was a better all-round musician than he
really was at this time.

Worse yet, the band was drinking—even on the job,
thanks to ringleader Condon—and smoking some pot,
thanks to dope-peddler Mezzrow, a clarinetist known
better for his legendary marijuana consumption than for
his improvisations. The end came after the band members
swam in a muddy New Hampshire lake, got terribly sun-
burned, and began the evening gig stiff, sore, and in a bad
mood. Red's patience lasted about two numbers before he
stomped angrily off the stand, yelling at Kaminsky to take
over. Some illegal joy juice and grass loosened them up,
and when Nichols returned the band was swinging like
mad—which made him angrier, thinking that they had
been holding out on him. Doubly incensed by what he
perceived as musical mutiny, and the manager's com-
plaints about the band's deportment, Red fired the whole
band on the spot and ended the tour.

Condon never forgave Nichols for this betrayal; it marked the end of their brief friendship. In later years, however, Kaminsky begrudgingly admitted that "the band was just as responsible for the whole fiasco as Red was—maybe more so, since he was the leader and it was his band."[1] This was the understatement of the year. Red wasn't running a clubhouse for little boys to get liquored up in; and if his reputation were ruined, there would be no chance at all to play jazz in between the commercial dates. Suffice it to say that this tour marked the end of his infatuation with Condon's boys. He never used any of them again.

RED NICHOLS & HIS FIVE PENNIES: Nichols, Weinstein, C. Teagarden, tp; J. Teagarden, G. Miller, George Stoll, tb; BG, cl; Stoneburn, a-sx; Binyon, fl/t-sx; J. Russin, p; A. Miller, bs; Krupa, dm; J. Teagarden and "The Foursome" (Marshall Smith, Ray Johnson, Del Porter, Dwight Snyder), voc. 26 September 1930.

While the band was still in rehearsal for *Girl Crazy,* they took to the Brunswick studios for one of those "white spirituals" that were all the rage in the 1920s. Even more embarrassingly, *On Revival Day* occupied two sides of a 10-inch 78, making it (to that point) the longest Nichols record yet made.

In all fairness, there are some good solos on the second

---

[1] Kaminsky, Max, *My Life in Jazz,* Harper & Row, 1963. It should be noted that Kaminsky's verbal biography places the incident in 1929; but this is a consistent error in this chapter, for instance placing Beiderbecke with the Goldkette band in February 1926 (rather than '27). In a telephone conversation with the author on 6 November 1992, Kaminsky insisted that 1929 was correct; but Woody Backensto, who knew Red in his late years, has equally insisted that this tour ended his relationship with the Condon musicians, Sullivan and Krupa excepted, but *especially Condon.* Since Condon is in the 8/29 Vitaphone short, and Russell and Freeman turn up on Nichols discs and transcriptions into late summer 1930, it had to be after that time; moreover, the photocopy of a 1961 letter from the Yale University Library to Backensto quotes the *Yale Daily News* announcing Red's appearance at the Freshman Promenade on 15 May 1931, undoubtedly with the band under discussion. When confronted with this additional information, Mr. Kaminsky admitted that he may have been wrong in insisting on 1929.

side; and I suppose one should not damn Nichols too much, considering that this tune was written by Andy Razaf, Fats Waller's partner, who was black himself. Yet the odor of racism hangs heavy over the moaning "chorus" and saccharine lyrics, despite the fact that most of these musicians were about as racist as Louis Bellson, Pearl Bailey's husband. (One apocryphal story, in fact, claims that Jack Teagarden begged Waller to let him tour with his band. When Fats refused, on the obvious grounds that the South and/or Midwest would strenuously object to a mixed band, Jack supposedly replied, "Aw hell, Fats, most people think I'm a spade anyway.") There is some interest to trivia buffs, however, that one of the Foursome's members—tenor Del Porter—later founded the band that would become Spike Jones and his City Slickers.

The band's next session, on October 23, omitted Big T and Stoll and added vocalist Dick Robertson (another one of those saccharine tenors) and two violins. It is particularly interesting for the two takes of *I Got Rhythm*, probably the first made of this now-standard. But to give one an idea of just how commercial this session really was, the last two cuts (*A Girl Friend of a Boy Friend of Mine*, from the 1930 Eddie Cantor musical film *Whoopee!*, and *Sweet Jennie Lee*) were released on the Melotone and Panachord labels as The Captivators—a band name that Red had long since abandoned. This supports the claim that Nichols was embarrassed by some of his records from this era, and wanted his name removed from them.

Surprisingly, there was a different version of *Rhythm* made six days later under the aegis of bandleader Freddie Rich, here using the pseudonym Harold Lem. Not only is the tempo much better, but the performance and arrangement are actually hotter, Venuti and Tommy Dorsey being especially good. At this point in time it is hard to determine which of the two versions more accurately reflect what the band played in its show performances, but both have historical interest.

After this came two straight commercial dates, featuring

vocals by Eddy Thomas and Harold Arlen. Both were tenors (surprise!), but Arlen at least had the advantage of being a musical and disciplined singer as well as a superb songwriter. The son of a cantor, he had played piano with a Nichols-based band called the Buffalodians under his real name of Hyman Arluck; and, though he is chiefly remembered today as the composer of the score for *The Wizard of Oz,* Arlen is scarcely as well-known as Berlin, Gershwin, or Porter, which is to say, not nearly as well-known as he should be.

In addition to *Over the Rainbow,* Arlen wrote numerous songs that became outstanding popular favorites and "jam tunes" for jazz musicians: *It's Only a Paper Moon, That Old Black Magic, I've Gotta Right to Sing the Blues, Ac-cent-chu-ate the Positive, Blues in the Night, Stormy Weather, I Love a Parade.* Unfortunately, most of these came after his association with Nichols, so there are no records of these Arlen tunes by Red, though Nichols did record a watered-down version of Arlen's greatest "jam tune," *Get Happy.*

RED NICHOLS & HIS FIVE PENNIES: Nichols, C. Teagarden, Manone, G. Miller, J. Dorsey, B. Russin, Sullivan, A. Miller, Krupa. 1 December 1930.

By the end of the year, Nichols and his bandmates were pretty well locked into performances of *Girl Crazy;* but the irrepressible Wingy Manone (1904-1982), a one-armed white trumpeter of the Armstrong school, rejuvenated the jazz wing briefly. *My Honey's Lovin' Arms,* another Miller masterpiece, begins with a brief intro; then Glenn plays the melody, with trumpet and clarinet behind him in thirds. The nice, swinging tempo features Babe Russin in an unusually relaxed groove—why is this man so underrated as a tenor player?—followed by Sullivan piano with Krupa's drums and soft brass chords behind him at one spot. JD's clarinet really swings before the ensemble finale, in which Nichols plays the melody straight.

Rockin' Chair eschews the "cutesy" vocal dialogue used by both Louis Armstrong, in the first recording of the tune, and Hoagy Carmichael in his own 1930 recording. Miller gives us a *Tin Roof Blues*-type intro, then a medium-slow Dixie statement of theme. Charlie Teagarden takes a fine solo, with Glenn on the break; then a two-clarinet break before Manone's vocal, which is more rhythmically inflected than actually sung, with a very nice Nichols muted obbligato before the ensemble finish.

Even better was the session made nine days later (December 10), when Weinstein was added on trumpet, Harold Arlen was added as vocalist, and Benny Goodman and Jack Russin replaced Jimmy Dorsey and Sullivan. *Bugaboo* is one of those quasi-racist songs that sounded so innocent in 1930 but so distasteful today, starting with a spoken intro "Say, boy, did you hear that? What *is* that? It sounds like nothin' I ever heard before!" and moving into a Manone vocal with lyrics like "sing Hallelujah, ya got the Bugaboo." All in all, however, it is relatively harmless; and like *Shine,* the music itself is quite good, being an uptempo, minor-key blues (by Nichols) with interesting changes.

Manone's "singing" is again rhythmic, but not much good tonally. He is followed, however, by muted trumpets, quite loud, with trombone interjections by Miller; then Goodman clarinet, digging and growling. Nichols plays next, then the ensemble, later joined by Goodman wailing a high Ab while they play hot syncopation behind him.

For some reason, the record everyone remembers from this session is *Corrinne, Corrina,* though it is no better or worse musically than *Bugaboo.* There is a four-trumpet intro with clarinet and trombone commentary, reviving (however briefly) the brass-ensemble-with-small-group concept that Red favored for a while in 1927-28. This is followed by a Manone vocal, a little better in pitch; then a trumpet section improvisation for three choruses, particularly good in the second, with Goodman's clarinet wailing overhead in the third. This is followed by a muted

Manone, then Glenn Miller on trombone, quite bluesy and good. After that is a typical Miller device, a trumpet-section riff with one trumpet holding a high Bb (Charlie Teagarden, it seems). After two choruses, an upward glissando smear to a high Bb ends it.

The third piece from this session, *How Come You Do Me Like You Do?*, is often unjustly neglected. The chart is even more clever than *Corrina,* starting with a baritone sax (Goodman!)-trombone intro, then one bar of trombone before the trumpet section plays the theme. Then comes a muted Charlie Teagarden solo, very good: Red became more and more enamored of Charlie's abilities as time went on. Too many critics take him for granted because of Jack's awesome abilities and accomplishments, but as his records show—even as late as 1963—"Little T" could swing and improvise with the best of them. His playing had a warmth similar to that of his older brother, plus a "flicker-vibrato" that Jack never possessed.

Goodman follows, in excellent form: this was certainly one of his best sessions with the Nichols bands. Then Arlen takes the vocal, and though it is a bit dated he is nonetheless highly musical, singing some particularly fine variations in the second chorus. The ride-out features the trumpets, with baritone and clarinet.

Unfortunately the next six sessions, ranging from 10 December 1930 to 24 April 1931, are all rather commer-cial dates with the occasional nice intro or hot solo, the lone exception being a superb Miller arrangement of *Keep a Song in Your Soul* on February 19 that centers around BG and Big T. Here, as elsewhere, Miller proves that he alone in his time knew how to write for strings in a jazz context. Most of them focus on the vocal abilites of Robertson, Lambert, Arlen, some creature named Paul Small, and Smith Ballew. Ballew was another one of those tenor-crooners who so dominated white pop; he was also quite handsome in a vanilla way, and became briefly popular as a bandleader and movie star in his own right. Particularly annoying, to me, was the April 24 recording

of *Singin' the Blues,* which I went out of my way to pro-
cure because I was curious to hear if Red did a tribute to
Beiderbecke in it (as the Fletcher Henderson band did that
same year, Rex Stewart taking Bix's solo note-for-note).
Imagine my chagrin when I discovered that *it wasn't even
the same tune,* but a mediocre melody framed around Ballew's sappy singing!

I should point out, in all fairness, that these commercial
dates that I disparage are, naturally, of some interest to
popular music historians. Red's bands still contained a
basic core of greatness, the Teagardens, Goodmans, Mill-
ers and Krupas still contributing some moments of excellence. But as *jazz* recordings, which is the scope of this
volume, their interest is negligible. One typical example
is the February 19 recording of *Things I Never Knew Til
Now,* a bland pop tune sung by Arlen and written by
gossip columnist Walter Winchell. Even that far back,
Winchell had considerable power to make or break perfor-
mers; in the midst of the Depression, it was wise from a
business standpoint to get on his good side, and recording
one of his songs was a sure-fire method; and, for that
reason (as well as the fact that Arlen holds considerable
interest for pop historians), the record is interesting. Yet
there is no escaping the fact that, as jazz, it is vapid. The
LP on which I have it is immediately followed by the 2
August 1930 take of *The Sheik of Araby,* into which I
accidentally let the album play after reviewing Winchell's
song. Even though this was a defective performance, and
less than a year older, my interest immediately picked up
when it started. Its contrast only went to show how low
the Nichols band had sunk in only eight months.

That Red himself was aware of this too-rapid plunge into
commercialism is borne out by a statement attributed to
him, that he didn't even want his name on some of these
records and in fact hesitated in re-signing with Brunswick
unless they allowed him some artistic freedom. He didn't
mind playing in Gershwin's shows, but the dearth of jazz
in those days was beginning to get to him. Nevertheless,

he did try to revive the patient from its coma occasionally, and the following session—on 26 May 1931—
brought young Ray McKinley in as a drummer-vocalist.
All sources list Red McKenzie as the singer on *You
Rascal You*, but that's Ray's voice, not Red's.

RED NICHOLS & HIS FIVE PENNIES: Nichols, C. Teagarden, G.
Miller, J. Dorsey, B. Russin, J. Russin, A. Miller; Perry Botkin, g;
Ray McKinley, dm/voc. 26 May 1931.

Just a Crazy Song (Hi-Hi-Hi) is not really a gem of a
tune, but it is infectious and Miller's arrangement is superb. After a hot trumpet intro, Glenn plays the melody
while trumpet and clarinet answer antiphonally with clever
yet swinging phrases (Example 1); then a break, and
return. Russin contributes a good tenor chorus, followed
by JD in a Goodman groove with Krupa's drums kicking
like mad. Gene responded so well to the Goodman approach that it's easy to see why he later left his commer-

Example 1: *Just a Crazy Song*, opening theme.

gig in Chicago to join Benny's big band. Nichols and
Miller then answer each other, but playing it straight.

You Rascal You was a surprise novelty "hit" of 1931;
there were excellent versions by Louis Armstrong, Big T
with Fats Waller, and Red McKenzie with JD, Coleman
Hawkins, and Muggsy Spanier. This one doesn't quite
come up to their level (especially Satchmo's superbly
rhythmic vocal and exciting trumpet), but McKinley does
the lyrics with tongue planted firmly in cheek and the
band responds with some scintillating blowing. *Moan,
You Moaners* again features a McKinley vocal, in another
one of those tainted minstrel-type numbers.

Ballew returned to sing three numbers on June 11, but two
weeks later the band turned in a particularly exciting
version of *Fan It,* with a vocal by McKenzie. After that
came what many consider the last great Nichols session.

RED NICHOLS & HIS FIVE PENNIES: Nichols, JD, Venuti, Lang,
Berton; Fulton McGrath, p. 16 Sept. 1931.

Vic Berton had spent the past two years gigging on the
West Coast, trying to break into movie work (partly suc-
cessfully, partly unsuccessfully). His surprise return to
New York, in September 1931, apparently inspired Red to
somewhat revive the old Five Pennies combo, this time
with Venuti and Lang in on the action. It would prove to
be the last time that these musicians were assembled
together in a studio, and the results were so superb that
they almost (but not quite) made up for almost a year of
commercialism.

Oh, Peter! You're So Nice kicks it off, in Bb, at a very
uptempo of ♩ =124 (2/4). It starts with a *Darktown Strutters' Ball*-type intro, in which we immediately notice with
delight that the "hot tympani" are back in action. The
opening ensemble is dominated by Venuti's violin, very
close-miked, though Nichols (and Berton) get their licks
in. There's a quick jump to C for Joe's solo, the first

chorus played in chorded style; the second chorus is particularly interesting, in that Venuti plays a single-string solo while accompanying himself! Then the tempo drops way down, to ♩=96 (4/4), and the key back to Bb, for a muted Nichols interlude, very pretty, with Lang accompaniment and Berton tympani. McGrath's barrelhouse piano brings the tempo back up, with Berton playing press rolls behind him; then Dorsey clarinet, hotter than we've ever heard him before, followed by Venuti leading the ride-out. They play an enticing diminuendo in the coda, then a quick crescendo for the finish.

The second number in this session was an excellent remake of *Honolulu Blues,* often overlooked by collectors, in which the band members play with almost equal fervor. Berton tympani is heard in the intro with guitar and piano, in a much slower tempo than the original; Venuti's violin plays the melody, straight, with tympani and guitar, Nichols's muted trumpet playing shuffle-rhythm in the middle eight. Then we hit double tempo for a nice break, ensemble with a McGrath piano solo. Jimmy Dorsey is very hot with tympani and rolling piano accompaniment, followed by Nichols growling, muted, with clarinet counterpoint and Berton tymp, followed in turn by a Venuti violin flutter, then out.

The band's next session, on October 2, was a more commercial date featuring some entirely new musicians: trombonist Wilbur Schwichtenberg, who later changed his name to Will Bradley; the superb bassist Artie Bernstein; the underrated drummer Victor Engle; and trumpeter-vocalist Johnny "Scat" Davis. I know some people who are crazy about Davis, and in fact he was quite popular in the 1930s, but in my view he was no more or less than yet another puerile singer trying to sound "hot." Unlike Lambert, Robertson, or even Ballew, Davis didn't just sing tenor—he sang falsetto, and a pretty bad falsetto at that. His pitch was almost always suspect, and his overrated "scatting" ability comes across as merely a laughable white imitation of Louis Armstrong. Even Cliff Edwards and Bing Crosby, who were really rhythmic pop singers rather than jazz artists, scatted better than Johnny Davis. The two songs made that day, *Get Cannibal* and *Junk Man Blues,* are almost embarrassingly racist and center too much around Davis's tenuous talents.

RED NICHOLS & HIS FIVE PENNIES: Nichols, tp; Johnny "Scat" Davis, tp/voc; Bradley, tb; JD, cl/a-sx; B. Russin, t-sx; J. Russin, p; Tony Starr, bj; Art Bernstein, bs; Vic Engle, dm. 2 Dec. 1931.

The following session, though still featuring Davis, was quite a bit better. Though Bradley (like Tommy Dorsey) was an accomplished trombone virtuoso, and in fact became one of Glenn Miller's idols when they played together in 1935 with Ray Noble's American big band, he always struck me as too emotionally cool to be a truly effective jazz soloist. Nevertheless, his adroit horn handling made him a valuable session and radio-date player; and, as Miller pointed out, he could do "more different things" than any other trombonist of his day. *Slow and Easy* starts off fast, but after admonition from Davis it lives up to its title, moving at a relaxed pace and featuring another Davis vocal and Jack Russin in a surprisingly good Fats Waller groove, Nichols doubling the tempo again at the end.

It is not noted who arranged *Waitin' for the Evening Mail,* and with Miller gone from the band since June I would be loath to credit him *in absentia;* yet the intro is particularly striking for its time. Taken at a relatively brisk ♩ =182 (4/4), the opening is played by trumpet and tenor sax in unison (Example 2)—or almost in unison, as the tenor departs from the trumpet on the last beat of bar 1 to play the 4th below. The ensuing passage of ascending and descending arpeggios in continuously descending chromatics is marvelously inspired, and in fact looks forward in both structure and orchestration to Duke Ellington's use of a trumpet-trombone-baritone sax unison section in his 1938 *Battle of Swing.*

Example 2: *Waitin' for the Evening Mail*, intro.

The opening theme is more Dixie-like, though one immediately notices the slicker swing of Bradley's trombone.
Indeed, this passage has a sound eerily reminiscent of the
manufactured Swing Era "Dixieland" of Bradley's own
band, rather than the "real" New Orleans, New York or
Chicago-styled Dixie of the 1920s, though Jimmy Dorsey
rides the beat well.   JD's solo, however, is a little disappointing, though there are some nice descending-ascending
chromatic figures in the background.   After a bridge,
Davis sings the vocal in his typically pathetic "hot" style,
but the situation is again saved by some really hot Nichols
trumpet with growl mute, and syncopated trombone on the
second and fourth beats of each bar.   Jack Russin's piano
follows, quite nice, with Engle excellent on drums, followed by brother Babe on tenor with syncopated figures
that Bradley would later recycle in his own band (e.g.,
Celery Stalks at Midnight).

Like the Miller arrangement of *Carolina in the Morning,*
Waitin' for the Evening Mail points forward to devices
that would be used *ad nauseum* in the Swing Era; but
again, Nichols failed to follow up (at that time) on them.
If he had, he might have maintained a position in the van-
guard of the new, emerging styles of jazz; but commercial
considerations again proved too overwhelming.   Indeed,
the following titles made at this date— *Yakka Hula Hickey*
Dula and *Haunting Blues*—are actually throwbacks to the
old Five Pennies style, using Artie Schutt in place of
McGrath, Lang instead of Starr, and Berton in place of

Engle. They are the last recorded examples of the "old"
Five Pennies combination, and are exciting discs often
overlooked by critics, but the performances are more
extroverted and less balanced than the 1925-28 discs.

The band's following two sessions were purely commercial dates, the first centering around Robertson's vocals
(December 15) and the second (15 February 1932) producing a dismal 12-inch pastiche called the "New Orleans
Medley, Part 2." There are, of course, "hot interludes,"
and a biting, one-and-a-half-minute rendition of *Milenberg
Joys* featuring Venuti and Red in scintillating form, but
singer Connee Boswell is the only New Orleans musician
present and neither the selection of tunes nor their
arrangements (*Milenberg* excepted) are really any good.

RED NICHOLS & THE FIVE PENNIES: Nichols, J. Dorsey, B.
Russin, McDonough, McGrath, Bernstein, Engle. 18 Feb. 1932.

No one probably knew it at the time, but this session
would turn out to be the last hurrah for Nichols's contribution to jazz. Again, the band is fairly small; in his liner
notes for the CD reissue of *Sweet Sue,* Brian Rust notes
that "the prevalent economic climate of depression"
caused a reduction "of the Nichols band to five or six,"[2]
but this is pure hogwash. As we have seen, Red continued
to record pure jazz arrangements every few months or so,
even in the midst of his larger-band commercial dates; and
in fact the remainder of his Brunswick output following
this session more often than not reverts to a ten- or
twelve- piece orchestra. Nevertheless, these numbers are
fine reminders that Red and his men had not forgotten
what it was like to play real jazz, even if the overall sound
is somewhat less jazzy than in the past.

Clarinet Marmalade begins with a slick intro and first
chorus, the ensemble continuing into the "B" theme.

2 From liner notes to *Rhythm of the Day,* ASV/Living Era CDAJA-5025-R.

McDonough plays a chorded guitar solo, really swinging; Nichols is pleasant if uninspired; and Jimmy Dorsey's clarinet is very nice. Then comes the bridge, with Engle's drums on the breaks, and a Dixie-styled ride-out in stop-time chords, with Bernstein's bass prominent, followed by a repeated riff to the finish.

Sweet Sue is not as hot as the January 1930 Louisiana Rhythm Kings version, but compared to most of the dreck surrounding this session it isn't bad. There is a clarinet-guitar opening with bowed bass, then trumpet with tenor sax cushion, the tenor coming up from behind in the middle section of the chorus. Nichols, muted, plays with shuffle-rhythm, sounding much like another band of the Swing Era—Jan Savitt and his Top Hatters—with Russin on the middle eight. When Red returns, the rhythm is a swinging 4. This is followed by McDonough guitar, single-note, with piano and sub-toned clarinet figures; then the clarinet trills while Nichols plays straight to the end.

The band's next session produced Part 1 of their "epic" *New Orleans Medley,* this time featuring the entire Boswell Sisters group, and Part 1 of their next gem, the *California Medley.* The Boswell Sisters were the first true jazz vocal group in history, but they made far better records than this effort with Nichols (or their one and only pairing with Don Redman's big band—a "concert arrangement" of the insipid *Lawd, You Made the Night Too Long* —and Bing Crosby also in on the action). Let us give Red Nichols some semblance of his dignity, and leave him here.

6. Postlude (1933-1965)

For all intents and purposes, Nichols's contribution to jazz was over. As we shall see, both he and the variegated members of his bands all had something more to say, and did, before their time was up; but the magical period which had started out so promisingly in 1925 had come to an end, not with a bang but a whimper, seven short years later. The first five were rich ones for Nichols and his groups; the last two were not as fruitful though, as we have seen, there was still much to admire.

Every good jazz buff knows what became of the Dorsey Brothers, Jack Teagarden, Pee Wee Russell, Joe Sullivan, Bud Freeman, Benny Goodman, Gene Krupa, Joe Venuti, Eddie Lang, Dick McDonough, Dave Tough, and especially Glenn Miller, so we won't recount their post-Nichols careers here. Suffice it to say that all of them, even Miller, made sizeable contributions to jazz in their later years, and all are legendary names among music-lovers.

Vic Berton and his family remained in California for many years, and in fact Vic was selected by Igor Stravinsky as the percussionist for a West Coast performance of his *L'Histoire du Soldat.* The original score called for multiple percussionists, but Vic told Igor that he could play all of the parts himself, simultaneously. Naturally, Stravinsky didn't believe him, so Vic set up a special audition and proved it. Thus did Igor Stravinsky, like the correspondent from *Melody Maker,* go away shaking his head in disbelief.

When the Swing Era got underway in 1935, Berton briefly led a recording-only big band of his own, one that played the then-popular mixture of pop tunes and hot jazz. They mark the last known recordings of the hot tympani. The best soloists on them were trumpeter Sterling Bose (1906-1958), a curious but talented musician who flitted briefly through the bands of Tommy Dorsey, Ray Noble, Goodman and Miller, in addition to this stint with Vic, and Pee

Wee Russell on a few titles. One of their very best collaborations was *A Smile Will Go a Long, Long Way,*
though *Dardanella* and *Taboo* (the latter with Henry "Hot
Lips" Levine replacing Bose) were also quite good.

Following the demise of his band, Vic became the principal percussionist of the Los Angeles Philharmonic; his
work can be heard on any number of air-checks and recordings made by the orchestra from the late 1930s to the
early 1950s. After World War II, Paul Whiteman reor-
ganized a "nostalgia" band playing updated versions of his
old hits, and asked Vic to join. The rancor of the "men's
room incident" of 1927 was long past, and Berton held no
hard feelings; but as he told Whiteman, "You'd have to
pay me an awful lot to make me give up this gig. This is
the first time I've eaten regularly in years!" He died in
Hollywood, on the day after Christmas, 1951.

Fud Livingston, for all his brilliance as an arranger, was
little involved in the Swing Era. Following his stints with
Nichols, he worked as an arranger for Whiteman; in 1936
he joined Jimmy Dorsey for two years as alto and tenor
saxist. Fud then retired completely from jazz, working for
music publishers and in Hollywood for motion pictures.
He died on 25 March 1957.

Leo McConville, the brilliant (and unsung) lead trumpeter
who sparked so many Nichols and Mole dates, also avoi-
ded Swing. He worked from 1928 to 1931 with Don
Voorhees, contributing to the latter's *Captain Henry's
Show Boat* radio program, and then did extensive studio
work until the mid-1930s. Then he dropped out of music,
moving to Reisertown, Maryland, where he began chicken
farming (and playing with local bands). The lure of
decent money brought him out of retirement for spells in
the little-known bands of Bob Craig and Bob Iula; but
once the big band days were bust, he went back to his
chickens. He died in Baltimore in February 1968.

Miff Mole was an all-purpose trombonist during his
decade-long stint with NBC, but jazz was only a small

part of it; more often than not, it was classical music or commercial and radio-show work. In 1938 he finally joined Paul Whiteman, and in 1942-43 played with Benny Goodman. He then led his own New York-Dixieland combo for two and a half years between 1943 and 1947 at Nick's in Greenwich Village, the haven for New York and Chicago musicians fed up with the big bands. During this period he recorded again, this time for Milt Gabler's legendary Commodore label; a year's free-lancing was followed by a trip to Chicago to join Muggsy Spanier, whose pre-Mole "Ragtimers" were a brief hit in 1939 before fizzling out in 1940. Mole settled in Chicago in 1948, and spent several years playing with small groups at the Blue Note, Jazz Ltd. and the Bee Hive. During the late 1950s he returned to New York, where he contributed to several Dixieland sessions, but by 1959 he was seriously ill and on crutches after several operations. He died in 1961.

Joe Tarto was also too good a musician to scuffle in jazz during the Depression years. After nearly working himself to death in the early 1930s, he quit his jobs in order to regain some semblance of sanity. He worked again with Nichols in 1935, on Red's weekly "College Prom" show, and then proceeded to play and record Italian, polka and hillbilly music for five years. In 1940 he joined Paul Whiteman, doubling as a jazz player Monday nights at Nick's in Greenwich Village. He played as a string bassist in Lionel Hampton's first Carnegie Hall concert (1945), then returned to tuba in Paul Lavalle's Cities Service Band of America for over a decade. He later joined the New Jersey Symphony Orchestra, and in 1980 published his treatise on *Basic Rhythms and the Art of Jazz Improvisation.* He died, full of years and honors, in 1986.

Artie Schutt was briefly a part of the first Benny Goodman band, in 1934, but he too ended up in Hollywood, where he worked as a staff musician at MGM for several years. After leaving MGM, he free-lanced around the Los Angeles area before his death in 1965.

Red Nichols continued to lead his pop band with occasional "hot interludes" on radio, records, and films until 1934, broadcasting regularly from the Golden Pheasant Restaurant in Cleveland. Then he migrated into radio, starring alongside singer Ruth Etting on a regular series for Kellogg's Corn Flakes; partly to see more of his daughter (Dorothy having been sent to boarding school), and partly because he admired him, Red featured Charlie Teagarden on trumpet more often than himself. A little later, he was the bandleader on Bob Hope's first radio program.

Then, in 1939, when most people had given up hope of ever seeing Nichols in a jazz context again, he organized his own big band. They were billed on their Bluebird and Columbia record labels as "Red Nichols and his Orchestra," but in their radio remotes announcers still called them "The Five Pennies." Little if any attention has been paid to the Nichols big band, but in retrospect it is fascinating to hear their performances.

Although their primary style was the expanded-Dixieland that had already been popularized by the Dorsey Brothers' 1934-35 orchestra, as well as by the bands of Bob Crosby and Will Bradley, it is interesting to note which features of his earlier music Red decided to retain. For one thing, there was a superb, atmospheric theme song, *Wail of the Winds,* which had Artie Schutt written all over it (and, in fact, was used by Red as a theme even during his Kellogg's Corn Flakes days). For another, his arrangements retained many Glenn Miller-isms, such as the riff-filled final choruses and extended introductions that Glenn had devised in 1929-30, as well as the elongated phrase-lengths and ooh-wah brass he introduced in the late 1930s. Red also sported an outstanding rhythmic female singer, Marion Redding; a wonderfully rollicking boogie-woogie pianist-arranger, Billy Maxted; a fine, relaxed drummer and singer, Harry Jaeger (who later graced several Goodman dates); and a sensational clarinetist, who later played with Tommy Dorsey, named Heinie Beau.

Apparently, Nichols had finally decided which elements of his "potpourri" years he wanted to incorporate into his own personal style, but it was too late. Though George T. Simon, then a young reporter for *Metronome* magazine, called Nichols's band "The Surprise of 1940," it became the big bust of 1941. As Simon put it, Nichols's "relaxed, gentlemanly horn blowing must have seemed almost like a novelty to the big band fans, most of whom had been weaned on the more aggressive, blaring styles of Harry James, Bunny Berigan, Ziggy Elman and the rest of the spectacular stylists featured with the era's top swing bands." By 1941 most of his good, seasoned musicians had already left him; and, as Simon (again) put it, "Red, who had seemed so relaxed and satisfied in front of the band at the Famous Door [in 1940], was trying to exhort his new set of youngsters to musical heights they seemed incapable of attaining. To show you just how hard Red was trying to impress, he even featured a singer, Penny Banks, who did little more than sound like Wee Bonnie Baker—quite a switch for a man who had made a name for himself starring only the best in music!"[1]

The collapse of the Nichols band, into which he had poured so much money, time and effort, left the man who was once "King of the Recording Studios" nearly broke. Out of work for the first time in twenty years, Red moved to San Meandro, California to settle down and be closer to his wife and crippled daughter: Dorothy contracted polio and spinal meningitis in 1940, and Red blamed himself. He worked during World War II as a welder in the shipyards, intending never to go back into music, but Dorothy asked him to start playing again for her sake. The tune she requested was *Battle Hymn of the Republic,* which became his big postwar hit.

From February to June 1944, Red played again as a side-man—for the first time since the Voorhees days—with Casa Loma, which by then was on a downslide of their own. The gig was important for him, however, in regaining both his chops and his confidence. Then, spurred by

---

[1] Simon, George T., *The Big Bands* (Macmillan, 1967), p. 381.

the early jazz or "Moldy Fig" revial, he formed a new Five Pennies band: a traditional sextet of trumpet, clarinet, trombone, bass sax, piano, and drums. But Joe Rushton was no Rollini, and it goes without saying that King Jackson, Rosy McHargue, Bob Hammack, and Rolly Culver didn't come within ten country miles of the star sidemen Red had in his late-1930s band, let alone the Moles, Russells, Schutts, and Bertons of fabled days. But, slowly, they caught on, and by the fall of 1944 they were recording for Capitol Records in a slick "Dixieland" style that bore only a superficial resemblance to the timeless music described in this volume.

Although this later period of Nichols' career lies outside the purview of this book, the appearance and continuance of this sextet (with personnel changes) into the early 1960s raises several tough questions. Firstly, what was Red doing? Didn't he know that this new Five Pennies could not compare with the past? Or was this just the best he could do completely on his own, without the musical support of a Mole, Berton, Schutt, Livingston, Venuti, Teagarden, Krupa, or Miller? And secondly, what of his solo style? Was there any way it could compare to his superb, Bix- and Louis-influenced playing of the 1925-32 era?

The answers to these questions are not as simple as the asking of them. Perhaps it would be best to point out that Nichols had always associated his name with commercial crossover music, even in the Roaring Twenties, and even when his bands didn't roar. His choices after World War II were essentially two: update his style, at least into the "progressive swing" format exemplified by Jonah Jones and Vic Dickenson, or continue in the "Nostalgia Dixieland" style he was already playing. Undoubtedly, the presence of faster musical company would have helped him tremendously; in the midst of his *Battle Hymns of the Republic, Three Blind Mice*, and other simple arrangements, several of them "telescriptions" for TV broadcast, are two film clips that are absolutely astounding. One is from the 1951 movie *Disc Jockey*, and features Red in the company of Joe Venuti, Ben Pollack, Red Norvo, trombonist Russ Morgan, and tenor saxist Vido Musso. The tune is a jump blues, and everyone is cooking—including Nichols. The other is a scene from the 1960 *Gene Krupa Story*, an otherwise ludicrous film starring Sal Mineo as Krupa. At an "informal jam session," Nichols and a bunch of ringers (two of whom are supposed to represent the Dorseys) suddenly update their style from 1930 jazz to 1950s progressive swing once "Krupa" sits down at the drums. Despite the idiocy of the scene, Red once again swings hard. This tells me two things: one, that Red really did need the inspiration of superior musicians to perform at his peak (he also sounds wonderful in a mixed band, with alto saxist Benny Carter and trombonist Dickinson, backing singer-pianist Julia Lee on a Capitol LP); and, two, that he chose not only less inspiration but the path of least resistance. He was an older man, now, who was just marking time, earning a living, resting on his laurels. He either felt that his reputation was secure, or didn't think much of that reputation to begin with.

That this is so may be seen in the October 1956 *This Is Your Life* show. Red is quiet and modest throughout; he has to be pumped by host Ralph Edwards to talk about himself, is genuinely stunned that so many of his old bandmates (JD, Schutt, Mole, Engle, and the Teagardens) showed up to honor him, and is speechless when Phil Harris presents him with a piano signed by musical celebrities including Bing Crosby. Aside from seeing his old friends, Red is most emotional when his grandchildren come out.

And that, perhaps, explains Red Nichols in a nutshell. He was a nice, white, middle-class family man who just happened to play good trumpet and lead one of the greatest jazz bands of all time. He liked playing for people, even if the best he had to offer them was *Dixie* or *Entrance of the Gladiators*. And that was why he kept up the Five Pennies the way they were, even after the silly fantasy of *The Red Nichols Story* in 1959. Red played the trumpet, Danny Kaye played Red, the money helped make him solvent and the film gave his sagging career a much-needed boost. He did overseas tours in 1960 and 1964, and played at such clubs as the Roundtable in New York where businessmen, baseball players and assorted Broadway celebrities became his new "hangers-on." He died on 28 June 1965—appropriately, on the road—in Las Vegas.

*   *   *   *   *

In a way, this book *had* to be written; for Red Nichols, like his friend and mentor Bix Beiderbecke, was actually very modest about his own talents. The fact that he could not swing as easily or improvise with the consistent brilliance of Beiderbecke led him to deprecate his own playing far too much; moreover, though he was always proud of the brilliant musicians with whom he had been associated, the entire latter stage of his career and musical directions often led jazz critics and scholars to overlook or negate the contributions his bands made to jazz as an art. Even Ralph Berton, Vic's younger brother, fell into the habit of considering Red merely the "poor man's Bix Beiderbecke," when in fact Red's artistic vision and abilities lay in an entirely different (though related) direction.

It is certainly true that Nichols never really developed a hot *style,* though his earlier records prove that he had hot *moments.* Perhaps he was too much of a thinker, too much of a pre-planner, to truly "become the music" as most great jazz musicians do; and in fact, it was this quality that he envied most in Beiderbecke and Armstrong. At the same time, however, he almost *had* to be a clear-thinking, non-drinking, pre-planning entepreneur in order to present as much superb jazz, both arranged and soloistic, as he did. The era in question was *not* as much of an amiable, wide-open free-for-all as some more romantic writers have tried to make it seem; and as we have seen, the more jazz became "big business" to the record companies, the more tightly they controlled, subdued, transformed or eliminated its output. What amazes one about Nichols's last period (late 1930-early 1932) is not the large amount of junk that his bands produced, but

the fact that he still had enough "pull" to get some genuine jazz past the hypercritical, commercially-adjusted ear
of Brunswick's recording director, Jack Kapp, a man who
even gave grief to his biggest-selling vocalists, The
Boswell Sisters.

The greatest irony of the 1925-32 years is not that Red
changed his style from what he liked to call "syncopated
chamber music" to a more extroverted form of jazz; as we
have seen, there was a great deal of good from that later
period, and different is not necessarily worse. The greatest irony was that he and his musicians, particularly Glenn
Miller, were continually devising and abandoning ideas,
riffs, rhythmic devices and entire styles with the abandon
of a brilliant but schizophrenic inventor. Had they been
able to sit back, view their output objectively, select the
stylistic devices that most appealed to them as musicians
and created a permanent (or at least semi-permanent)
organization out of all this chaos, they might have had
something really going for them, Depression or no Depression. After all, this was exactly what Gene Gifford and
Glen Gray did in 1930; and though their devices wore thin
and had to be replaced by the late 1930s, the Casa Loma
Orchestra *did* at least have continuous work, playing hot
arrangements, at a time when Nichols and his band members were forced to diversify into other work.

The main point of this entire thesis, then, is that consci-
ously or unconsciously, directly or indirectly, the music
created by the various Red Nichols groups (especially
between 1925 and 1930) was not only important in and of
its own time, but highly important to the overall history of
jazz. It was, in fact, *just as important though in a different way* as the music of Jelly Roll Morton or early Duke
Ellington. Despite being an entirely "white" concept of
jazz, utilizing the heat and swing of the black musicians at
a second-hand remove, it nevertheless left in its wake a
profound use of and appreciation for harmonic devices and
virtuosic playing within a jazz context. If Vic Berton
could not quite swing with the looseness and aggressive-

ness of, say, a Baby Dodds or a Chick Webb, he nevertheless played his cymbals and hot tympani in a way that no
drummer, black or white, has ever duplicated. If Miff
Mole lacked the funky saunter on his trombone that
Charlie Green or Joe "Tricky Sam" Nanton possessed, he
could negotiate octave-leaps and twists of phrase that
those musicians could never have played in a million
years. If Artie Schutt never quite possessed the electric
drive of Jimmy Blythe or Tiny Parham, he nevertheless
played with more fire, greater swing and imagination than
most other band pianists of his time.

And Red—poor Red!—seemed always to be in the shadow
of some other, finer, greater white trumpeter or cornetist,
much in the same way that Glenn Miller was with trombonists. First it was Bix Beiderbecke; then it was Charlie
Teagarden; then Bunny Berigan, then Billy May and
Harry James and Ziggy Elman and—even within his own
style, and in his own circle—Max Kaminsky and Bobby
Hackett. No matter the era or situation, it was always a
case of, "Well, Red's not bad, BUT." And Red, ever
modest about his own talents (though naturally proud of
his accomplishments), was right there to agree with them.
One might say that Red Nichols never really emerged
from the shadows of his peers, but in a real sense he never
really emerged from the shadow of Red Nichols.

And yet, quite aside from the marvelously complex
creations that Red and his bands produced, was there another trumpeter or cornetist who could have played what he
did on *Get With, Alabama Stomp, Boneyard Shuffle, Davenport Blues, That's No Bargain, Waitin' for the Evening
Mail,* or the Edison version of *Hurricane*—not to mention
the Whiteman recording of *I'm Coming, Virginia?* I don't
think so. For all his stylistic debt to Beiderecke—and it
was considerable, no mistake about that—Nichols emerged
from these and other sessions with his own personality,
and integrity, intact. He was no mere imitator, regardless
of how deeply the Bix influence ran; and considering how
easy it would have been for a player of his technical prow-

ess to do so, we must laud his attempts (even when they failed) to play his own stuff. As Max Kaminsky put it, "Red was a fabulous trumpet player. Though he would have sold his soul to the devil to swing as hard as Bix, he could play more different things, and more *difficult* things, than any trumpeter I ever heard."[2] Amen to that!

It is impossible, for me, to even think of the late-1940s and early-1950s bands of Miles Davis, Gerry Mulligan, and Shorty Rogers without noticing stylistic or structural resemblances to the Nichols bands of the late 1920s and early 1930s. Beiderbecke (and, to a lesser extent, Trumbauer) may have influenced the *solo* styles of later jazz to a greater degree, but there are only rare Bix-Tram records—usually arranged by Challis, Satterfield or Livingston—where one comes away with the same feeling of group accomplishment. In addition, those Bix-Tram exceptions are usually well-organized arrangements with occasional solos, e.g., *Humpty Dumpty,* or well-organized arrangements that "take off" from the principal ideas, e.g., *Three Blind Mice.* Very rarely, if ever, do they *integrate* the solos into the overall tune or arrangement structure, as Nichols did so well and continued to attempt even to the very end. For all the direct or near-direct stylistic links between, say, Beiderbecke and Miles Davis (via Hackett), or Trumbauer and Lee Konitz (via Lester Young), the orchestration, harmonic and song structures of the various Cool School bands owe their very souls to Red Nichols.

And don't you ever forget that.

---

2 From a telephone conversation with the author, 6 November 1992.

Bibliography

There is not much literature on, by, or about Red Nichols, but here are some sources you might check out:

FEATHER, LEONARD. *The Encyclopedia of Jazz.* Horizon Press, 1960/1972.

HARRISON, MAX; FOX, CHARLES; THACKER, ERIC. *The Essential Jazz Records, Vol. 1: Ragtime to Swing.* Greenwood Press, 1984.

HARRISON, MAX. *Jazz Retrospect.* Crescendo Publishing Co., 1976/1991.

HENTOFF, NAT & SHAPIRO, NAT. *Hear Me Talkin' To Ya.* Dover, 1966.

SCHULLER, GUNTHER. *The Swing Era.* Oxford University Press, 1989.

SIMON, GEORGE T. *The Big Bands.* Macmillan, 1967.

STROFF, STEPHEN M. *Discovering Great Jazz.* Newmarket Press, 1992.

It might also be mentioned, in passing, that James Lincoln Collier's *The Making of Jazz* (Delta, 1978), though containing a few references to Nichols, omits any intelligent discussion of the Five Pennies, and in fact laughably gives more space to foreign knock-off Fred Elizalde than to Red himself. Also, Britisher Barry McRae's *The Jazz Handbook* (G.K. Hall & Co., 1989) relegates Red to two tiny mentions, not even giving him a spot of his own in discussing '20s jazz.

Selected Discography

With all the records Red made, filling out a complete discography is something I would much rather leave to the Brian Rusts and Stan Hesters of the world; and, as we have seen, no one's fact-tracking (unfortunately, not even mine) is always perfect in any case. I would, however, like to mention the Red Nichols discs that are in print (at least, at the time of publication), and then list those recordings I surveyed in the course of preparing this book.

The two LP sets on Sunbeam Records (13821 Calvert St., Van Nuys, CA 91401) may not still be in print, but they are listed in the Schwann Spectrum catalog and are worth seeking out. **Red Nichols & his Five Pennies, 1929-31 with Benny Goodman** (Sunbeam SB-137) contains the marvelous performances of *Carolina in the Morning, Chinatown My Chinatown, Alice Blue Gown, Bugaboo, Corrinne Corrina,* and *How Come You Do Me Like You Do,* among others; and the 2-disc **Popular Concert, 1928-32** mixes such pop ephemera as the *New Orleans Medley* and *California Medley* with interesting hybrids like *Poor Butterfly, Limehouse Blues,* and *Sally, Won't You Come Back.*

An MCA LP, **Rarest Brunswick Masters 1926-31** (MCA-1518), contains the superb recordings of *That's No Bargain* and *The New Yorkers,* but also such highly commercial material as *I Got Rhythm, Sometimes I'm Happy* and *Things I Never Knew,* and the defective later "takes" of *Original Dixieland One-Step* and *The Sheik of Araby.*

On American CDs, the outlook is rather skimpy. Bluebird's **The Jazz Age: New York in the Twenties** (RCA 3136-2-RB) has the great 1927-28 versions of *Davenport Blues, Delirium, Slippin' Around, Feelin' No Pain, Harlem Twist,* and the rather dismal *Five Pennies,* along with discs by Venuti, Ben Pollack, and Phil Napoleon. The lone Nichols entry (so far) in GRP's Decca Jazz Series is **B.G. and Big Tea in NYC** (GRP GRD-609), which presents

Dinah, Indiana, On the Alamo, Peg O' My Heart, Sweet Georgia Brown, China Boy, The Sheik of Araby (the good take), and *Keep a Song in Your Soul.* **New York Jazz in the Roaring Twenties** (Biograph BCD-129) has four of Red's Edisons in great sound (including *Hurricane)* and a marvelous uptempo performance of *Five Pennies* by Phil Napoleon's band. Also, a company called EPM has an album of combined Nichols and Napoleon material, which I haven't seen or heard, on EPM ZET-745.

The British, however, have jumped into the fray with two good collections. **Red Nichols & Miff Mole** (BBC CD-664) features *Darktown Strutters' Ball, Hurricane, Someday Swetheart, Wabash Blues, Davenport Blues* (Molers), *Hot Time in the Old Town Tonight, Delirium, Riverboat Shuffle, Feelin' No Pain, Honolulu Blues, Shim-Me-Sha-Wabble* (Teschemacher version), *That's A-Plenty,* and others. **Rhythm of the Day** (ASV/Living Era CDAJA-5025-R) contains the title track, plus *Buddy's Habits, Original Dixieland One-Step, Boneyard Shuffle, Alexander's Ragtime Band, Cornfed, Mean Dog Blues, Eccentric, There'll Come a Time, Waitin' for the Evening Mail* and the 1932 *Sweet Sue. Imagination* is on **New York,** BBC CD-590; and **Joe Venuti and Eddie Lang,** BBC CD-644, contains *Bugle Call Rag* and *Oh, Peter! You're So Nice,* though the latter track sounds much more solid on Living Era. There are also a few great sides available on Broadway and Intermission LPs (P.O. Box 100, Brighton, MI 48116), especially on **Real Rare Red** (BR-110) which includes the 1922 "Syncopated Five" cuts and the superb 10 September 1929 Louisiana Rhythm Kings session.

All record labels and numbers listed are of original issues. In most cases this means 78s, though the first issue of some alternate takes was on LP or CD. To reiterate, I've omitted unissued recordings; this was merely my way of keeping track of Red's musical evolution, which I have added here as an appendix to correct Rust's errors and give the reader a reference guide. (Again, my warmest thanks to Stan Hester for helping me with the corrections.)

RED NICHOLS-MIFF MOLE RECORDINGS: Master List

Labels: Ap=Apex; ARC=American Record Corp; Ba=Banner; By=Broadway; Br=Brunswick; BM=Bon Marche; Ca=Cameo; Cl=Clarion; Col=Columbia; Cr=Crown; Dca=Decatur; De= Decca; Do=Domino; Ed=Edison; El=Electrola; Em=Embassy; Gr=Grafton; Ha=Harmony; HJC=Hot Jazz Club; HRS=Hot Record Society; Im=Imperial; JA=Jazz Archives; Lin=Linton; LS=Lucky Strike; Mf=Mayfair; Mx=Maxsa; Mt=Melotone; Mic=Microphone; NML=Nat'l Music Lovers; Od=Odeon; OK=OKeh; Or=Oriole; Pan=Panachord; Pam=Paramount; Par=Parlo- phone; PA=Pathe Actuelle; Pe=Perfect; RCA=RCA Bluebird/Victor; RB=Radio Broadcast; Re=Regal; Ro=Romeo; Sal=Salabert; SD=Steiner-Davis; Sun=Sunbeam; Sup=Supertone; Sk=Starck; St=Starr; UHCA=United Hot Clubs of America; VT=Velvet Tone; Vic=Victor Talk- ing Machine Co; Vo=Vocalion; Zon=Zonophone.

GEORGE OLSEN AND HIS MUSIC   26 June 1924
Red Nichols, tp; Floyd Rice, tp/mel/a-sx; Chuck Campbell, tb; George Henkel, s-sx/fl/ a-sx; Buck Yoder, cl/a-sx; Dave Phennig, t-sx/vln; Eddie Kilfeather, p/arr; Billy Priest, bj/ a-sx; Jack Hansen, tu; George Olsen, dm.

30327-2	YOU'LL NEVER GET TO HEAVEN (With Those Eyes) (Clark-Leslie)	
		Vic 19405; HMV B-1880; Zon 3787

LANIN'S RED HEADS   26 February 1925
Nichols, Hymie Farberman, ct; Herb Winfield, tb; Chuck Muller, cl/a-sx; Dick Johnson, Lucien Smith, cl/t-sx; Bill Krenz, p; Tony Colucci, bj; Joe Tarto, tu; Vic Berton, dm.

140397-1	JIMTOWN BLUES (Charles Davis)	Col 327-D
140398-2	KING PORTER STOMP (Morton)	Col 327-D, 3669

		4 May 1925
140579-3	I WOULDN'T BE WHERE I AM (Rose-Henderson)	Col 376-D, 3715
140580-3	FLAG THAT TRAIN (To Alabam') (Richmond-McPhail)	As above

GOLDIE'S SYNCOPATORS   4 May 1925
Nichols, Frank Cush, ct; Tommy Dorsey, tb; Jimmy Dorsey, Arnold Brilhart, cl/a-sx; Fred Cusick, t-sx; Adrian Rollini, bs-sx; Irv Brodsky, p; Tom Felline, bj; Stan King, dm.

106004	DUSTIN' THE DONKEY (Quicksell)	PA 036260; Pe 14441
106005	TIGER RAG (La Rocca-Shields)	Ap 8644; Do 4011, 21303; PA
		03266; Pam 6853; Ba 6049; Or 984, 1544; Pe 14447;
		Re 8380; LS 24120; Mic 22197; St 10272; Sal 197

THE COTTON PICKERS   21 August 1925
Nichols, ct; Mickey Bloom, tp/mel; Miff Mole, tb; Chuck Muller, cl; Alfie Evans, C-sx; Rube Bloom, p; Harry Reser, bj; Tarto, tu; Phil Role, dm.

16191	MILENBERG JOYS (Morton-Roppolo-Mares)	Br 2937
16192	MILENBERG JOYS (Morton-Roppolo-Mares)	By BR-120 (LP)
16195	IF YOU HADN'T GONE AWAY (Brown-Rose-Henderson)	Br 2937

LANIN'S RED HEADS   19 October 1925
Nichols, Mole, Muller, Tarto, Berton; L. Smith, t-sx/vln; Dick Johnson, cl/a-sx; Roy Smeck, bj; George Crozier, arr; Art Gillham, p/voc.

141155-2	I'M GONNA HANG AROUND MY SUGAR (Palmer-Williams)	Col 483-D
141156-3	FIVE FOOT TWO (Lewis-Young) vocAG	Col 483-D

UKELELE IKE & HIS HOT COMBINATION   October 1925
Nichols, ct; Mole, tb; Bobby Davis, a-sx; Arthur Schutt, p; Dick McDonough, bj; Tarto, tu; Ber- ton, dm; Cliff Edwards (Ukelele Ike), uk/voc.

106315-A-B	OH! LOVEY, BE MINE (Donaldson)	PA 025159,11039; Pe 11593; Sk 159
106316-A-B	SAY! WHO IS THAT BABY DOLL? (Turk-Maceo-Pinkard)	Same

ROSS GORMAN & HIS EARL CARROLL ORCH.   29 October 1925
Nichols, ct; Donald Lindley, James Kozak, tp; Mole, tb; Ross Gorman, cl/a-sx/br-sx; Alfie Evans, cl/a-sx/vln; Harold Noble, cl/a-sx/t-sx; Billy McGill, cl/t-sx; Barney Acquelina, bs-sx;

Nick Koupoukis, fl/pic; Jack Harris, Saul Sharrow, vln; Schutt, p; McDonough, bj; Tony Colic-
chio, g; David Grupp, dm.

141214-3	I'M SITTING ON TOP OF THE WORLD (Henderson)	Col 498-D, 3862
141215-2	RHYTHM OF THE DAY (Murphy-Lindley)	Col 498-D, 3958

THE HOTTENTOTS 11 November 1925
Nichols, Mole, Bloom, Berton; Dick Johnson, cl.

E-1678/80	DOWN AND OUT BLUES (Farrell-Sizemore)	Vo 15161
E-1682	THE CAMEL WALK (Schaper-Mack-Trymm)	Vo 15161; Aco G-16060

THE RED HEADS 15 November 1925
Nichols, Mole, Schutt, Berton; Bobby Davis, Fred Morrow, cl/a-sx.

106400	FALLEN ARCHES (Ponce)	PA 36384, 11456; Pe 14565; Par X-6848; Sal 329
106401	NERVOUS CHARLIE (Nichols)	PA 36347; Pe 14528
106402	HEADIN' FOR LOUISVILLE (Meyer-DeSylva)	PA 36347, 11069; Pe 14528

THE HOTTENTOTS 8 January 1926
Nichols, Mole, D. Johnson, L. Smith, Bloom, Colucci, Berton.

E-2077/9	PENSACOLA (Rose)	Vo 15209
E-2080/3	NOBODY'S ROSE (Rose)	Same

ORIGINAL MEMPHIS FIVE 21 January 1926
Nichols, ct; Mole, tb; Jimmy Lytell, cl; Frank Signorelli, p; Jack Roth, dm.

E-17613	CHINESE BLUES (Waller-Mills)	Br 3039

Same personnel, but add Joe Tarto (tu). 23 January 1926

E-17656/9	'TAIN'T COLD (Barris)	Br 3039

Next two selections released as **THE HOTTENTOTS**

E-2206/8	CHINESE BLUES (Waller-Mills)	Vo 15234
E-2209/11	BASS ALE BLUES (Napoleon-Signorelli)	Same

THE RED HEADS 4 February 1926
Nichols, ct; Mole, tb; J. Dorsey, Evans, cl/t-sx; Bloom, p; Berton, dm; Arthur Fields, voc.

106602	POOR PAPA (Rose-Woods) vocAF	PA 36387, 11134; Pe 14568; Gr 9217 (as Windsor Orch); Sal 262
106787	'TAIN'T COLD (Barris)	PA 36419, 11396; Pe 14600
106788	HANGOVER (Nichols-Mole)	As above

WE THREE Nichols, Schutt, Berton; Eddie Lang, g*. 24 March 1926

106746	PLENTY OFF CENTER (Nichols)	PA 36492, 11206; Pe 14673; Sal 383
106787	TRUMPET SOBS (Nichols)*	PA 36464; Pe 14645

THE RED HEADS 7 April 1926
Same as February 4, but Evans (cl/a-sx) omitted; Schutt (p) repl. Bloom.

106786	WILD AND FOOLISH (Smith-Redman)	PA 36492, 11206; Pe 14673
106787	HI-DIDDLE-DIDDLE (Coon)	PA 36458, 11234; Pe 14639; Ap 752; Par X-6900; Sal 382; Do 21520; LS 24504; Mic 22517; St 23042
106788	DYNAMITE (Henderson)	PA 36458, 11456; Pe 14639; Par X-6903; Sal 378

THE HOTTENTOTS Same as January 8. May 1926

2519-1	LOTS O' MAMA (Weber-Meyers-Schoebel)	Pam 12359

ANNETTE HANSHAW & THE CHARLESTON CHASERS 12 September 1926
Nichols, Mole; Jimmy Lytell, cl; Brodsky, p/bj/tu; Annette Hanshaw, voc.

E-2518-C	BLACK BOTTOM (DeSylva-Brown)	PA 32207, 11248; Pe 12286
E-2519-D	SIX FEET OF PAPA (Moll-Sizemore)	PA 32211; Pe 12290; Ap 774

THE RED HEADS   14 September 1926
Nichols, Leo McConville, tp; Mole, tb; J. Dorsey, cl/a-sx; Evans, cl/t-sx; Schutt, p; Dick McDonough, bj/g; Berton, dm.

107094-B	ALABAMA STOMP (Creamer-Johnson)	PA 36527, 11236; Sal 471;
		Pe 14708; Par X-6946
107095-A-B	THE HURRICANE (Mertz-Nichols)	PA 36536, 11331; Pe 14717;
	Ap 26009; Do 21580 (as Red Dandies); Leo/St 23093; Sal 467
107096-C	BROWN SUGAR (Barris)	PA 36527, 11236; Pe 14708

RED AND MIFF'S STOMPERS   13 October 1926
Nichols, Mole, J. Dorsey, Evans, Schutt, Tarto, Berton.

| 11245-A-B-C | ALABAMA STOMP (Creamer-Johnson) | Ed 51854; SD 106 |
| 11246-A-B-C | STAMPEDE (Henderson) | Same as above |

THE RED HEADS Nichols, Schutt, Lang, Berton.   4 November 1926

| 107192 | GET WITH (Nichols) | PA 11347 |
| 107193 | GET A LOAD OF THIS (Nichols-Lang) | Same |

RED & MIFF'S STOMPERS Same as October 13.   10 November 1926

| 11291 | HURRICANE (Mertz-Nichols) | Ed 51878; SD 105 |
| 11292 | BLACK BOTTOM STOMP (Morton) | Same |

THE RED HEADS   11 November 1926
Nichols, McConville, Mole, J. Dorsey, Schutt, McDonough, Berton; Brad Gowans, ct.*

107204	THAT'S NO BARGAIN (Nichols)	PA 36576, 11331; Pe 14757
107205	HEEBIE JEEBIES (Atkins)*	PA 36557, 11289; Pe 14738;
		Par X-6963; Sal 565
107206-A-B	BLACK BOTTOM STOMP (Morton)	As above, but add Par X-6965

RED NICHOLS & HIS FIVE PENNIES   8 December 1926
Nichols, J. Dorsey, Schutt, Lang, Berton.
Note: Certain sessions bear two matrix numbers: four digits for release on Vocalion, five for release on Brunswick. Vocalion mx. nos. follow the title, in parentheses.

E-20992	WASHBOARD BLUES (Carmichael)(E4178)	Br 40608; Vo 15498
E-20993	WASHBOARD BLUES (E4179)	Br 3407, 6814, 80072, 01801,
		A-222; Vo 1069
E-20994	THAT'S NO BARGAIN (Nichols)(E4180)	Br 3407, 40608
E-20995	THAT'S NO BARGAIN (E4181)	Same as E-20993, add Vo 15498

Miff Mole (tb) added.   20 December 1926

E-21594	BUDDY'S HABITS (Straight-Nelson)(E4263)	Br 80071, 01802,
		3477, 6815, A-358; Vo 1076, 15573
E-21597	BONEYARD SHUFFLE (Carmichael)(E4260)	Same as above

THE ARKANSAS TRAVELERS   4 January 1927
Nichols, Mole, J. Dorsey, Schutt, Berton; Fred Morrow, a-sx.

143260-3	WASHBOARD BLUES	Ha 332-H; VT 1332-V; Diva 2332-G
143261-1	THAT'S NO BARGAIN	Ha 383-H; VT 1383-V; Diva 2383-G
143262-3	BONEYARD SHUFFLE (Carmichael)	Same as 143260

RED NICHOLS & HIS FIVE PENNIES Same as Dec. 20.   12 January 1927

E-22981	ALABAMA STOMP (E4382)	Br 3550, 6817, 01904, A-456
E-22982	ALABAMA STOMP (Creamer-Johnson)(E4383)	Vo 15566
E-22983	ALABAMA STOMP (Creamer-Johnson)(E4384)	Br 3550
E-22984	HURRICANE (Mertz-Nichols)(E4385)	Same as E-22981
E-22985/6	HURRICANE (Mertz-Nichols)(E4386/7)	Br 3550

THE CHARLESTON CHASERS   17 January 1927
Nichols, Mole, J. Dorsey, Schutt, McDonough, Tarto, Berton.

143258-5	SOMEDAY, SWEETHEART (Spikes)	Col 861-D, DB-5005,
		4419, CQ-1416, DW-4361, 0920
143259-5	AFTER YOU'VE GONE (Creamer)	Col 861-D, 4453, FB-1108

THE RED HEADS   18 January 1927
Nichols, Mole, J. Dorsey, Schutt, Berton; Frank Gould, voc.

107350-B-D	TELL ME TONIGHT (Little) vocFG	PA 36583; Pe 14764
107351-A-C	HERE OR THERE (Davis-Greer) vocFG	As above, add PA 11376
107352-A-B-C	YOU SHOULD SEE MY TOOTSIE (Yellen-Ager) voc FG	
		PA 36593, 11376; Pe 14774

MIFF MOLE'S (LITTLE) MOLERS   26 January 1927
Nichols, Mole, Schutt, McDonough, Berton.

80338-A	ALEXANDER'S RAGTIME BAND (Berlin)	OK 40758; Col 36280,
		C-6179; Par R-3320, A-2155; Od 165090, 193042
80339-A	SOME SWEET DAY (Rose)	OK 40758; Par R-3320, R-2506,
		A-2155; Od 193042
80340-A	HURRICANE (Mertz)	OK 40848; Par R-3362; Od 193053, A-189176

RED & MIFF'S STOMPERS   11 February 1927
Nichols, Mole, JD, Schutt, Berton; Tony Colucci, bj.

37768-2	DELIRIUM (Schutt)	Vic 20778
37768-3	DELIRIUM (Schutt)	JA 21 (LP)
37769-2	DAVENPORT BLUES (Beiderbecke)	Vic 20778
37769-3	DAVENPORT BLUES (Beiderbecke)	JA 21 (LP)

CHARLESTON CHASERS As Jan. 17, but add Kate Smith (voc).   14 February 1927

143476-3	ONE SWEET LETTER FROM YOU (Warren) vocKS	Col 911-D
143477-3	I'M GONNA MEET MY SWEETIE (Davis-Greer) vocKS	Col 911-D

Same personnel as January 17.   25 February 1927

143533-1	FAREWELL BLUES (Meyers-Rappolo-Schoebel)	Col 1539-D
143534-2	DAVENPORT BLUES (Beiderbecke)	Col 909-D, 4453, FB-1108
143537-2	WABASH BLUES (Meinken-Ringle)	Col 909-D, 4419; Par R-2211,
		A-6510, B-71143; Od D-517

RED NICHOLS & HIS FIVE PENNIES   3 March 1927
Nichols, Mole, J. Dorsey, Schutt, Lang, Berton; Joe Venuti, vln.

E-21718	BUGLE CALL RAG (Pettis-Meyers-Schoebel)(E4643)	Br 3490,
		3510, 6816, 01803, A-7556; Vo 15536
E-21721	BACK BEATS (Guarante)(E4640)	Same as above

MIFF MOLE'S (LITTLE) MOLERS   7 March 1927

80501-B	DAVENPORT BLUES	OK 40848; Par R-3362; Od 193053, A-189176
80502-A	THE DARKTOWN STRUTTERS' BALL (Brooks)	OK 40784; Vo 3041;
		Par R-3326, A-2188, A-4903; Od 193008, 194865
80503-A	HOT TIME IN THE OLD TOWN TONIGHT (Mertz)	As above, but
		omit Par A-2188, Od 194865

THE SIX HOTTENTOTS   23 March 1927
Nichols, Mole, JD, Schutt, Tarto, Berton; Irving Kaufman ("George Crane"), voc.

7173-1-2	I'M IN LOVE AGAIN (Porter) voclK	Ban 1964; By 1069; Do
		3935, 21279; Or 880; Pam 20511; PA 36643; Pe 14824, P-106; Re
		8289; Ap 8624; Leo 10256; LS 24097; Imp 1803; BM 240; Max 1623
7174-2-3	SOMETIMES I'M HAPPY (Berlin) voclK	Ban 6008; Do 21274, 3975;
		NML 1208; Or 933; PA 36643, 11477; Pe 14824, P-306; Re 8333; Ap
		8614, 26050; Leo 10249; LS 24091; Mic 22165; Imp 1845; Mx 1622
7175-1	ROSY CHEEKS (Whiting)	Ban 1962; By 1070; Do 3931, 21275; Or
		883; Pam 20512; Re 8289; Ap 8614; Leo 10250; Mx 1622; Jewel 5002

ROGER WOLFE KAHN & HIS ORCHESTRA
14 April 1927

Roger Wolfe Kahn, a-sx/t-sx (according to Brian Rust; possibly just leader); McConville, Tom Gott, tp; Mole, tb; Evans, cl/a-sx; Arnold Brilhart, cl/a-sx/fl; Harold Sturr, cl/t-sx; Venuti, Joe Raymond, vln; Brodsky, p; Colucci, bj; Lang, g; Arthur Campbell, tu; Berton, dm.

38469-1	JUST THE SAME (Donaldson-Burke)	Vic 20634; HMV K-5286

PAUL WHITEMAN & HIS ORCHESTRA
29 April 1927

Nichols, Henry Busse, Ted Bartell, unknown, tp; Vincent Grande, Wilbur Hall, tb; Max Farley, Hal McLean, Chester Hazlett, cl/a-sx; Charles Strickfadden, a-sx/br-sx; Mischa Russell, Kurt Dieterle, Mario Perry, vln; Matty Malneck, vln/vla; Harry Perella, p; Mike Pingatore, bj; Lang, g; Al Armer, bs; Berton, dm; Bing Crosby & the Rhythm Boys (Al Rinker, Harry Barris), voc.

38135-7	I'M COMING, VIRGINIA (Heywood-Cook) vocBC,RB	Vic LPM-2071, LVA-1000, LX-995 (LP)
38135-9	I'M COMING, VIRGINIA vocBC,RB	Vic 20751; El EG-614
38378-1	SIDE BY SIDE (Woods) vocBC,RB	Vic LPV-570 (LP)
38378-4	SIDE BY SIDE (Woods) vocBC,RB	Vic 20627; HMV B-5318, K-5223; El EG-709; Dca 505

THE SIX HOTTENTOTS Same as March 23.
2 May 1927

7241-2	MEMPHIS BLUES (Norton)	Ba 1986; Do 3956; Or 952
		(as Dixie Jazz Band); Re 8310, 8335

THE ARKANSAS TRAVELERS Same as January 4.
10 May 1927

144119-3	JA-DA (Carlton)	Ha 421-H
144120-2	SENSATION (Edwards)	Ha 421-H
144121-2	STOMPIN' FOOL (Ford)	Ha 459-H

THE SIX HOTTENTOTS Same as May 2.
16 May 1927

7264-1-3	MELANCHOLY CHARLIE (Crum)	Ba 6009; Do 3975; Or 931; Re 8333; MF 103
7265-1	HURRICANE	Ba 6009; Do 3976, 21580; Or 931; Re 8335; MF 103

THE CHARLESTON CHASERS Same as Feb. 25.
18 May 1927

144168-2	MY GAL SAL (Dresser)	Col 1539-D, J-577
144169-3	DELIRIUM (Schutt)	Col 1076-D, 4562; Par R-2540; Od D-517

RED NICHOLS & HIS FIVE PENNIES
20 June 1927

Same as March 3, but add Adrian Rollini (bs-sx).

E-23665	CORNFED (Effros-Wall)(E6302)	Br 3597, 6818; Vo 15602
E-23666	CORNFED (Effros-Wall)	Br 3597, 01805, A-7543
E-23668	FIVE PENNIES (Nichols) Br 3855, 3819, 6821, 01851, 4844; Col DO-1354	

Same as above.
25 June 1927

E-23755	MEAN DOG BLUES (Jackson)(E6300)	Br 3597, 6818, 01805, A-7543; Vo 15602

15 August 1927

Nichols, McConville, Manny Klein*, tp; Mole, tb; Pee Wee Russell, cl/t-sx; Fud Livingston, arr/t-sx; Rollini, bs-sx; Lennie Hayton, p/cel/arr; McDonough, g; Berton, dm.

E-24224	RIVERBOAT SHUFFLE (Carmichael-Mills)* arrFL	Br 3627
E-24225	RIVERBOAT SHUFFLE (Carmichael)* arrFL	Br 3627, 3698, 6820, 01806, A-7601, A-500400
E-24228	ECCENTRIC (Robinson) arrFL	As above, plus Col DO-1354
E-24230	IDA, SWEET AS APPLE CIDER (Leonard) arrLH	Br 3626
E-24232	IDA, SWEET AS APPLE CIDER arrLH	Br 3626, 6819, 80069, 01536, A-7559, A-500401; Coral 91015; Mt M-12443; Pe 15648; Vo 4654, 15622; Ba 32517
E-24235	FEELIN' NO PAIN (Livingston) arrFL	Same as above

HARRY RESER'S SYNCOPATORS   29 August 1927
Harry Reser, bj; Nichols, Farberman, tp; Sam Lewis, tb; Larry Abbott, cl/a-sx; unknown cl/t-sx;
Bill Wirges, p; Tarto, tu; Tom Stacks, dm; Franklyn Bauer, voc.

| 144584-? | SHAKING THE BLUES AWAY (Berlin) vocFB | Col 1109-D |
| 144585-? | OOH! MAYBE IT'S YOU (Berlin) vocFB | Col 1109-D |

MIFF MOLE'S (LITTLE) MOLERS   30 August 1927
Nichols, Mole, Russell, Livingston, Rollini, Schutt, McDonough, Lang, Berton.

81296-B   IMAGINATION (Livingston)   OK 40890; Col 35687; Par R-3420,
                                            R-2286, A-7618; Od 165192, 193092, A-189145
81297-B   FEELIN' NO PAIN (Livingston)   OK 40890; Col 35687; Par R-3420,
                                            R-2269, A-7600; Vo 3074; Od 165192, A-189145, 193092, 028536
81298-B   ORIGINAL DIXIELAND ONE-STEP (LaRocca-Shields)   OK 40932;
                                            Col 36010; Br 8243; Par R-3530; Od 165276, A-189106

Same personnel as above.   1 September 1927
81413-B   MY GAL SAL (Dresser)   OK 40932; Par R-3530; Od 165276, A-189106
81414-B   HONOLULU BLUES (Goldstein-Gunsky)   OK 40984; Par R-3441;
                                            Br 8243; Od 165328, 193171, A-189122
81415-C   THE NEW TWISTER (Lillard-Krise)   As above: omit Br, add Vo 3074

THE CHARLESTON CHASERS   6 September 1927
Nichols, McConville, Mole, Russell, Hayton, McDonough, Berton; Jack Hanse, tu; Craig
Leitch, voc.

| 144625-2 | FIVE PENNIES (Nichols) arrFL | Col 1229-D, 4797 |
| 144626-3 | SUGAR FOOT STRUT (Pierce-Schwab) vocCL | Col 1260-D, 4877 |

DON VOORHEES & HIS ORCHESTRA   7 September 1927
Nichols, McConville, unknown, tp; Mole, tb; Bill Trone, mel; Morrow, Phil Gleason, cl/s-sx/a-sx;
Paul Cartwright, cl/s-sx/t-sx; Raymond, vln; Hayton, p; McDonough, bj/g; Hansen, tu; Berton,
dm; Billy Day, Irving Kaufman (as "Vincent van Tuyl"), voc.

144634-3   DAWNING (Silver-Pinkard) vocBD   Col 1131-D, 4873, 0889
144636-3   RAIN (Ford) vocBD   Col 1126-D, 4684, CS-8
144637-3   WHEN THE MORNING GLORIES WAKE UP (Fisher-Rose) vocIK
                                                    Col 1124-D, 4683

THE CHARLESTON CHASERS   8 September 1927
Same as Sept. 6, but add Livingston (cl/a-sx), Kress (g); omit Leitch (voc).

| 144649-2 | IMAGINATION (Livingston) | Col 1260-D, 4877 |
| 144650-2 | FEELIN' NO PAIN (Livingston) | Col 1229-D, 4797 |

DON VOORHEES & HIS ORCHESTRA   9 September 1927
Same as September 7, but Lewis James repl. Day and Kaufman (voc) on both titles.

| 144651-3 | MY BLUE HEAVEN (Whiting-Donaldson) | Col 1129-D, 4684, 0836 |
| 144652-2 | A SHADY TREE (Donaldson) | Col 1131-D, 0889 |

                                                                10 September 1927
As above, but Kaufman (as "Frank Harris," voc) & Lang (g) repl. James & McDonough.

144641-2   BABY'S BLUE (Hupfeld) vocIK   Col 1123-D, 4682, 0981, CS-8
144642-3   CLEMENTINE (Creamer-Warren) vocIK   Col 1180-D

THE ARKANSAS TRAVELERS   14 September 1927
Nichols, Mole, Russell, Morrow, Bloom, Berton.

144667-2   BIRMINGHAM BREAKDOWN (Ellington)   Ha 505-H; Rex 25070
144668-2   RED HEAD BLUES (Germain-Lillard)   Ha 601-H
144669-2   I AIN'T GOT NOBODY (Graham-Williams)   Ha 505-H; Rex 25070

THE RED HEADS   16 September 1927
Nichols, Mole, Russell, Schutt, Berton; Wingy Manone, ct*.

107782-1-2   A GOOD MAN IS HARD TO FIND (Green)   PA 36701; Pe 14882;

Ca 1260; Lin 2725; Ro494; Sal 765; Mf 101
107783   NOTHIN' DOES-DOES IT LIKE IT USED TO DO-DO (Kahal)
PA 36707, 11515; Pe 14888
107784-1-2   BALTIMORE (McHugh-Healy)*   PA 36701, 11515; Pe 14882; Sal 764

MEYER'S DANCE ORCHESTRA (Possibly Lou Gold)   10 October 1927
Nichols, Lytell, Morrow, Schutt, McDonopugh, Berton.
107830   EVERYBODY LOVES MY GIRL (Lewis-Young)   Pe P-378

RED & MIFF'S STOMPERS   12 October 1927
Nichols, Mole, Russell, Livingston, Hayton, Kress, Hansen; Berton, dm & harpophone.
40168-1   SLIPPIN' AROUND (Mole)   Vic 21397
40169-2   FEELIN' NO PAIN (Livingston)   Vic 21183

RED NICHOLS' STOMPERS   26 October 1927
Nichols, Bo Ashford, tp; Bill Rank, Glenn Miller, tb; Max Farley, a-sx; Frank Trumbauer, C-sx;
Russell, cl/a-sx; Rollini, bs-sx; Schutt, p; Kress, g; Hansen, tu; Chauncey Morehouse, dm; Jim
Miller, Charlie Farrell, voc (both titles).
40512-1   SUGAR (Nichols-Yellen-Ager)   Vic 21056; HMV B-5433, AM-1211
40513-1   MAKE MY COT WHERE COT-COT-COTTON GROWS (LeSoir) As above

THE BLUEBIRDS   26 January 1928
Nichols, tp; Lewis, tb; Abbott, cl/a-sx/kazoo; Norman Yorke, t-sx; Jimmy Johnson, bs-sx; un-
known vln; Reser, bj/g; Wirges, p; Stacks, dm/voc.
E-7035   LET'S MISBEHAVE (Porter) vocTS   Vo 15682
E-7038   MINE, ALL MINE (Stept-Ruby-Cowan) vocTS   As above

RED NICHOLS & HIS FIVE PENNIES   27 February 1928
Nichols, McConville, Klein, tp; Mole, tb; Dudley Fosdick, mel; Livingston, cl/t-sx; Hayton, p;
Kress, g; Berton, dm.
E-26693   AVALON (Rose-Jolson-DeSylva)   Br 3854, 3801, 6681, 80070,
                01569, 4867, A-7707, A-500402; Ba 32550; Or 2555; Pe 15688
E-26694   JAPANESE SANDMAN (Egan-Whiting)   Br 3855, 3819, 6821, 01851, 4844
E-26695   JAPANESE SANDMAN (Egan-Whiting)   Br 3855

As above, but omit Klein; add Russell (cl/a-sx).   1 March 1928
E-26749   NOBODY'S SWEETHEART (Myers-Schoebel-Kahn)(E7168) As for 26693
E-26750   NOBODY'S SWEETHEART (Myers-Schoebel)(E7169)   MCA 1518 (LP)

2 March 1928
Nichols, McConville, Klein, Mole, Fosdick, Livingston, Schutt, Kress, Berton; Murray Kellner
(Kel Murray), vln; Art Miller, bs; Scrappy Lambert, voc; William Grant Still, arr.
XE-26772   POOR BUTTERFLY (Hubbell-Godlen) vocSL   Br 20062
XE-26773   POOR BUTTERFLY (Hubbell-Godlen) vocSL   Br 20062, 20066
XE-26774   POOR BUTTERFLY (Hubbell-Godlen)   Br A-5044
XE-26775   CAN'T YOU HEAR ME CALLING, CAROLINE (Gardner) vocSL
                                                              Br 20062, 20066
XE-26776   CAN'T YOU HEAR ME CALLING, CAROLINE (Gardner)   Br A-5044

THE CHARLESTON CHASERS   7 March 1928
Nichols, McConville, Mole, Livingston, Hayton, Kress, Berton, Lambert.
145726-2   MY MELANCHOLY BABY (Norton) vocSL   Col 1335-D; Re G20294
145727-2   MISSISSIPPI MUD (Barris) vocSL   Same as above

RED NICHOLS & HIS FIVE PENNIES   29 May 1928
Nichols, McConville, Mole, Livingston, Hayton, Kress, Berton.
E-27605   PANAMA (Tyers)   Br 3961, 03499; UHCA 20; Dec BM-1197
E-27606-A   THERE'LL COME A TIME (Manone-Mole)   Br 3955, 3850, 6822,
                                                              A-7849, A-9932

Same as March 2, but Lang (g) & Venuti (vln) repl. Kress & Kellner.   31 May 1928
  XE-27621   DEAR OLD SOUTHLAND vocSL   Br 20070, 20075, 0125
  XE-27621-G DEAR OLD SOUTHLAND (Creamer-Layton)   Br A-5081
  XE-27622   LIMEHOUSE BLUES (Furber-Braham) vocSL   Same as 27621
  XE-27622-G LIMEHOUSE BLUES (Furber-Braham)   Br A-5081

As above, but omit Klein, Lang (& McConville on 27624).   31 May 1928
  E-27623-A WHISPERING (Schoenberger-Colburn-Rose)   Br 3955, 3850,
                                       6822, 01852, A-7849, A-9932
  E-27624   I CAN'T GIVE YOU ANYTHING BUT LOVE (Fields)   Vo 15710

Klein returns; add Kress (g); Morehouse (dm/vib) repl. Berton.   1 June 1928
  E-27625   MARGIE (Conrad-Davis)   Br 3961, 03499; UHCA 10; De BM-1197
  E-27626-A IMAGINATION (Livingston)   Br 3989, 3871, 6823, 01855
  E-27627   ORIGINAL DIXIELAND ONE-STEP (LaRocca-Shields)   As above

RED NICHOLS & HIS ORCHESTRA   21 June 1928
Nichols, McConville, Mole, Fosdick, Livingston, Schutt, Kress, Morehouse; G. Miller,arr.
  45814-1   HARLEM TWIST (Livingston-Morehouse) vocCM; arrGM
                                     RCA 3136-2-RB (CD)
  45814-2   HARLEM TWIST (Livingston) vocCM; arrGM   Vic 21560
  45814-3   HARLEM TWIST vocCM; arrGM   Vic 21560; HMV EA-467
  45815-1   FIVE PENNIES (Nichols)   RCA 3136-2-RB (CD)
  45815-2   FIVE PENNIES (Nichols)   Vic 21560; HMV EA-467
NOTE: Nichols himself requested that 45814-3 be used after -2 was issued on 78.

MIFF MOLE'S (LITTLE) MOLERS   6 July 1928
Nichols, tp; Mole, tb; Fosdick, mel; Frank Teschemacher, cl; Joe Sullivan, p; Eddie Condon,
bj; Gene Krupa, dm.
  400849-C   ONE STEP TO HEAVEN (Klages-Greer)   Col 35953; HRS 15
  400850-A   SHIM-ME-SHA-WABBLE (Williams)   OK 41445; Cl 5474-C; Ha 1427-H;
                    VT 2534-V; UHCA 23; Col 35953; Par R-2506; Od 238185, 279713

                                              27 July 1928
Nichols, McConville, Mole, Fosdick, Livingston, Schutt, Kress, Tarto; Stan King, dm.
  400895-B   CRAZY RHYTHM (Meyer-Kahn)   OK 41098; Par R-230; Od
                                    165412, 193237, A-189188
  400896-A   YOU TOOK ADVANTAGE OF ME (Rodgers-Hart)   OK 41098; Par
                    R-1157; Od 165412, 193237, A-189188, A-296057

RED NICHOLS & HIS FIVE PENNIES   2 October 1928
Nichols, Klein, Fosdick, Livingston, J. Dorsey, Schutt, Kress, Berton.
  E-28326-A A PRETTY GIRL IS LIKE A MELODY (Berlin)   Br 4456, 6826,
                                    01854, 1033, A-8337

                                            1 February 1929
Add G. Miller (tb); Morehouse (dm) & Benny Goodman (cl/a-sx) repl. Berton & Dorsey.
  E-29209   I NEVER KNEW (Kahn-Fiorito)   Br 4243, 3931, 02356
  E-29210   WHO'S SORRY NOW? (Kalmar-Ruby)   Same as above

                                            5 February 1929
Nichols, Klein, G. Miller, Fosdick, Goodman, Livingston, Hayton, Kress, Berton.
  E-29222   CHINATOWN, MY CHINATOWN (Schwartz-Jerome)   Br 4363, 5019,
                                  6825, 01856, 1029, A-8298, A-500403

As for October 2, but add G. Miller (tb) & Rollini (bs-sx).   16 February 1929
  E-29294   ALICE BLUE GOWN (Tierney-McCarthy)   Br 4456, 1033
  E-29294-A ALICE BLUE GOWN (Tierney-McCarthy)   Br 6826, 01854, A-8337
  E-29295-A ALLAH'S HOLIDAY (Hauerbach-Friml)   Br 4286, 3960, 01853,
                                    1002, A-8264

172   RED HEAD

| E-29295-B | ALLAH'S HOLIDAY (Hauerbach-Friml) | Br A-8258 |
| E-29296 | ROSES OF PICARDY (Wood) | As for 29295-A, but add Br 6824 |

LOUISIANA RHYTHM KINGS   20 February 1929
Nichols, Mole, Fosdick, Livingston, Schutt, Berton; Nichols, arr. (all three titles).

E-29319	FUTURISTIC RHYTHM (Fields-McHugh)	Vo 15779
E-29320	OUT WHERE THE BLUES BEGIN (Fields-McHugh)	Vo 15779
E-29321	THAT'S A-PLENTY (Pollack) Vo 15784; Br 02731; De M-30216; Dca 510

THE CAPTIVATORS, Directed by RED NICHOLS   20 March 1929
Nichols, tp/dir; Klein, tp; G. Miller, tb; Evans, Pete Pumiglio, cl/a-sx; Jimmy Crossnan, cl/t-sx; Schutt, p; Kress, g; A. Miller, bs; Chick Condon, dm; Lambert, voc/vocaphone.

E-29507	I'M MARCHING HOME TO YOU (Silver-Sherman) vocSL	Br 4308, 3991
E-29507-G	I'M MARCHING HOME TO YOU (Silver-Sherman)	Br A-8257
E-29508	BUILDING A NEST FOR MARY vocSL	Br 4321, 5014, 1019
E-29508-G	BUILDING A NEST FOR MARY (Rose-Greer)	Br A-8258
E-29509	I USED TO LOVE HER IN THE MOONLIGHT (Lewis-Young) vocSL	
		Br 4308, 3991
E-29509-G	I USED TO LOVE HER etc. (Lewis-Young)	Br A-8257

RED NICHOLS & HIS FIVE PENNIES   18 April 1929
Nichols, McConville, Klein, tp; G. Miller, Jack Teagarden, tb; Benny Goodman, cl/a-sx/ br-sx; Babe Russin, t-sx; Schutt, p; Kress, g; A. Miller, bs; Krupa, dm; Lambert, voc; G. Miller, Fred van Eps Jr., arr..

E-29708-A	INDIANA (Hanley-MacDonald) arrGM	Br 4373, 6718, 01591, A-9206,
		A-500404; Vo 4599; Col DO-1236
E-29708-B	INDIANA (Hanley-MacDonald) arrGM	Br 80006
E-29709-A	DINAH (Akst-Lewis-Young) arrGM	Br 4373, 6718, 01591, 80006,
		A-9206, A-500404; Vo 4599; Lucky S-28
E-29710-A	ON THE ALAMO (Kahn) vocSL; arr FvE Jr.	Br 4363, 5019
E-29710-B	ON THE ALAMO (Kahn) arrFvE Jr.	Br 6825, 01856, 1029,
		A-8298, A-500403

MIFF MOLE'S (LITTLE) MOLERS   19 April 1929
McConville, Klein, Mole, J. Dorsey, Schutt, Lang, King.

401815-C	I'VE GOT A FEELING I'M FALLING (Waller-Rose)	OK 41232; Par
		PNY-41232, R-421, R-2355, A-2976; Od 279695, A-189260
401816-A	THAT'S A-PLENTY (Pollack)	Od 279695
401816-B	THAT'S A-PLENTY OK 41232; Par PNY-41232, R-421, R-2336, A-2964
401816-C	THAT'S A-PLENTY (Pollack)	Od A-189260

LOUISIANA RHYTHM KINGS   23 April 1929
Nichols, G. Miller, Goodman, Schutt; Dave Tough, dm.

| E-29689 | BALLIN' THE JACK (Smith-Europe) | Vo 15828; HRS 15; HJCA 612 |
| E-29691 | I'M WALKIN' THROUGH CLOVER (Friend-Pollack) | Vo 15810 |

RED NICHOLS & HIS FIVE PENNIES   20 May 1929
Nichols, McConville, Klein, tp; J. Teagarden, G. Miller, Trone, tb; J. Dorsey, Evans, Brilhart, cl/a-sx/bsn/fl; Larry Binyon, fl/t-sx; Kellner, Raymond, Henry Whiteman, Lou Raderman, vln; L. Schmidt, cel; Schutt, p; Kress, g; Tarto, tu; Berton, dm; J. Teagarden, Lambert, voc.

| XE-29957-A | SALLY, WON'T YOU COME BACK? (Buck-Stamper) vocSL, JT | |
| | | Br 20092, 0101 |

                                                             7 June 1929
As above, but Tommy Thunen (tp), Herb Taylor (tb) and Jimmy Crossnan (t-sx/bsn) replace McConville, Trone and Evans.

XE-29994-A	IT HAD TO BE YOU (Kahn) vocSL	Br 20092, 0101
XE-29995-A	I'LL SEE YOU IN MY DREAMS (Kahn) vocSL	Br 20091
XE-29996-A	SOME OF THESE DAYS (Brooks) vocJT, SL	Br 20091

LOUISIANA RHYTHM KINGS 11 June 1929
Nichols, J. Teagarden, Russell, Freeman, Sullivan, Tough.

E-30029-C	THAT DA-DA STRAIN (Medina)	Vo 15828; Br 02731; HRS 7; De M-30216; HJCA 612
E-30030-A	BASIN STREET BLUES (Williams) vocJT	Vo 15815; HJCA 613; Br 02506
E-30031-C	LAST CENT (Austin-Prince)	Same as above

RED NICHOLS & HIS FIVE PENNIES 12 June 1929
Nichols, Klein, Thunen, tp; J. Teagarden, G. Miller, Taylor, tb; Russell, cl; Bud Freeman, t-sx; Sullivan, p; Tommy Felline, bj; A. Miller, bs; Tough, dm; Red McKenzie, voc.

E-30056-A	WHO CARES? (Yellen-Ager) vocRM	Br 4778, 6831
E-30057-A	ROSE OF WASHINGTON SQUARE (Hanley-McDonald)	Br 4778, 6831, 01204, 4730, 500200

20 August 1929
Nichols, Thunen, John Egan, tp; J. Teagarden, G. Miller, Taylor, tb; J. Dorsey, Russell, cl; Livingston, t-sx; H. Whiteman, Moe Goffin, vln; Brodsky, p; Felline, bj; Hansen, bs; George Beebe, dm; Lambert, McKenzie, voc.

E-30502-A	I MAY BE WRONG BUT I THINK YOU'RE WONDERFUL (Ruskin-Sullivan) vocSL	Br 4500, 6753
E-30502-B	I MAY BE WRONG etc. vocSL	Br 4500, 6753, 4891, A-8493
E-30503-G	I MAY BE WRONG etc. (Ruskin-Sullivan)	Br A-9520
E-30504-A	THE NEW YORKERS (Ruskin-Sullivan) vocRM	Br 4500, A-8493
E-30504-B	THE NEW YORKERS (Ruskin-Sullivan) vocRM	MCA 1518 (LP)
E-30504-G	THE NEW YORKERS (Ruskin-Sullivan)	Br A-9520

As above, but omit strings. 27 August 1929

E-30712-A-B	THEY DIDN'T BELIEVE ME (Ruskin-Sullivan) vocSL	Br 4651, 6827
E-30713-G	THEY DIDN'T BELIEVE ME (Ruskin-Sullivan)	Br A-8655
XE-30714-A-B	THEY DIDN'T BELIEVE ME (Ruskin-Sullivan)	RB 29
XE-30715-A-B	I MAY BE WRONG etc. (Ruskin-Sullivan)	RB 30
XE-30716-A-B	THE NEW YORKERS (Ruskin-Sullivan)	RB 31
XE-30717-A-B	ON THE ALAMO (Kahn)	RB 32
XE-30718-A-B	THAT'S A-PLENTY (Pollack)	RB 33

Add H. Whiteman, Goffin, (vln), Dick Robertson (voc). 6 September 1929

E-30531-A-B	WAITING FOR THE HAPPY ENDING (Ager) vocSL	Br 4510, 1043
E-30533-A-B	CAN'T WE BE FRIENDS? (James-Swift) vocDR	Br 4510, 6827, 1043

9 September 1929
Nichols, Thunen, Mickey Bloom, tp; J. Teagarden, G. Miller, Trone, tb; Goodman, J. Dorsey, cl/a-sx; Rube Bloom, p; Felline, bj; Tarto, tu; Tough, dm; Lambert, voc.

E-30538-A	NOBODY KNOWS (And Nobody Seems to Care)(Berlin) vocSL	Br 4790, 6832, 02505
E-30539-G	NOBODY KNOWS (Berlin)	Br A-8744
E-30540-A	SMILES (Callahan-Roberts) vocSL	Br 4790, 6832
E-30541-G	SMILES (Callahan-Roberts)	Br A-8744

LOUISIANA RHYTHM KINGS 10 September 1929
Nichols, Thunen, G. Miller, J. Dorsey, Brodsky, Tough.

E-30544	WAITING AT THE END OF THE ROAD (Berlin)	Vo 15833
E-30545	LITTLE BY LITTLE (O'Keefe-Dolan)	Vo 15841
E-30546	MARIANNE (Turk-Ahlert)	Vo 15833

THE CAPTIVATORS, Directed by RED NICHOLS 22 October 1929
Nichols, Thunen, M. Bloom, J. Teagarden, Taylor, G. Miller, J. Dorsey, R. Bloom, Tarto, Felline, Tough, Lambert.

E-31266	GET HAPPY (Kohler-Arlen) vocSL	Br 4591
E-31267-G	GET HAPPY (Kohler-Arlen)	Br A-8615

E-31268	SOMEBODY TO LOVE ME (Klages-Greer) vocSL	Br 4591
E-31269-G	SOMEBODY TO LOVE ME (Klages-Greer)	Br A-8615
E-31270	SAY IT WITH MUSIC (Berlin) vocSL	Br 4651
E-31271-G	SAY IT WITH MUSIC (Berlin)	Br A-8655

RED NICHOLS & HIS "STRIKE UP THE BAND" ORCH. 17 January 1930
Nichols, Ruby Weinstein, Charlie Teagarden, tp; T. Dorsey, G. Miller, tb; J. Dorsey, cl/a-sx; Sid Stoneburn, a-sx; Russin, Binyon, t-sx; Tarto, tu; Jack Russin, p; Teg Brown, bj; Krupa, dm/voc.

E-31882-B	STRIKE UP THE BAND (Gershwin) vocGK	Br 4695, 6753
E-31883-G	STRIKE UP THE BAND (Gershwin)	Br A-8659
E-31884	SOON (Gershwin) vocGK	Br 4695
E-31885-G	SOON (Gershwin)	Br A-8659

LOUISIANA RHYTHM KINGS 20 January 1930
Nichols, Thunen, tp; G. Miller, tb; J. Dorsey, cl/a-sx; B. Russin, t-sx; Rollini, bs-sx; Wes Vaughan, bj; J. Russin, p; Krupa, dm.

E-31943	SWANEE (Gershwin-Caesar)	Br 4845, 6834, A-500325
E-31944	SQUEEZE ME (Waller-Razaf)	Br 4953, 03282
E-31945	OH, LADY BE GOOD (Gershwin)	Br 4706, 6829, 02676, 03324, A-8687
E-31946	SWEET SUE, JUST YOU (Harris-Young)	Br 4953, 03282
E-31947	THE MEANEST KIND OF BLUES (Jackson)	Br 4845, 6834, 03324, A-8687
E-31948	I HAVE TO HAVE YOU (Robin-Whiting)	Br 4706, 6829, 02676

RED NICHOLS & HIS FIVE PENNIES 24 January 1930
As for January 17, but C. Teagarden, G. Miller, Stoneburn, Binyon omitted; add Rollini, bs-sx.

E-31903	SOMETIMES I'M HAPPY (Youmans-Caesar)	Br 4701, 6828, A-8673
E-31903-A	SOMETIMES I'M HAPPY (Youmans-Caesar)	MCA 1518 (LP)
E-31904-A-B	HALLELUJAH! (Youmans-Caesar)	Same as 31903

LOUISIANA RHYTHM KINGS 27 January 1930
Nichols, Thunen, G. Miller, J. Dorsey, B. Russin, Rollini, J. Russin, Vaughan, Krupa.

E-31911	O'ER THE BILLOWY SEA (Nowlin-Smith)	Br 4908, 6837; Lucky 5077
E-31912-A	LAZY DADDY (Ragas-Shields)	Br 4923, 6838
E-31913	KARAVAN (Wiedoft-Olman)	Same as 31911
E-31914	PRETTY BABY (Kahn-Jackson-Van Alstyne)	Br 4938, 6840, A-81260
E-31915	TELL ME (Callahan-Kortlander)	Br 4938, 6840, A-81260, A-500325
E-31916	THERE'S EGYPT IN YOUR DREAMY EYES (Brown)	Br 4923, 6838

RED NICHOLS & HIS FIVE PENNIES 3 February 1930
Nichols, Thunen, Klein, tp; J. Teagarden, G. Miller, tb; J. Dorsey, cl/a-sx; B. Russin, t-sx; Rollini, bs-sx; J. Russin, p; Vaughan, g; Krupa, dm.

E-31923-A	I'M JUST WILD ABOUT HARRY (Sissle-Blake)	Br 4839, 6833, 01121, A-500405
E-31924-A	AFTER YOU'VE GONE (Creamer-Layton) vocJT	Br 4839, 6833, 01104, A-500405

Same as above. 14 February 1930

E-32040-A	I WANT TO BE HAPPY (Youmans)	Br 4724, 6830, 80007, 01302, A-8832, 3005
E-32041-A	TEA FOR TWO (Youmans)	Same as above

2 July 1930
Nichols, Weinstein, C. Teagarden, tp; J. Teagarden, G. Miller, tb; Goodman, cl; Sullivan, p; B. Russin, t-sx; Stoneburn, a-sx; Brown, bj; A. Miller, bs; Krupa, dm.

E-33304-A	PEG O' MY HEART (Bryan-Fisher)	Br 4877, 6835, 01019, A-8962; De BM-1166
E-33304-B	PEG O' MY HEART (Bryan-Fisher)	Br 80004

E-33305-A   SWEET GEORGIA BROWN (Bernie-Pinkard-Casey)   Br 4944, 6841,
                                                                  01048, A-8997
E-33306-A   CHINA BOY (Winfree-Bouteljie)   As 33304-A, add Br 80004, De 49014

J. Teagarden, T. Brown, voc.   3 July 1930
E-33333-A   THE SHEIK OF ARABY (Smith-Wheeler-Snyder) vocJT, TB   Br 4885,
                                                6836, 80005, 01104, A-8866, A-500403
E-33334-A   SHIM-ME-SHA-WABBLE (Williams)   Br 4885, 6836, 01204,
                                                                     A-8866, A-500200
E-33334-B   SHIM-ME-SHA-WABBLE (Williams)   Br 80005

Omit vocals.   2 August 1930
XE-33549-B   CALL OF THE FREAKS (Barbarin)   Intermission BR-101 (LP)
XE-33550-B   THE SHEIK OF ARABY (Smith-Wheeler-Snyder)   MCA 1518 (LP)

                                                                  3 August 1930
XE-33559-B   SWEET GEORGIA BROWN/I AIN'T GOT NOBODY   MCA 1518 (LP)

                                                                 25 August 1930
Omit J. Teagarden; Russell (cl) & Freeman (cl/t-sx) repl. Goodman & B. Russin.
XE-34058   BALLIN' THE JACK/WALKIN' THE DOG   Intermission BR-101 (LP)

                                                                 27 August 1930
Nichols, C. Teagarden, tp; G. Miller, Charlie Butterfield, tb; Goodman, cl; Freeman, t-sx;
Rollini, bs-sx; Sullivan, p; Krupa, dm.
E-34109-A   CAROLINA IN THE MORNING (Kahn-Donaldson)   Br 4925, 6839, 01062
E-34111-A   WHO? (Harbach-Hammerstein-Kern)   Same as above
E-34112-A   BY THE SHALIMAR (Magine-Delbridge-Kochler)   Br 4944, 6841,
                                                                  01048, A-8997

                                                              26 September 1930
Nichols, Weinstein, C. Teagarden, tp; J. Teagarden, G. Miller, George Stoll, tb; Goodman, cl;
Stoneburn, a-sx; Binyon, fl/t-sx; J. Russin, p; A Miller, bs; Krupa, dm; J. Teagarden, The Four-
some (Marshall Smith, Ray Johnson, Del Porter, Dwight Snyder), voc.
E-34626-A   ON REVIVAL DAY, Pt. 1 (Razaf) vocJT, F   Br 6026, 6843, 01087, A9008
E-34627-A   ON REVIVAL DAY, Pt. 1 (Razaf) vocJT, F   Sunbeam SB-137 (LP)
E-34628-A   ON REVIVAL DAY, Pt. 2 (Razaf) vocJT, F   Same as E-34626

LORING "RED" NICHOLS & HIS ORCHESTRA   23 October 1930
As above, but JT & Stoll omitted. Add: Bergman, Selinsky, vln; Brown, bj; Robertson, voc.
E-34958   EMBRACEABLE YOU (Gershwin) vocDR   Br 4957, 6842, A-8963
E-34959   I GOT RHYTHM (Gershwin) vocDR   Br 4872, 4957, 6711,
                                                                  A-8963, 01300
E-34959-A   I GOT RHYTHM (Gershwin) voc DR   MCA 1518 (LP)
E-34960   A GIRL FRIEND OF A BOY FRIEND OF MINE (Kahn) vocDR Mel 12005
E-34961   SWEET JENNIE LEE (Donaldson) vocDR   Mel M-12005; Em E-125;
                                                             Pan 25001, P-12005

NOTE: E-34960/61 issued as THE CAPTIVATORS.

HAROLD LEM (FRED RICH) & HIS ORCHESTRA   29 October 1930
Nichols, ldr; Klein, C. Teagarden, tp; T. Dorsey, tb; J. Dorsey, cl/a-sx; Goodman, a-sx; B.
Russin, t-sx; J. Russin, p; Venuti, vln; Lang, g; Tarto, tu; Krupa, dm; Smith Ballew, voc.
150908-2   I GOT RHYTHM (Gershwin) vocSB   Ha 1234-H; Cl 5104-C
404533-A   I GOT RHYTHM (Gershwin) vocSB   OK 41465; Par PNY-34149;
                                                             Od ONY-36158

LORING "RED" NICHOLS & HIS ORCHESTRA   6 November 1930
Nichols, C. Teagarden, Snub Pollard, tp; J. Teagarden, tb; Binyon, Stoneburn, cl/sxs; Wladimir
Selinski, Lou Raderman, vln; Roger Edens, p; A. Miller, bs; Krupa, dm; Harold Arlen, Eddy
Thomas, voc.

E-35214-A   LINDA (Arlen-Kohler) vocHA   Br 4982, 6844, A-9003
E-35215-A   YOURS AND MINE (Nelson-Burke) vocET   As above

RED AND HIS BIG TEN   18 November 1930
Nichols, Weinstein, G. Miller, Goodman, Pumiglio, Stoneburn, J. Russin, Kress, A. Miller, Krupa, Robertson.
64623-1   THAT'S WHERE SOUTH BEGINS (Yellen-Shapiro) vocDR   Vic 23026
64624-3   I'M TICKLED PINK WITH A BLUE-EYED BABY (O'Flynn) vocDR
                                                                     Vic 23026; HMV B-5977

RED NICHOLS & HIS FIVE PENNIES   1 December 1930
Nichols, C. Teagarden, Manone, G. Miller, J. Dorsey, B. Russin, Sullivan, A. Miller, Krupa.
E-35618-A   MY HONEY'S LOVIN' ARMS (Ruby-Meyer)   Br 6012, 01121, A-9005
E-35619-A   ROCKIN' CHAIR (Carmichael) vocWM   Br 6012, 01852, A-9005

Add Weinstein, Arlen; Goodman (cl) & J.Russin (p) repl. JD & Sullivan.   10 December 1930
E-35733-A   BUGABOO (Nichols) vocWM   Br 6058, 01120, A-9024;
                                              Mt M-12495; Or 2574; Pe 15684; Ro 1120
E-35734-A   CORRINNE CORRINA (McCoy-Chatman) vocWM   Same as above
E-35735-A   HOW COME YOU DO ME LIKE YOU DO? (Austin-Bergers) vocHA
                                                          Br 6149, 01180, A-9099

LORING "RED" NICHOLS & HIS ORCHESTRA   12 December 1930
Nichols, Weinstein, G. Miller, Goodman, Lambert, Robertson; Gil Rodin, a-sx; Nappy Lamare, g; Eddie Miller, t-sx; Harry Goodman, bs; Ray Bauduc, dm.
E-35738-B   BLUE AGAIN (Fields) vocDR   Br 6014, 01082, 4764, A-9002; Sup S2167
E-35739-B   WHEN KENTUCKY BIDS WORLD GOOD MORNING (Wayne) vocDR
                                                   As above, plus Pan P-11988
E-35740   WHAT GOOD AM I WITHOUT YOU? (Ager) vocSL   Mt M-12049; Pan
                                                   25015, P-12049; Mf G-2003
E-35741   WE'RE FRIENDS AGAIN (Turk-Ahlert) vocSL   Mt M-12049
NOTE: Mt M-12049 issued as THE CAPTIVATORS.

RED AND HIS BIG TEN   5 January 1931
Nichols, Weinstein, G. & A. Miller, B. Goodman, Stoneburn, Pumiglio, Kress, Krupa; Fulton McGrath, p; Paul Small, voc.
67760-1   AT LAST I'M HAPPY (Friend-Conrad) vocPS   Vic 23033; HMV R-14590
67761-1   IF YOU HAVEN'T GOT A GIRL (Vallee) vocPS   Vic 23022; Zon EE-252

RED NICHOLS & HIS FIVE PENNIES   16 January 1931
Nichols, Weinstein, C. Teagarden, J. Teagarden, G. Miller, B. Goodman, Stoneburn, Binyon, Bergman, Selinsky, J. Russin, T. Brown, A. Miller, Krupa, Arlen.
E-35167-A   YOU SAID IT (Arlen) vocHA   Br 6029, 6842, A-9007
E-35168-A   SWEET AND HOT (Arlen-Yellen) vocHA   Br 6029, 6711, A-9007,
                                                   4872, 01300; Col DO-1236

Omit GM, Brown, vlns; add 3 Cuban drummers & Small (voc).   23 January 1931
E-35954-A   THE PEANUT VENDOR (Simons-Gilbert) vocPS   Br 6035, 01076,
                                                              A-9000; Sup S-2196
E-35955-A   SWEET ROSITA (Mills-Gilbert) vocPS   Same as above

LORING "RED" NICHOLS & HIS ORCHESTRA   19 February 1931
Same personnel as January 16, but omit Brown.
E-36108-A   THINGS I NEVER KNEW TIL NOW (Winchell-Vann) vocHA
                                                             Br 6068, A-9032
E-36109-A   TEARDROPS AND KISSES (Little-Kenny) vocHA   Br 6070, A-9046;
                                                             Sup S-2191
E-36110-A   WERE YOU SINCERE? (Meskill-Rose) vocHA   Same as above
E-36111-A   KEEP A SONG IN YOUR SOUL (Waller-Hill) vocJT   Br 6068, 6845,
                                                             6069, A-9032

As for January 16, but Stoll (tb) & McGrath (p) repl. J. Teagarden & J. Russin; Brown plays g; add Smith Ballew, voc.

E-36728-B	IT'S THE DARNDEST THING (Fields-McHugh) vocSB	Br 6191, 01275
E-36729-A	SINGIN' THE BLUES (Fields-McHugh) vocSB	Br 6191, 6845, 01275
E-36730-A	LOVE IS LIKE THAT (Russell) vocSB	Br 6118, A-9055, 6098

RED NICHOLS & HIS FIVE PENNIES   26 May 1931
Nichols, C. Teagarden, G. Miller, J. Dorsey, B. Russin, J. Russin, A. Miller; Perry Botkin, g; Ray McKinley, dm/voc.

E-36830-A	JUST A CRAZY SONG (Smith-Williams)	Br 6133, 01163, A-9090
E-36831-A	YOU RASCAL, YOU (Theard) vocRayM	Same as above
E-36832-A	MOAN, YOU MOANERS (Williams) vocRayM	Br 6149, 01180, A-9099

11 June 1931
Nichols, Weinstein, C. Teagarden, G. Miller, Stoll, J. Dorsey, Stoneburn, Binyon, Bergman, Selinsky, T. Brown, A. Miller, Krupa, Ballew; Paul Mertz, p/arr.

E-36855-A	SLOW BUT SURE (Newman-Agnew) vocSB	Br 6138, A-9094
E-36856-A	LITTLE GIRL (Arlen) vocSB	Br 6138, A-9094
E-36857-A	HOW TIME CAN FLY (Donaldson) vocSB	Br 6164, A-9140

NOTE: Br 6138 issued as LORING NICHOLS & HIS ORCHESTRA.

As for May 26, but omit C. Teagarden (tp); add Red McKenzie (voc).   24 June 1931
| E-36877-A | HOW LONG BLUES (Carr) vocRM | Br 6160, 01213, A-9117 |
| E-36878-A | FAN IT (Jaxon) vocRM | Same as above |

Nichols, J. Dorsey, Venuti, Lang, McGrath, Berton.   16 September 1931
| E-37204-A | OH, PETER! YOU'RE SO NICE (Wiedoft-Rose) | Br 6198, 01233, A-9170 |
| E-37205-B | HONOLULU BLUES (Goldstein-Gunsky) | Same as above |

2 October 1931
Nichols, Don Moore, tp; Johnny "Scat" Davis, tp/voc; Will Bradley, tb; J. Dorsey, cl/a-sx; Russ Lyon, B. Russin, t-sx; McGrath, p; Tony Starr, bj; Artie Bernstein, bs; Vic Engle, dm.

| E-37233-A | GET CANNIBAL (Weems-Nichols) vocJD | Br 6219, 01281, 4875, A-9192; Lucky 3046 |
| E-37234-A | JUNK MAN BLUES (Nichols-Dooley) vocJD Br 6219, 01225, 4875, A9192 |

Omit Moore (tp) & Lyon (t-sx); J. Russin (p) repl. McGrath.   2 December 1931
E-37436-A	SLOW AND EASY (Williams) vocJD	Br 6767, 01312
E-37437-A	WAITING FOR THE EVENING MAIL (Baskette) vocJD	
		Br 6767, 01312, 4896

As for September 16, but Schutt (p) repl. McGrath.   2 December 1931
| E-37438-A | YAKKA HULA HICKEY DULA (Coatz-Wendling) | Br 6234, 01262, A-9199 |
| E-37439-A | HAUNTING BLUES (Busse-Hirsh) | Same as above |

As for E-37436/7, but omit Starr; add D. Robertson (voc).   15 December 1931
| E-37462-A-B | TWENTY-ONE YEARS (Miller) vocDR | Br 6241, 01293, A-9203 |
| E-37463-A | MY SWEETIE WENT AWAY (Turk-Handman) | Same as above |

15 February 1932
Nichols, J. Davis, Bradley, J. Dorsey, B. Russin, Binyon, J. Russin, McDonough, Bernstein, King; Venuti, Harry Hoffman, vln; Connie Boswell, Art Jarrett, voc.

| BX-11283-A | NEW ORLEANS MEDLEY, Part 2 vocCB, AJ | Br 20110, 0118 |

Nichols, J. Dorsey, B. Russin, McDonough, McGrath, Bernstein, Engle.   18 February 1932
B-11314-A	CLARINET MARMALADE (LaRocca-Shields)	Br 6266, 01301, A-500176; Par R-2598, B-71157
B-11315-A	SWEET SUE, JUST YOU (Harris-Young)	Same as above
B-11315-B	SWEET SUE, JUST YOU	ARC F-152 (for theater use only)

Nichols, Davis, T. Dorsey, J. Dorsey, B. Russin, Binyon, Venuti, J. Russin, McDonough, Bernstein, King; Sid Garry, Art Jarrett, The Boswell Sisters, voc.

BX-11427-A	NEW ORLEANS MEDLEY, Part 1 vocSG, AJ, BS	Br 20010, 0118
BX-11432-A	CALIFORNIA MEDLEY, Part 1 vocSG, AJ, BS	Br 20107, 0108

RED NICHOLS & HIS ORCHESTRA   June 1939

Nichols, tp/dir; Don Stevens, J. Douglas Wood, tp; Martin Croy, Robert Gebhart, tb; Harry Yolonsky, Ray Schultz, cl/a-sx; Bobby Jones, Bill Shepard, cl/t-sx; Billy Maxted, p/arr; Tony Colucci, g; Jack Fay, bs; Vic Engle, dm; Marion Redding, voc.

WAIL OF THE WINDS (Theme Song)(Nichols)	Blue Lantern LP-1000
WELL, ALL RIGHT! (Don Raye) vocMR	Blue Lantern LP-1000
DIXIELAND BLUES (Maxted-Nichols)	Blue Lantern LP-1000
SCATTERBRAIN (Koene-Masters-Burke)	Blue Lantern LP-1000

Earlier I spoke of Nichols's thousands of recording dates from 1922 to 1930, and of the various bands he played with and for. The following list, running from September 1924 to March 1926, is no more than one-eighth of those sessions, and does not include song titles or personnel; but it shows just how busy this very young man was, and why his jazz dates may have occasionally suffered in quality. When you play this much commercial dance music, you have to put your creative faculties on hold, or at least on reserve, for those eight or sixteen bars where you might do your own material. (Thanks to Stan Hester for the information.)

September 1924

4--Sam Lanin session, Plaza Records.
6--Ben Selvin session, Plaza Records.
7--S. Lanin session (Plaza)
11--S. Lanin session (Cameo)
12--Nathan Glantz session (Plaza)
15--N. Glantz session (Plaza
18--S. Lanin session (OKeh)
19--S. Lanin session (Cameo)
Late Sept. (exact date unknown)--B.
  Selvin session for Plaza.

October 1924

9--S. Lanin session (Plaza)
10--Barney Rapp session (?), Victor
13--Al Jockers session (Cameo)
15--S. Lanin session (Perfect)
17--S. Lanin session (OKeh)
20--Max Terr session (Perfect)
22--George Olsen session (Victor)
23--Joe Samuels session (Paramount)
27--Adrian Schubert session (Plaza)
31--Billy Wynne session (Edison)
October (day unknown)--B. Selvin (as
  "Newport Society Orch.") for Triangle.

November 1924

2--B. Selvin session (Plaza)
5--S. Lanin session (Plaza)
10--S. Lanin session (Cameo)
12--S. Lanin session (Plaza)
14--S. Lanin session for Cameo
  A. Schubert session (Plaza)
20--Frank Silver session (Edison)
24--Charleston 7 session (Edison)
25--Goofus Five session (OKeh)
26--S. Lanin session (Plaza)
28--S. Lanin session (Perfect)
  B. Wynne session (Edison)
Late November (exact date unknown)--
  Ambassadors session (Vocalion)

December 1924

3--Max Terr session (Plaza)
12--Joe Samuels session (Plaza)
18--S. Lanin session (OKeh
23--S. Lanin session (Gennett)
  Tennessee Tooters (Gennett)
24--S. Lanin session (Gennett)
28--B. Wynne session (Edison)
Early December (exact date unknown)
  --B. Selvin session (Bell)

January 1925
1--S. Lanin session (Gennett)
4--Bill James session (Plaza)
10--B. Wynne session (Edison)
  S. Lanin session (OKeh)
13--S. Lanin session (Emerson)
14--S. Lanin session (Cameo)
15--S. Lanin session (Perfect)
  S. Lanin session (OKeh)
16--B. Wynne session (Edison)
  S. Lanin session (Columbia)
22--S. Lanin session (Columbia)
23--Tennessee Tooters (Vocalion)
27--B. Selvin session (Plaza)

February 1925
5--B. Wynne session (Edison)
11--S. Lanin session (Columbia)
13--S. Lanin session (Plaza)
17--Tennesse Tooters (Vocalion)
20--S. Lanin session (Gennett)
  Harry Reser (?) for Columbia
26--Lanin's Red Heads (Columbia)
27--S. Lanin session (Plaza)
  H. Reser session (Gennett)

March 1925
2--S. Lanin session (Edison)
3--S. Lanin session (Columbia)
10--B. Wynne session (Edison)
11--B. Wynne session (Perfect)
12--S. Lanin session (Perfect)
13--S. Lanin session (OKeh)
  Joe Smith session (?), OKeh
  (sounds like Nichols on solo)
16--California Ramblers (Columbia)
19--A. Schubert session (Plaza)
23--California Ramblers (Columbia)
24--N. Glantz session (?), Gennett
25--S. Lanin session (Plaza)
30--California Ramblers (Columbia)

April 1925
1--California Ramblers (Paramount)
2--California Ramblers (Edison)
3--California Ramblers (Cameo)
  Ernie Golden session (Plaza)
  S. Lanin session (OKeh)
6--Lou Gold session (Plaza)
  L. Gold session (Cameo)
  S. Lanin session (Cameo)
7--California Ramblers (Cameo)
  S. Lanin session (Cameo)
8--S. Lanin session (Cameo)
  L. Gold session (Cameo)
9--S. Lanin session (Columbia)
10--L. Gold session (Pathe/Perfect)
  Fred Silver session (Edison)
13--California Ramblers (Perfect)
14--California Ramblers (Perfect)

15--S. Lanin session (Gennett)
20--Mike Speciale session (Cameo)
21--B. Wynne session (Edison)
22--S. Lanin session (Columbia)
23--California Ramblers (Edison)
27--N. Glantz session (Plaza)
28--California Ramblers (Cameo)
During this month Columbia issued a
special 12" Vivi-Tonal (electrical) disc
by various artists; Fred Rich Orch. led
off the record with a Nichols solo. Exact date unknown.

May 1925
1--Southerners (?) on Gennett
4--S. Lanin session (OKeh)
  S. Lanin session (Columbia)
5--L. Gold session (Plaza)
6--N. Glantz session (Plaza)
7--Arthur Fields session (Vocalion)
8--S. Lanin session (Plaza)
11--California Ramblers (Edison)
12--B. Selvin session (Plaza)
13--California Ramblers (Cameo)
14--California Ramblers (Columbia)
15--S. Lanin session (Cameo)
18--L. Gold session (Cameo)
  H. Reser session (Columbia)
20--S. Lanin session (Columbia)
  L. Gold session (Plaza)
21--S. Lanin session (Gennett)
22--B. Wynne session (Edison)
  M. Speciale session (Pathe/Perf.)
On May 23 Red took a leave of absence from the California Ramblers,
and went to Chicago to see Hannah
Williams as well as Beiderbecke with
Charlie Straight.
30--S. Lanin session (OKeh)

June 1925
2--Little Ramblers (Columbia)
  Bill Wirges session (Perfect)
3--S. Lanin session (Columbia)
  Bob Haring session (Cameo)
4--California Ramblers (Columbia)
8--S. Lanin session (Perfect)
9--California Ramblers (Columbia)
12--California Ramblers (OKeh)
18--B. Wynne session (Edison)
19--S. Lanin session (Gennett)
  S. Lanin session (Plaza)
20--The Georgians (Columbia)
23--California Ramblers (Edison)
24--Paul van Loan session (Cameo)
25--S. Lanin session (Columbia)
26--M. Speciale session (Perfect)
  Howard Lanin session (Victor)

July 1925
2--S. Lanin session (OKeh)
3--S. Lanin session (Cameo)
20--B. Wynne session (Edison)
21--Max Terr session (Perfect)
24--L. Gold session (Cameo)
27--B. Wynne session (Edison)
28--L. Gold session (Cameo)
31--S. Lanin session (Columbia)
A slow month for Red.

August 1925
1--S. Lanin session (Cameo)
   P. van Loan session (Cameo)
3--S. Lanin session (Cameo)
   Ross Gorman session (Columbia)
   (This is Red and Miff's first recording together.)
4--P. van Loan session (Cameo)
5--S. Lanin session (Plaza)
7--Mark Strand session (Columbia)
   R. Gorman session (Columbia)
10--L. Gold session (Cameo)
11-L. Gold session (Perfect)
12--Tennessee Tooters (Vocalion)
   P. van Loan session (Cameo)
13--Tennessee Tooters (Vocalion)
17--S. Lanin session (Gennett)
18--R. Gorman session (Col rejected)
19--S. Lanin session (Gennett)
20--The Cotton Pickers (Brunswick)
24--S. Lanin session (Cameo)
26--B. Haring session (Cameo)
   The Ambassadors (Vocalion)
27--S. Lanin session (Columbia)

September 1925
1--M. Speciale session (Edison)
3--S. Lanin session (Perfect)
7--M. Speciale session (Perfect)
9--R. Gorman session (Columbia)
10--P. van Loan session (Cameo)
11--R. Gorman session (Columbia)
   M. Soeciale session (Perfect)
   S. Lanin session (Gennett)
15--B. Selvin session (Vocalion)
   S. Lanin session (OKeh)
   B. Wynne session (Edison)
16--L. Gold session (Plaza)
   S. Lanin session (Cameo)
   Peggy English session (Vocalion)
18--L. Gold session (Plaza)
   The Hottentots (Vocalion)
21--The Cotton Pickers (Brunswick)
   "Red Sanders" (Speciale), Gennett
22--L. Gold session (Plaza)
23--S. Lanin session (Plaza)
25--S. Lanin session (Gennett)
27--S. Lanin session (Columbia)
29--Howard Lanin session (Victor)

October 1925
Two sessions backing Ukelele Ike (Cliff
Edwards), dates unknown (Perfect).
2--Harry Reser session (Columbia)
5--L. Gold session (Cameo)
6--B. Selvin session (Plaza)
7--M. Speciale session (Cameo)
   S. Lanin session (Plaza)
8--S. Lanin session (Gen, rejected)
   Jack Albin session (Edison)
9--M. Speciale session (Perfect)
   L. Gold session (Perfect)
10--"Red Sanders" (Speciale), Gennett
13--Al Jockers session (Cameo)
   Bob Haring session (Cameo)
14--Jack Shilkret session (Victor)
15--"7 Missing Links" (M. Terr), Perfect
16--Hotel Biltmore Orch. (? playing gig)
17--S. Lanin session (Plaza)
19--S. Lanin session (Cameo)
   Lanin's Red Heads (Columbia)
22--H. Reser session (Columbia)
23--Bob Haring session (Cameo)
   S. Lanin session (Gennett)
   B. Wynne session (Edison)
28--Fred Rich session (Harmony)
   S. Lanin session (Perfect)
29--R. Gorman session (Columbia)
   B. Haring session (Cameo)
30--"Ipana Troubadors" (S. Lanin), Col
   L. Gold session (Harmony)

November 1925
3--S. Lanin session (Perfect)
5--S. Lanin session (Plaza)
   R. Sanders session (Gennett)
   B. Haring session (?) (Cameo)
11--The Dixie Daisies (Lanin)(Cameo)
   The Hottentots (Vocalion)
13--S. Lanin session (Gennett)
   B. Selvin session (Plaza)
   The Cotton Pickers (Brunswick)
15--The Red Heads (Pathe/Perfect)
16--S. Lanin session (Gennett)
17--L. Gold session (Plaza)
18--The Georgians (Columbia)
19--Ernie Golden session (Edison)
20--L. Gold session (Perfect)
24--Dixie Daisies (Lanin)(Cameo)
25--M. Speciale session (Perfect)
27--S. Lanin session (Perfect)
30--P. van Loan session (Cameo)
Nichols also made sessions this month
with Walter Davison (Cameo) and Cliff
Edwards (Perfect), dates unknown.

December 1925
1--S. Lanin session (OKeh)
   S. Lanin session (Plaza)
   L. Gold session (Cameo)

2--S. Lanin session (Gennett)
S. Lanin session (Cameo)
4--Fred Rich session (Perfect)
7--L. Gold session (Cameo)
S. Lanin session (Cameo)
9--E. Golden session (Edison)
10--S. Lanin session (Columbia)
11-S. Lanin session (Gennett)
17--M. Speciale session (Edison)
21--F. Rich session (Harmony)
23--B. Haring session (Cameo)
24--L. Gold session (Cameo)
E. Golden session (Edison)
S. Lanin session (Gennett)
27--S. Lanin session (Cameo)
29--R. Gorman session (Columbia)
S. Lanin session (Columbia)
30--E. Golden session (Plaza)
Also two sessions (exact dates unknown) for Jack Stillman (Perfect) and Gloria Greer (Cameo).

January 1926
1--B. Haring session (Cameo)
4--S. Lanin session (Plaza)
R. Gorman session (Columbia)
6--L. Gold session (Perfect)
7--L. Gold session (Harmony)
8--The Hottentots (Vocalion)
11--S. Lanin session (Perfect)
12--M. Speciale session (Harmony)
13--M. Speciale session (Perfect)
15--S. Lanin session (Gennett)
S. Lanin session (Plaza)
16--S. Lanin session (Cameo)
19--Fred Rich session (Cameo)
20--S. Lanin session (OKeh)
H. Reser session (Columbia)
21--Original Memphis Five (Brunswick)
22--R. Gorman session (Columbia)
23--Original Memphis 5 (Brun/Vocalion)
26--L. Gold session (Perfect)
S. Lanin session (Cameo)
27--S. Lanin session (Columbia)
Also this month, sessions with Cliff Edwards (Perfect), N. Glantz (Puritan) and H. Reser (Columbia), dates unknown.

February 1926
1--S. Lanin session (Gennett)
Jack Stillman session (Gennett)
2--Fred Rich session (Harmony)
3--F. Rich session (Harmony)
F. Rich session (Perfect)
4--M. Speciale session (Perfect)
The Red Heads (Pathe/Perfect)

5--M. Speciale session (Perfect)
9--S. Lanin session (Plaza)
10--S. Lanin session (Harmony)
11--S. Lanin session (Perfect)
15--S. Lanin session (Cameo)
16--A. Schubert session (Plaza)
L. Gold session (Harmony)
18--S. Lanin session (Columbia)
23--Tennessee Happy Boys (Plaza)
25--H. Reser session (Columbia)
27--S. Lanin session (OKeh)
Also this month, sessions for L. Gold (Plaza), S. Lanin (Plaza) and the Grey Gull label, exact dates unknown.

March 1926
4--B. Haring session (Cameo)
5--B. Haring session (Cameo)
S. Lanin session (Columbia)
Red Heads (Pathe, unissued)
9--S. Lanin session (Perfect)
10--S. Lanin session (Plaza)
11--S. Lanin session (Harmony)
12--A. Schubert session (Plaza)
15--Vincent Lopez session (OKeh)
16--Murray's Greengable Orch.
(Gennett)
L. Gold session (Perfect)
18--Royal Troubadors (Gennett)
19--S. Lanin session (Plaza)
22--S. Lanin session (Columbia)
S. Lanin session (Cameo)
24--R. Gorman session (Columbia)
We Three (Pathe/Perfect)
29--J. Stillman session (Edison)
30--F. Rich session (Cameo)
Dates unknown for following sessions made in March 1926: Arkansaw Serenaders (Puritan); Dixie Jazz Band (Plaza, two sessions); Majestic Dance Orch. (Plaza); "Phil Hughes" (H, Reser, Perfect); Esther Walker (vocalist, Brunswick).

Index

NOTE: The following index does not include song titles, or names given in discographical data. Also, since Nichols' name appears on almost every page, I have reduced his listings to subheadings of important moments in his career.

About the Author

Stephen M. Stroff is a writer, pianist, and music historian of both jazz and classical music. He was born in Shamokin, Pennsylania, grew up in New Jersey, and moved to Ohio in 1977. He graduated from Seton Hall University in 1972 with degrees in English and Music, and in fact his first ambition was to be a teacher. Since 1975 he has built a career as a free-lance music critic, and in 1978 was one of only six young critics nationwide selected to attend a seminar at the Aspen Music Festival.

Since 1974 Mr. Stroff has written for a variety of publications great and small, including *High Fidelity, Opera News, Ovation, Cincinnati Magazine, No Name Jazz News, Letter from Evans,* and *Le Grand Baton.* From 1983 to 1986 he was both jazz and classical editor for *Goldmine,* and from 1991 to 1994 he edited and published his own magazine, *The Music Box,* which featured Jack Walrath, Terry Teachout, Sean Petrahn, and the late Ralph Berton among its contributors.

Mr. Stroff has had three other books on music published: *Guldstrupan (Golden Throat,* Bokad & Co., 1981), a biodiscography of Swedish tenor Jussi Björling; *Discovering Great Jazz* (Newmarket Press, 1991), a beginner's guide to the history of the music; and *Opera: An Informal Guide* (A Capella Books, 1993), another introductory volume for novices. In addition, he self-published *Methods of Singing,* an historical surey of singing methods and their relationship to classical vocal music through the centuries, in 1985. He has recently finished work on *The Zen of Music,* a holistic listening guide that examines jazz, folk, classical, and world music from the viewpoint of spiritual realization. He currently lives in Cincinnati with his wife and four cats.